EUPHORIA

Elin Cullhed is a Swedish author who made her debut in 2016. *Euphoria* is her first novel for adults. It won the 2021 August Prize, Sweden's most prestigious literary award, and was a finalist for the Strega European Prize.

Jennifer Hayashida is a poet, translator and artist. She is the recipient of awards from the New York Foundation for the Arts, PEN and the Jerome Foundation among others. Her translations from the Swedish include work by Ida Börjel, Athena Farrokhzad and Iman Mohammed.

By the same author

The Gods (published in Sweden as *Gudarna*)

EUPHORIA

ELIN CULLHED
TRANSLATED BY JENNIFER HAYASHIDA

CANONGATE

This paperback edition published in Great Britain, the USA and Canada
in 2023 by Canongate Books

First published in Great Britain, the USA and Canada in 2022
by Canongate Books Ltd, 14 High Street, Edinburgh EH1 1TE

Distributed in the USA by Publishers Group West
and in Canada by Publishers Group Canada

canongate.co.uk

1

Translated from the Swedish by Jennifer Hayashida

Published under agreement with Ahlander Agency

The cost of this translation was supported by a subsidy from the
Swedish Arts Council, gratefully acknowledged
For permission credits please see p. 293

British Library Cataloguing-in-Publication Data
A catalogue record for this book is available on
request from the British Library

ISBN 978 1 83885 599 4

Typeset in Bembo by Palimpsest Book Production Ltd,
Falkirk, Stirlingshire

Printed and bound in Great Britain by Clays Ltd, Elcograf S.p.A.

For Mom

Euphoria is a work of fiction about Sylvia Plath that should not be read as a biography. Events and characters in the book, which may correspond with reality, are transformed into fiction and literary fantasy in the context of the novel. Thus, Sylvia Plath also becomes a fictive character in this work.

7 December 1962, Devon

7 REASONS NOT TO DIE:

1. Skin. To never again feel the skin of one's beloved child. Nicholas when he becomes a clown in bed and I nuzzle his behind. Frieda who needs to be tickled in order to feel alive and grows calm with a laughter that cleanses her, afterwards. My skin as it strains against theirs and knows that we are the same flesh for ever and ever in all eternity Amen. Oh, to never again feel their throbbing pulses that sprang from me. I can never cease to live for them no matter how much of Ted's skin they also possess, Ted's snakeskin, he who opens his maw and presses the prey whole into his mouth until you choke.

2. Time. I want to see my children grow up and scrub their knees as they learn how to cycle, I want to pull the noose off my neck and laugh in his face as he is already (and very alone, snakes are pathologically self-absorbed) on his way to the next prey and I am busy living. I want to lick a lollipop and feel how sugar and time dissolve inside me, I want to wake to a summer's day, coffee in hand and an urge to write like hell until time also stops and is preserved and ebbs like seawater and forgives me. Time, I want you to forgive me. I also want to feel how time makes everything so fucking forgiving, how

it makes strawberries plop out yet again (even though death is so close, decomposition next), makes people awaken on their pillows and once again imagine that everything is just fine.

God, I feel so good now, now when I am going to die. I see everything more clearly than ever before. I should always live to die; it's like heroin, like the kick of seeing one's former beloved run out of oxygen since he has consumed all the air that surrounded him in his armour. Snakeskin is something you shed; the skin pales like a forgotten rag on a British beach. I prefer immolation: I am convinced of the superiority of fire as a metaphor for my own life. Oh, fire that could not be greeted with open arms. Oh, alarm, as the fire got hold of a living man's writing which he mistakes for Nobel Prize material. I say: the future will remember me. So, I don't have to be skin and time and the early sixties, since time will be transformed into me but without my involvement. Pristine, like a sublime word on a gleaming page of poetry. Ted will wash my book pages as I have washed his ugly shirts. He will shrivel like a paradise apple in the autumn dirt. One of the Japanese crab apples we have here.

3. Never to fuck again, to feel the heat of the stake as it pushes into my flesh and turns me into animal and obliteration. If someone wanted to fuck me every day, I wouldn't have to die, haha. Don't quote me on that, but feel free to show my mother, the most unfucked human in history (and therefore so sour, so parched, so banal to see through, like a glass of water; my mother is a glass of water, impossible to go without but so thoroughly boring and blandly predictable and who has made me so contemptuous of death, so hateful of other women when women are the ones who could possibly help me; she has made me feel as though I do not need water, as though I am beyond water, I am not a water-needing creature not a mammal, I stand above you with your common

mortal thirst for water, I hate water, spare me my daily glass of water!).

4. GIVE him that. Give him that I die and all his prophecies come true. 'It would be easier if you were dead,' as he hissed at me this summer in order to get set to dare to leave me. 'You and your death ray, you have a particular bite for death' – all his groaning that I kill everything. I don't want to give him that. I want to stand at the centre of the circle and glow and live. If not me in my life, who else? I don't want to give him the story of my life. For him to declare: *Yes, children, your mother was a special person, she was not always well, she loved life when it flowed toward her like gold but life is also hard edges and cold and bacteria in March and being broke. We must tend to her memory, children, we must tell her stories and every year when the daffodils emerge from the ground we can pick a bouquet in her honour. Your mother Sylvia's voice was deep and strong but it never managed to make its way out of her body and onto the page, that is why she so badly wanted to turn off her body and only let the spirit live on. What she has written for posterity was worth more to her than life with us.* Blah blah. Fuck that! I don't want to give him the finest pieces of cake from my life. For Olwyn his older sister to stand there on her iron legs with her arms crossed and assert: Oh yes, I've said it since the first time I saw her, you won't get far with that woman, Ted. Her fragile strength, that mourning veil across her face so temptingly easy to pull away with a sarcasm that makes her entire self-image crumble, the wide smile grow into a grin. A little devil-girl, Ted, a little hottie, a weak American with cellophane wrapped around her heart. You'll keep her for a while, then she will melt like sugar in rain. Trust me!

And he will listen to his sister and grow stronger and think: Yes, I was a fool to try to love her, for she could not be loved.

When the truth is that it's his home that has no room for love. His home, where he comes from, where you work and grin and bear it, where the senses and aesthetics and the way you interact DO NOT MATTER. There is no culture in his home, nothing noble, no refinement; there, you are coarse and foul-mouthed and have bad manners and how is it my fault that I was someone who could love and could be beautiful and who entered his house, his home, his England, his crude inheritance of coal and stained clothes.

I wanted to give of what I had, of my wit my knowledge my gift for words and for things you see. Observations. But see: the world does not want beautiful hard-working girls made of gold. The world cannot bear them. The world wants hard wicked Olwyn-girls, the kind of girls not loved by men, who are born to make their own way in the world, European post-war women who know what it means to dig in, but not what it is to be intellectually refined and teach girls at Smith and write astonishingly cool poems in their spare time. They are jealous, oh, how they are jealous of someone like me, and still they are the ones who come out on top – those who win at life, even though they themselves will never bear a man any children and carry on the royal lineage, splay their legs wide on the bed and push glowing magma out into the world. She won't sacrifice shit, Olwyn, for she will never burn. She will stand there and grin and bear it grin and bear it and let life sweep through her until she dies. She will never step into life itself, reshape it, dictate it, steep it in beautiful shapes, give it new children. Therefore, she also manages to avoid feeling how the world cannot stand her strength her crushing beauty her genius. She will laugh at my death, she will sigh at my death, she will also envy my death, for no, she will never be that brave!

5. The ocean, and the rocks. To walk in the sheer light one afternoon in Winthrop and gather rocks for my father, be

seven years old and feel how the nature I find for him bonds us more firmly than anything else in the world. The mysteries I give him are ours to discover and carefully tend, like the heart's own secrets. The ocean licks my tanned legs, and it smells of furious salt and wet seaweed in heat, and he asks me to go for a walk to find the most beautiful shells, the smoothest rocks, which he will then tell me something about. The beach and my father, the ocean, his eternity. I love my father. I know that I was born of him, that he gave me sincerity: mystery and language. When I have returned to Winthrop I no longer see the grandeur of the beaches, and the ocean bores me – I know that I have other tasks that await me. I think that I will rediscover the calm and shimmer of childhood, but the result is simply that I see through and betray it with my new eyes. So, perhaps this is not actually a reason to live. Even if my children would love the ocean as I do, they would never get to meet my father, their grandfather, have his big enormous paws in which to place small round rocks. He both is and is not a reason to live, my father. I want to tend to his memory, stand up for him and let my body be transported to the end of time as if an anchor for his shipwrecked boat. But I also want to be spared from seeing the ocean, the rocks, the seashells turn into ghosts. And feel the rattle of death around my neck.

6. Frieda, oh Frieda.

7. Nicholas.

ONE YEAR EARLIER

ONE YEAR EARLIER

It was my life that was the writing.

It was my body, my skin, my white shimmering wrists that took me cycling through Devon. When I met a person I recognised, I trembled. It was as if my nerves and veins hung in a fine mesh outside my body, and the heart was my mouth; it was my heart which spoke and shot out a 'Hello!' on meeting a neighbour (the bank director's wife), who happily eyed me to assess if I was normal.

My heart thrashed there at my centre. My mouth. My red mouth. I was the subject, the theme itself. How could I then reach outside of myself and create themes of my own? How could I situate myself far away from the centre of the motif?

Ted knew this, that's why he was married to me: I was the nerves, I was the blood, I was the heart, I was the white skin, I was the string of pearls, I was the marble, I was the dove, I was the deer, I was the dead mole we found on the ground, I was the girl, I was the woman, I was the mother of his children. I was America, I was an entire continent, I was the future, I was the subject he wanted to discover, I was a person he wanted to colonise, he wanted to eat me, he wanted to shelter me, he wanted to conserve me. He wanted to fetch me home from America where I was born and let me feel the pulse of London in my heart and then he wanted to place me in a house in the countryside, in Devon among all the daffodils and birds. He bought me a bicycle. He fucked me hard on the sofa in the cold living room. I was a warm wet puddle beneath him that he came inside. It smelled of meat and blood. Sperm. Afterwards he felt almighty. He had conquered America, he had stretched his own limits, he had perfected the motif: the woman who must die.

The woman sentenced to death.

He had created me.

I lifted myself out of the puddle and washed myself, smiling happily. I was fertilised with his children his dream his promises. England. I stood on his land. His hare hunts. His apple trees, seventy-one of them (I counted seventy-two). His words, his trees, his writing. His voice. I completed life for him. I let one of his children fall to the universe from my flesh. Frieda. An apple from the tree. Red mouth, red heart, red pulse. Then I also felt that I was alive. 'Nothing has made me happier than the children,' I wrote in a letter home to my mother. But I also knew that everything I said and wrote (MY ENTIRE VOICE; WHAT I WAS) would one day be used against me. My reality shape-shifted by the minute, Ted knew; one minute I was content, the next I was happy, the third I was in despair, the fourth I wept, sweated, I longed, I wished and hoped.

None of this could really be taken seriously.

So when the bank director's wife ran into me downtown, once I had managed to wiggle off the seat (I was very pregnant again), I wished that I was her, that I was the one looking at HER, not her looking at me. I, Sylvia, must be so much more beautiful to look at, and still I could not see myself!

I smiled tightly out of my breathlessness, wiped a bead of sweat from my face. Warm in the warm clothes. Downtown was decorated: Christmas was just a few weeks away. The bank director's wife had bought something I also should have bought. I noticed how I did not at all let her take up space in her own right but how I also, subtly, had already colonised her, helped myself to her priggish appearance downtown and given her the power to fire up anxiety and stress inside me.

'Package to pick up?' she asked.

'Indeed, I want to make sure to keep up certain subscriptions from the US,' I replied and regretted giving such a long and elaborate answer to something which was actually quite simple.

I wondered what it would be like to be her friend but dismissed the thought with a new thought: God, what a hideous coat.

'And where is Frieda?' she asked.

I smiled sharply out from beneath my sweatiness.

'At home with her father,' I replied proudly.

'He's good, your husband,' said the bank director's wife.

'Ted,' I reminded her. 'Ted Hughes.'

The bank director's wife nodded. She looked as if she were mulling something over.

'Would you care to come over for dinner some evening? Just to share a meal with us. I thought it might be time for us neighbours to get to know each other. Would . . . tomorrow work?'

So . . . so *prudent*. Of course. She caught me – see, how clever she was in taking the opportunity! Dealings between people were not at all as they were in my home country, where you could easily say the words I Love You to someone with whom you had merely shared a half-hearted dull meal. I Love You – you simply broke off a piece of your heart, it did not need to imply that you were entering into a particularly intimate alliance. But here in England it seemed as if socialising had to follow a strict regulatory framework: you did not socialise out of desire, but out of a peculiar sense of obligation. *It might be time for us neighbours. We must. We cannot live next door and see each other daily without also showing each other who we are, the old dusty furniture we keep at home*. Oh, I couldn't bear it. But I also could not bear to look her in the eye and say: No. No! I don't want to! Forget it!

I retrieved the package from the young man behind the counter, and there was something about my being that made his eyes wobble, or was it nerves, mouth like a heart, the red pounding and pounding. The nervousness.

I turned toward the woman:

'Sure,' I glittered. 'We've got nothing else going on.'

The bank director's wife smiled smugly from inside her fur coat. She was *bubbly*. So be it, I thought: Now I'd made somebody happy.

'Lovely, dear!' she shouted as she headed off across the square.

Why didn't I ever learn! Fetch packages, do everyday tasks, ride a bicycle, fire off words like 'hello' and 'thank you', as if it was the most strenuous thing in the world. On a daily basis, people did things far more demanding and all I did was: 1. be pregnant, and 2. bicycle and fetch a package downtown and not even *that* could I manage, not even that could I manage without leaving some kind of imprint on the world.

Must I? Must I really? Must I be a living circus? Must I have to have a heart? Do I have to remind people of something – of their own feelings and motives? Do I have to be a living, breathing era cycling around?

I had my package on the bicycle rack, the handlebars swaying. I was disappointed because the errand downtown had already come to an end and what I'd had in mind – for something to happen, for a thought to appear, a line of poetry to start into motion from the exertion, or for something hilarious to happen, something silly – nothing. Not a word in my head, no opening of a chapter, no novel, no character took shape. Nothing.

★

It was two o'clock when I stepped onto the porch, heavy and enormous in my troll-like body. I was home again. Home in the kingdom I shared with Ted Hughes.

And Frieda. She approached me, leaned her little one-year-old body against mine. I preempted her and said: Mommy can't carry you now; you're too heavy. I nearly kicked her off while struggling out of my coat, kept my woollen sweater on.

I realised that Ted was writing, in my studio.

He hadn't discovered me yet, but now he got up from the chair in front of the typewriter and shuffled down the stairs.

'Are you writing?' I asked. He looked caught red-handed. I wore my amazed smile, the one that juts out so sharply.

'I wrote a few lines, yes,' he confessed. 'They want me to turn in more material for the BBC.'

This tall, burly man. Brown hair, long face, sharp nose. Our house was cold, freezing upstairs and down; we needed to light a fire. It was wrong to have been writing while I was out, free; it was I who should have been free at that moment, free downtown on my bicycle. And still . . .? Still, he had written?

'How do you do it?' I asked and bent down toward our daughter, blew her nose. 'As soon as I do something else for a mere second, she comes and tugs at me.'

Ted shrugged.

'Like I said, I was just going to get a line down.'

Frieda had parental affection and love to catch up on. I thought I could sense that she had been alone for a long while. Now she needed someone. She hung at my hip, but I was too tired after the bicycle ride.

'Do you have a package?' Ted asked.

I sniffed at the package – it had lost its charm. So what?

'Eh,' I said dismissively. 'Just some magazines from my mother.'

'Sounds lovely,' Ted said. 'Good to have something that gives you pleasure.'

Was he serious? I looked up at him. He must be kidding. He must be ironic. He couldn't be serious . . . Would a bunch of ladies' magazines from America really give me pleasure?

'Like I said, it's nothing,' I said and stood up with a violent urge to throw Frieda to the side, her body clamped to my hip like a puppy to its bone.

'We're invited to dinner tomorrow night,' I moaned while seated on a chair, wrestling on my woollen stockings. 'Maybe their house is warmer. The Tyrers'. I ran into the bank director's wife downtown.'

'I see,' Ted replied. 'Then I can review my BBC projects with someone who might show some interest.'

What did he mean? What kind of blackmuddy galaxy was contained by what he had just uttered? Was he tired? Was he upset? Was it not my prerogative to be tired and upset? An anxious butterfly fluttered through me. It had been lying in wait all day and now its brittle wings made my insides tremble. The butterfly was locked up and searching for the right exit and rushed straight into my flesh. I searched for a word.

'Has Frieda slept?' I asked instead.

'No, go ahead and put her down,' Ted said.

'Has she eaten lunch? It's two o'clock!'

'There's bacon.'

'What did you eat?'

'I wasn't hungry for lunch.'

I sighed, opened the hatch to the fireplace in the living room and tossed a log onto the bed of coals, but it did not spark a fire as I had hoped: instead, the log squelched the flames, the fireplace went black. It was freezing in our house – the midwife had told us that we needed to have it warmer by January, when the baby arrived.

'SHE ATE BACON FOR BREAKFAST!' I shouted so the child in my stomach did a somersault from the exertion.

'So give her wax paper, then! Bacon is what we have!'

I had no reply.

'I'm finishing this poem now!' Ted continued impatiently, got up and closed the attic door behind him.

'Bacon,' I said to Frieda and felt how I was suddenly starving. I took the pan off the hook, surrendered to hunger. A small part of me poured out. I wore my large cobalt-blue sweater, bulky like a tent across my stomach; it did not do me justice. Atop the large mountain (that was me) a large, greasy stain was forming. I stood and watched as it spread across the wool. I began to cry, grimacing away my tears but the weeping was there, and it stung. Damn poem! The long slice of bacon had lain wiggling in the pan for a while, now it was stiff and hard on the plate. I cut it up for Frieda. She chewed and recoiled in disgust since the meat was acrid and far too salty. I had cooked it for too long. I grabbed her plate, impaled another slice of flaccid bacon and fried it again, lowering the heat on the fluttering flame beneath the pan.

It was my responsibility to set things right.

Once, she had been pure and innocent and ate only milk from inside me, milk that streamed from my breasts and that I was not entirely clear as to where it came from. Milk. White, warm milk. Now my breasts were large and sensitive again, and I had been so horny this last trimester, I had wanted it every night. But Ted had not quite comprehended what I was doing. I spooned him, but since my belly pressed against his back we never made actual contact. He would sigh, turn away. I dragged myself after him, my arms and legs hot and sweaty even though our bedroom was cold.

So, eat now, child. I gave Frieda the softer slice of bacon. She sucked on it, laughed. It was as if her smile was etched into her: perhaps as a defence, I thought, as armour against the darkness she sees in her parents, against which the smile bars entry like a guard. I also thought: Frieda is hard as rock. She will outlive us all.

Why was I not happy today? Why had I woken up with the grey sky in my head? Today was just a day like all the rest. What made this day think it was so damned special? How could one person, a single person's movement through the day (the bank director's wife downtown), so completely sabotage my reality? She was stuck in me, her smug smile, so full of herself and at the same time *wanting to know*. She wanted to know things about me and Ted and Frieda. It was never like that in London: there, we were alone and protected by the streets. Here, everything was raw, bare, and it was unpleasant on the verge of dirty to be in the hands of others like that. I was a rat scuttling about, wanting to remain undetected, and they wanted to capture me. Would I persevere? It was crowded here in the English countryside; I was from Boston, which by comparison was like living by the ocean.

I sat down on the sofa to read the first issue of *Ladies' Home Journal*. Red sofa, dark room, pale winter light from the windows. In a letter to Mother I had written that I suddenly loved to sew and do crafts, that this was what the pregnancy did to me: made me lazy and lovable. I wanted to read ladies' magazines and not at all devote myself to any intellectual activity. But now, as I opened the magazine, that was not so. Now I opened the magazine and in that moment I betrayed my mother.

The magazine's slick pages and colourful pictures of potted plants and yellow and green sofa upholstery made me feel nauseous and empty. This was what I had written that I loved. This was what I had asked my mother for. This care. A freshly baked fluffy white bread swelled up in one of the pictures. A white loaf one could bake on one's own. It tugged at me, it was a greeting from home, it was a sign: oh, how delicious homemade white bread would be, something delectable to toast in the oven in the morning. The recipes in England were dreadful: they put cinnamon and nuts in everything – currants, lemon peel, it was so *ugh*. I would bake a loaf of white bread.

Ted was down from upstairs: he was opening an envelope in the kitchen. Three letters had arrived for him. He sounded happy: he had been contacted by the Writers' Guild. Grant awarded. He brayed with sudden joy at the kitchen table. I paged through the magazine, but did not look at the spread, did not read the letters. It was good news for the family! Why, then, was it as if something froze in place inside of me? What was this worry I couldn't rid myself of? NOW HERE I WAS IN MY OWN STILL-LIFE, TIMELESS PERFECTION, I WAS SITTING HERE. Be happy! I was the pregnant wife of my author husband, wasn't that what I wanted? I uttered the words 'Congratulations, how wonderful,' and got up and kissed him with great effort since my body was so enormous. I thought: I will write about this to Mother. I will blaze the words out, send them out like little ice-skating princesses on fresh ice. My words will wear little bows tied to them. Letters were my strongest suit in this regard: there, I could remain in how things ought to appear. I could represent, linger in the glory of everything being stable and complete, where the reality the words pointed to was still possible. My letters contained existence as it should be, not like this idiotic day that did not at all want to obey me – and then this was still just a day like any other day.

And yesterday, when no notices had arrived – I had slept worse during the night and had really only stayed at home and cooked with Frieda while Ted was in London working – then I had been completely blissful. The day to me was exactly as days ought to be: I felt a promise in my chest, I felt the chugging along of December, I tied little red silk ribbons around the curtains, I played games with Frieda that actually *amused* me, I decided that this was how my days as Ted's wife at home ought to be.

I frantically tried to write yesterday's recipe in my head. What was it I had pulled off? Why didn't worry leave me as it had yesterday? Was it that I had simply cooked the cod with parsley sauce and not baked a cake for dessert? Was that what had broken into pieces today, that I had completely worn myself out by bicycling downtown? Was it Ted's absence yesterday that had been so delicious? Why could I not bear it when he was here? Was it the pregnancy, that I had slept much longer and deeper last night, and in a way never wanted to stop sleeping – if I gave myself up to sleep I discovered how tired I was – was it Frieda's fault, who was much needier and whinier and clingier today? Was it that Ted was writing? Yes, it was probably that Ted was writing, and that his writing reminded me of the awful hole I had in my head, from which wonderful literature would never again pour forth.

The phone that had been unplugged had now been plugged back in by Ted, and he stood in the hallway talking to someone in his soft, considerate voice – the kind of prosody you always wanted to be on the right side of. He had called someone, he spoke, recounted: the entire house would fill with his voice.

I felt Ted's grant erode my own, the one I had received in late summer and whose commissioned production I had completed in advance. An entire novel, which I titled *The Bell Jar*, for lack of anything better. Next summer, the money would be gone . . . And I had baked a son for us in the oven of my body; that was what I had been up to, nothing else, no writing.

Ted finished the conversation and returned with a hand to the small of my back, because he had realised that I was moaning on the couch and then he wanted to be of help.

'Shouldn't you lie down and rest?' he asked.

'I was going to bake bread.'

Ted sighed.

'You don't need to bake bread now,' he said.

'But we have no bread at home. It's Friday. You want bread for breakfast too, don't you?'

'Let me do it,' he said. 'You stay here.'

I lay down on the sofa, beaten. I thought: he won't do it. I wanted to bake bread for my family, period. The family must have bread! Was I the only one who understood this? In a way, I longed for the baby to arrive and for us to become a real family, a real family of four. Right now, we were a couple with a child. When the baby was born, Ted would have his hands full – then he would be *forced* to bake, forced to take care of me . . . I looked forward to it.

The kitchen cupboards rattled. I pushed away my desire to waddle into the kitchen and meddle with Ted's baking. What kind of bread would he bake? A bad one, surely. Not a white, fluffy loaf. Why couldn't I be the one to bake the bread? Why wasn't I happy today? Why didn't pregnancy work on me? Why did I just feel musty and overripe? All of me had grown mouldy. There was no *I* left, only the transformation itself, the volcanic eruption. Sometimes that was what was so lovely about expecting: flying under the radar of the person one was normally treated as, becoming another, with other motives and expressions. A completely different apparition. But today.

I tried to retrieve another voice inside me, my mother's, my aunt's, my brother's: *Rest now, Sivvy. Let go and let yourself rest.*

I exhaled deeply. But I couldn't even manage that. Why should I rest if I didn't even want to? I wanted to write! I wanted to bake bread! I wanted to live like Ted!

And while Ted filled the kitchen with the most glorious life smells and topics of conversation ('I shall become a literary mogul. I love that word, "mogul": we will become moguls you and I, Sylvia, literary moguls'), I sat next to him humming and gnawing at his reality. I did it even though my ass hurt from sitting and even though I hated every inch of his brown British loaf, something I would barely be able to conceal tomorrow at breakfast, but that was a later problem.

What did the guilt consist of? Not feeling well? I took a frosty walk in the afternoon. The sun had released its last light onto the earth. The birds were awake even though the month of December did them nothing but harm. I dragged myself around; I thought, oxygen. Oxygen in my body. Oxygen in my hips. I was in service here on earth, I was a body with a body inside: I was two. And still I dragged my feet and regretted saying yes to that dinner tonight.

I had a piece of Ted's bread in my pocket, Frieda's breakfast, which I crumbled to bits between my fingers. The tall British bushes were a protective blanket between me and the homesteads. Frost, I thought. Frost-nipped. I walked here and still I was not dressed to greet what the world wanted to serve me. I was an ungrateful child. I had been given everything I ever wanted. I was soon in the home stretch of the Plathian dream: two children of four. Husband who wrote. Me who wrote. Grant recipient. Mother on the other side of the planet. Had the nerve to walk around and see everything that was so grand in a different light entirely. Why was I someone who went fishing in death and its murky waters? Me – old moth-eater, old fish – what business did I even have there? Get up and clean yourself of weeds, tear off the heaviness of your days. I was here, I was English, I was healthy and steady with a child in my belly. No reason. No reason!

I had a husband, crow, a husband and crow at home who wanted me. He took care of me. He desired me. He was attached to me . . . we were inseparable, of earth joined together. His coal-black damp fox-fur-bristly England, green with Irish grass. My enamel-white strained-pearlescent America, long-legged. And my mouth, once a wide cherry to sink your teeth into, red and juicy, now mostly resembling a fish, washed out, pulled out of the water – a sardine, the more Ted looked at me.

We were we. Why this guilt . . . why this feeling of guilt I now carried? It was just a walk, nothing else! It was just paving stones, it was just bushes, it was just weather. The walk made me awfully nervous about squandering time and not being productive. I walked and was material. Therefore, the guilt? I was not gathering material: I *was* material, but how could I assess the distance to my own material (which was me) and begin to create on those grounds? It was all I had ever wanted to do, it was all I had ever done, but it had never been enough. No one had really wanted it, and when someone had wanted it, it had not been exactly what I had wanted them to want. (THEM: *MADEMOISELLE, THE NEW YORKER*, MAGAZINES.) If only I had been allowed to decide! Then it would have become another poem, another short story or novel or essay, it would have been on my terms. But no one ever did as I wished.

I was wasted time. The pregnancy walking around and living in my body was the perfect example of my being adrift. I had even loaned out myself.

Guilt.

Once the day was like this I knew how it would reproduce itself. It was like dropping a bottle of black ink on the floor. It spilled out, contaminated, stained Ted, began to eat at him, finally it made him furious. There was no point in going to dinner. We would sit there and be lost since I was lost on this day, and Frieda would gnaw like a maddening eruption of guilt in me (she unravelled because I unravelled, because I felt like shit), and Ted would wish himself far away, perhaps even together with another woman.

North Tawton – sigh! The decay unfolded right before my eyes as the brown autumn leaves stuck to the bottom of my shoes. The villagers had me like a little doll in the palms of their hands and I knew I needed to dance. I needed to dance and sew and knit in front of them. Ted was a man: he could vanish upstairs to the little attic room and write as he wanted. I was public property, I was material. I was woman. Me, they wanted to capture.

Was that why I had sought out the Anglican church, our neighbours? Stood knocking on the large wooden door in order to be guided into the chapel. I had no desire whatsoever to play Christian, I did not proclaim any faith and I definitely didn't listen to anyone yammering on from the pulpit who did not take life and humanity seriously. Those priests never said anything meaningful, they spoke with straw in their mouths! Straw and blotting paper. They were dimwits disguised as important people and they boasted, for oh, how important and good they were. Blech! It disgusted me.

I took a few steps back on the gravel in order to look up at the church, so grey and mundane, hoisting its spear into the air. A perverse erection in the middle of all that oatmeal-grey Englishness. But then why had I sought them out, why was I so set on Frieda attending Sunday school? I wanted her to have a good childhood. I wanted to raise her into some kind of culture. In London, culture lived in the faces of the interested and well-travelled and urbane, the things they chose to speak about. Here in Devon, desire for knowledge was dead, the spiritual extinguished – church was where you had to turn.

I almost forced my way in when the rector opened: he had to back up in the face of my monstrous apparition. I stood in the freezing cold stone-lined vestibule with helpless eyes and regarded him. Will you take on my daughter? It does nothing but rain in England and she will grow quiet and mute like a doll with two writerly parents as her only source of inspiration. Someone has to help her, someone who is not me.

'My daughter will soon be two,' I managed to say and shivered, most audibly. 'Do you have any activities for her?'

'Are you the couple that just moved in?' asked the rector, who had a peculiar side-parting and picked at a sheet of music stuck into the worn psalm book.

'We live on Court Green.'

'Oh, the old vicarage.' His face lit up.

'We are the new promise,' I laughed and here was my smile, the smile I offered so unconditionally to priests and others who needed it. My smile that began in my mouth and could extend endlessly out onto my face. I wasn't always able to stay with the smile and offer *only* that, I needed to, as if dragged by a compulsion, follow the smile into its deepest, most distant corners . . . into the darkness. I needed to discharge the darkness. I needed to give away the joy and sorrow of my soul. I needed to force another human being to react against, *interact* with my darkness. I needed to make someone else perplexed, crestfallen. Here was someone who smiled with so much effort that she was impossible to take seriously! I undermined my own smile while pushing it out with such force; indeed, I hollowed out my entire being. And then I came crawling and needed to patch myself back together again before the other person. Needed to beg and plead that they still absolutely had to take me seriously, take my smile, I am someone, I really am a real person, take me.

I had to constantly put this circus of the self on display.

I couldn't stop the movement in my own blood.

Now I grew afraid, afraid that the rector would see the failure in my hollow American face, afraid that he could see that I wasn't actually happy.

Afraid of being sad in front of him. Maybe it's me, I thought, maybe I'm the one who needs a church, maybe I'm the one who needs a priest.

To confess.

Maybe I was the one who needed Sunday school, who was the child here.

I was handed a brochure from the rector's ceremonious hand that had surely never touched any such vibrating piece of flesh as what I consisted of, who had surely never sinned. Oh, could I not have an ounce of his dull meekness!

The rector looked into my brown eyes.

'You are very welcome to attend, as well,' he said and pointed to my belly. 'We have Evensong, Tuesday and Thursday.'

I felt how my nose of course dripped, and here I stood offering my violent smile.

'Thank you!' I curtsied, and realised how awful it was to curtsy before a priest. Were there other gestures? I extended my hand toward him.

'Frieda will benefit so from going to Sunday school,' I said and shook the rector's hand over and over. 'She really is in need of spirituality these days, and of discipline of course.'

'We don't discipline the children, perhaps we educate them,' the rector objected.

'Of course! Naturally.' Now I changed course. I wanted the rector to love what I had to say.

'Christian education,' I said, lying. 'That's really what we are searching for.'

The rector placed a ceremonious hand on my shoulder and showed me the way out.

'It will be nice to get acquainted with you at the vicarage,' he said and I smiled at the word, smiled at the moment and the nicety: nice.

'Very nice,' I replied. 'Thank you, sir, for seeing me in the afternoon like this. You have no idea how grateful I am.'

'There, there, no need to overdo things. We are here for whoever seeks us out, no more, no less. Frieda is very welcome with you or with your husband.'

He tired of me! He tired, right in front of me! I couldn't believe it was true! I hunched over with shame – I had missed the mark, I had exaggerated, I had squandered the opportunity to appear restrained and stable in his eyes. Capricious – I had revealed my capriciousness to a priest. Damn! When I got home I would appeal to Ted to allow me to rest against his chest and mock this damn English priest and his sense of his own perfection. Blah! I could throw up.

I smiled at the rector and waved. I stumbled out onto the gravel like a drunkard and wanted to go back home, home to the other who would save me from myself – Ted.

And at home with Ted I cried. I cried long, slowly sliding tears. We sat on the sofa and Frieda was still asleep. I felt anxious about the fact that she would soon wake up. 'It's so much,' I said. 'It's so much.' He asked if I was sad?

'I don't know,' I replied.

'But you're crying.'

'I'm just angry at that priest.'

'Why did you go there?'

I felt attacked by Ted's question. It froze and settled beneath the words that had just now comforted; like a cold dagger it lay there picking at me with its sharp blade. I didn't want more attacks, no more strenuous movement today – I'd had enough – we were already going to leave in a few hours, I needed rest, comfort. I needed to just lie and fall into Ted's beautiful arms.

Maybe it could suffice to remain here with him.

I felt my heart slow down.

His warm hand, that was what I had fallen for in Cambridge in February of 1956. His infinitely long fingers had almost wrapped themselves around my entire body, they could reach that far. They reached through the night. The heat never ended. I counted on them. I knew that I could not affect these fingers. I could not break them. Ted: you tall, beautiful bird, a large and enormous raven that extended its strong wings and wrapped me in them. Let me be held there. England was full of black birds who flew in flocks, small lost black birds who did not know where to go if they did not turn to each other. They looked like a swarm of bees high up in the sky, a lost corpse that desperately tried to gather its black limbs in the air. But Ted. Ted was immense, he was stronger than that. He was alone. He was the bird kingdom's giant, master of his own fate, a great poet, and all that swarmed in him was just that, words: the teeming black characters he filled the typewriter pages with. His own interior world, the one I was bolstered and fascinated by and which he was so calm and assured of that it had its own proper place in the universe, so he could afford to hear me out. Listen to my tentative formulations and hoarse cracked words.

I could see that encounter every time I looked into his grey, sometimes blackening post-war gaze. I could never forget it. We had followed each other through so many questions and together we had found answers. Ted had given me permission. Ted had forgiven me. Ted had held me. Ted had left me. Ted had returned. Ted had placed demands on me. Ted had asked me. Ted had stood beside me. Ted had come and gone. Ted had continued to be my friend. Ted had seen my depths and my difficulties. Ted had stood by my side and looked on. Ted had condemned me. Ted had come back anyway. Ted had changed me. For this, I had loved him the most. That Ted, slowly, had changed my way of seeing, speaking, and understanding things. Ted had permeated me, marked me. I had lain close beside him like a piece of glass on the shore, sanded smooth by rough waves. And now he got up and walked away.

Now he walked away from me. Such emptiness.

My jealousy of Ted knew no bounds. This was my greatest challenge, and I knew it. When he got up from our gentle moment on the sofa, when he wrestled out of our pit of consolation in order to help Frieda, who had woken up in bed.

Then I reached for him. I wanted to step into his body and for a few seconds be him. It was not enough to live alongside him. I wanted to live inside him. I wanted to get at his very core, I wanted to copy it or just get permission and access, maybe a key, to his body so that I could step into it and feel what it was like to be him when he walked, to be him when he stood large and powerful straight up and down on the living-room floor, resolute, assured of what he would now do. The heart in him beat so firmly and calmly, and conviction ran through him as smoothly as did his blood: he would go in to Frieda. He was father, he was raven, he had two legs which long and steady carried him through reality and now he had separated himself from me, whose body lay maimed on the sofa.

Maimed. The cadaver on the sofa.

It was an assault. It was an assault to leave me alone like this.

'How's my girl?' I asked Frieda, who had flown on Ted's strong arms out of the nursery. She rubbed her eyes sleepily.

'Mommy,' she said and reached her thin arms toward me, fell away from her father and requested my embrace.

Frieda's soft defenceless trusting childbody. I breathed in the weight of her lightness. Soft cottonperfect. Her radiant hair. I had an angel here in my arms and it also made my heart rear and pause. I held her for a moment full of suddenness, of unguarded joy. It was a moment also full of Ted – he remained and regarded us, the meeting of cheek with another cheek. He smiled at us. I burrowed into her with everything I had.

It was at moments like this that Ted mustn't leave me. And that was what he always did. He thought Frieda was all I needed, that motherhood was enough – I couldn't possibly need him and his blessed energy? Yes! If I could trip him, ensure that he had to walk with a cane! If only he wasn't always on his way away from me! My body was too heavy to stand here in the hallway and carry a one-year-old as well. It had just been a fun kiss on the cheek, now life had to go on. I also wanted to sit down, if only for a moment today, and look at my papers. I also had a letter to *The New Yorker* that I wanted to write. Did this entire house think that I didn't work? That I didn't bring in money? I would remind him that I had, in fact, been awarded a grant, which we were living on, and that the book already was written, the book that would shock the world (maybe) or at least entertain some lost soul (likely) or at least sit on a bookstore shelf and have *potential*.

Away, Frieda, away! I pushed her to the side, told her that she must be extra careful now that my belly was huge like a mountain.

'Whoth thewe?' Frieda asked and poked a finger into me. I had to smile, briefly.

'A little human being,' I replied. 'A heavenly little baby dove.'

'Whoth thewe?'

I wanted to call Ted back – his ears should also listen to

this. Frieda's amazement, her playful chatter and already so developed language. There should be two of us for each and every moment.

'Oh, my child,' I said. 'A fox lives here.'

I lay down in Frieda's little bed while she played. The light from the window fell differently in here: it was like a never-ending, sharp bolt of lightning. I closed my eyes while Frieda picked up toys to chew on or hand to me with equal parts childish expectation and solemnity. This was where I belonged – here, in the sweet, in the meaningless. I also wanted to go up to the attic and be important like Ted, but I knew that someone had to lie here and be infinite before their child. Extended in time, behind a belly high like a hill at a rundown playground. Someone needed to lie still and open wide while Frieda put a duckie in my mouth. It tasted of rubber.

I would like to cease, so fully become one with Frieda that the other grating of my intellect would not insist. I would like to hand in my letter of resignation to writing. If I opened my eyes I would see in Frieda's gaze that she thought it would be a fine idea. I knew that Ted felt the same way. I knew that the words I wrote to Mother when I asked for *Ladies' Home Journal* really were true. I meant it: *I love to just do crafts, sew clothes for Frieda and the baby and help myself to cookies and glossy ladies' magazines.* I knew that everyone loved it when my writing fell silent, because then also the wolf would fall silent (mostly).

I could live in the blessing of my body. Live at the complete mercy of my child.

She handed me a music box.

'Pway, Mommy,' she said.

'No, we might disturb Daddy.'

'Pway!'

And I played: it was 'The Internationale', I knew it was

the wolf's eyes darkly glimmering deep inside me. I felt that it wanted to bother Ted. I cranked the little handle, following Frieda's orders, faster and faster, until I heard steps upstairs: he would come down soon, he would come down soon—

Until he came with heaviness and wage labour in his steps and without glancing at me took over looking after Frieda.

Not a word.

I waddled upstairs while Frieda protested wildly.

The window just above our double bed had white, homemade curtains. Sewn by my hand. Now I would lie down here and write something. In the light that stretched its thin rays through the fabric: Devon's measly December light. I sank down on the covers, on my side so that the baby wouldn't stop the flow of blood and air to my lungs. My heart beat quickly. I felt with my hand – bangs – forehead – eyes – I was still here. Breathe slowly and deeply, I thought. Breathe into your heart.

I needed a respite for at least half an hour before I got dressed and ready for dinner.

It was these moments: I wished time were elastic and the wolf tame, that they would do what I wanted. If time obeyed me. If the wolf was tied up. Then the possibility would appear to both rest and write the letter to *The New Yorker* and get dressed up like a beautiful prima donna tonight, for Ted. But I just needed to survive time. Accept that it had its course, regardless of what I so heatedly wished for. I disliked being steered. The baby began to kick: that was what always happened when I settled in. It would come to life. It made my stomach bob, like ripples on an ocean, and I detected heartburn – my stomach was pushed so far up that its juices rode a carousel in my throat and into my mouth. I swallowed acid.

Opened the closet: would this do? This one? The clothes were cold, and my body was large and warm. Inflated. Inert. I pulled on some soft long underwear, black, it would have to serve as nylons, and I had let out the elastic in the waist so that it wouldn't press against my lower belly, where there needed to be room.

My thighs had swollen and they rubbed against each other as I walked. I was not beautiful: I could see it in the mirror. I had swelled up. Who lived in me? I moaned. I pulled on a dress-like item that mostly resembled an apron. It was sky blue. I would take it apart, I would sew a vest for Frieda instead. I tore off the clothes. I needed to wear something else. Why wouldn't anyone sew clothes for me? Why wasn't my mother here? Did Ted not understand how devastatingly gorgeous his wife would be if only she had slightly more stylish clothes?

I had felt a coolness from Ted for a while: the desire that my being had previously elicited had recently been replaced by a silence, a far-away quality to his eyes, as if he saw me but did not take me in, did not in his seeing take me in fully. He couldn't build a wall now, I thought. I couldn't handle walls. And I would only tear walls down, even if it called for claws. For there would be a bloody war between Ted's walls and my sabre-sharp claws.

I turned around in the mirror – now I was wearing something black instead, I looked bound for a funeral but it was a dress that attested to my dignity, which made at least my arms and legs look respectable. I painted a red heart on my large, swollen pregnancy lips. It looked like a heart someone had stepped on.

A young girl with a bouncy, dark bob opened the neighbours' door. She was soaked in a caustic perfume. How old might she be, sixteen? And she looked straight at Ted and then down at my large belly. I wanted to extend my hands and turn her gaze right, grip her chin and steer her until she looked me properly in the eyes. 'Nicola,' the girl greeted us politely. I took hold of the collar of Frieda's light-blue over-alls, which I just a moment ago had wiped clean with spit on my fingers. She tore at the baby hat until the string tightened around her neck. Right away, I was there helping her loosen it.

Ted said hello to the hosts in his half-polite manner. They had entered the foyer to greet us: the Tyrers, the young girl's parents.

'Pleasure, pleasure,' he said ironically with his long arm above me as I squatted below.

Why did he have to say it as if he didn't mean it? Now it was as if he was making a mockery of the Tyrers right to their faces, letting them know it was an inconvenience for us to come over. Enough, I had to take over, with my blazing, magazine-glossy smile, as I rose from Frieda's position on the floor and shot up like a doll from a TV advertisement.

Marjorie Tyrer kissed my cheek and took my coat before

shrieking with joy at the adorable and toddling Frieda. So adorable!

Frieda was handed an antique teddy bear to hold. She put her mouth to its nose and made the entire group exhale in unison, 'Oooh . . .'

My girl, I thought. Good girl. Half an hour ago I had sat hunched over her pee puddles on the floor, rubbing the rough cold rag across her behind until she screamed.

There, now. This was how things should be: representation.

The young girl Nicola gave us each a glass of sherry as a welcome drink; she carried them clumsily one in each hand – she could have used a tray. All the while she looked at Ted, brash, sassy, dumb. She had a stupid gaze, I thought, and studied her carefully. Clumsy, thick legs in white tights and an irritatingly short brown skirt. Her parents were older, advanced in age to have a teen in the house.

'Nicola's last Christmas at home,' Marjorie explained and carefully turned to me. I didn't want to converse about little Nicola so that she would feel talked about, so I just hummed and stared at a meaningless painting on the wall. Nicola had bent down to help Frieda turn the bear's head right. Marjorie's husband the bank director was eager to claim Ted: he had prepared by placing a stack of books on the glass table. Now he wanted Ted to withdraw from the quintet: a hand on his back, old George, in green with his collar out beneath his pullover, lifting the top book and letting Ted take over. It was apparently Auden, my old Auden who once made me begin to write. Now Ted was going to talk about poetry while I entered the kitchen with Marjorie, who stuck a fork in a roast and began carving.

A disgusting odour rose from the meat. I had to turn away in sheer misery, keeping an eye out for the daughter Nicola's exploits in the adjoining room. Through the cracked door I could see how she got involved in the two men's conversation:

entertaining Frieda was a mere excuse. She had already let go of Frieda's hand. I exited Marjorie's iron grip – naturally, she wanted to discuss various ailing women in the neighbourhood and explain their particular illnesses to me in detail – and took my glass of sherry into the living room. Bent down to the floor. I was Frieda's. Frieda lit up. Someone to play with me—

And Nicola?

She had one leg raised in a right angle to the easy chair, which made her body assume a peculiar sexual authority even though she was stupid and clumsy and a mere sixteen-year-old. Ted had begun to include her in the conversation. I could hardly believe it. He was going to speak with *her*? About poetry?

I needed to get a grip.

It was rare for a twenty-nine-year-old wife with one child and another on the way to need to make an excursion to the swampy darkness of jealousy.

She spoke of her desire for real poetry. To write. She would like to learn how.

I eavesdropped. I felt her perfume all the way to where I was sitting. Stranded on the floor with Frieda. Now Ted had turned his entire body toward her: he was talking to the brat. The brat's mouth hung open as she nodded. Had a tiny irritating tongue that smacked against her upper lip as she spoke. God, George, Marjorie: can't you shut her up?

How dare he . . . Ted?

My husband?

The person I reached for at night?

How could he bear to stand and speak with a teenage brat about poetry?

Couldn't anyone see that I sat sacrificed on the floor?

Was no one going to ask me to rise?

Why was I even sitting here?

I was invited to dinner! I was an adult! I was the woman

in the Plath-Hughes family. I was modern. I ought to be treated with interest and respect.

I gasped for air . . .

I needed to write about this!

All at once, that thought saved me. I pulled myself up – Frieda entertained herself with the bear – I fell back onto the squeaky leather sofa, cold against my behind. I exhaled.

Ted was deep inside his talking – 'I can read your poetry and give you feedback if that would be of interest to you' – as he turned around to regard me for a second.

He does not see me, I thought. He is inside his own words. He is inside the affirmation he gets from the young girl.

And George said something about a fox hunt. The girl giggled.

Was that what this was about: origins? Did these three have something in common that I was on the outside of? England, the British, so vague, for me so exhausting, so diffi-cult to grasp. A field full of grass. Swampland, boots for wading, the eternally gusty, damp air. Did the girl strike a chord in my husband because she came from a backwater similar to the one he . . .? My God. I could have interrupted and entered the conversation myself. It could have been she and I, deeply engrossed in a conversation about sisterly poetry. I felt a sting of sadness that things did not work that way. She was not the least bit interested in me.

The young girl stuck her stubby fingers into her glass. She pulled out a candied cherry and placed it in her mouth. She withdrew from the group and stomped into the kitchen, to her mother:

'Mother, I've been encouraged by Ted Hughes to work on my poems! It's great!'

'How wonderful!' her mother exclaimed in the kitchen, quickly kissing the girl's cheek. 'So brave of you! We're so grateful, Ted!'

We sat down at the table. I was closest to Frieda so that I could place things in her mouth. Ted sat the furthest away from me. He had the spot next to Marjorie and across from the old man George and diagonally across from the young girl Nicola, who also sat next to me.

I cut off pieces of the baked potato, mashed them with my fork and poured little green peas over the potato mountain Frieda would eat. If I had been at home, I would have done what I did when we ate steak: I would have chewed the beef myself and spat it out for Frieda, the way people did during the Stone Age. Ted thought I was disgusting when I did it, but I actually had a relative in America who had choked to death on a piece of meat, and I saw it as a point of pride to protect my children from death. But at a dinner party I of course felt it necessary to stick to a fork and knife.

During the rest of the meal, I sat listening to Nicola's chatter about girl things – this was the subject she had saved for me. She was very fond of going to the movies, she sighed.

'Really?' I asked, my hands covered in mashed-up food and shreds of beef, which I stuffed into Frieda's smeared mouth.

'Yes, and it's fun to imagine becoming an actress one day,' she went on.

'Is that so,' I casually replied, 'weren't you just talking about wanting to become a poet?'

She did not reply.

She wanted to talk about fashion, about Brigitte Bardot, about her plans to escape this damn backwater once and for all and become somebody famous, and I felt wounded to my very core since *I*, soon thirty years old and from glorious America, had just settled in this backwater, it was now mine, while I of course was gladdened by her plans to leave and agreed that she couldn't realise them soon enough.

On the way home from our neighbours' I couldn't help but congratulate myself that: 1. I could check the box that I had come to know the neighbours and, to boot, had managed it splendidly, and 2. I now had enough material to virtually complete a novel.

'It's my weapon,' I said while walking hand in hand with Ted along the black night street. 'It's my weapon, it's how I will persevere: I will write about them. I will write about these peculiar British neighbours. Don't they understand what parodies of themselves they are? George – his monotonous, hoarse, booming voice, as if he has swallowed a stack of bills down at the bank and can't cough them back up.'

Ted laughed: I saw his eyes sparkle, so I went on.

'Those greying hairs protruding from his nose and his complete disregard for anything other than manly things, and himself. Fox hunting – travelling to the south – souvenirs from trips to the south – weapons and ammunition. Bank business.'

I squeezed Ted's hand. We entered the foyer. The large vicarage had been our property for nearly six months but had never quite felt like home, until now. Ted carefully carried Frieda into the nursery and snuck back and gently removed my coat and hung it on a hanger. We giggled as he kissed me: we were colluding because the neighbours who lived nearby were utterly, utterly insane! Ted blew gently against my ear and was in a good mood – three glasses of beer, two sherries, one whisky with George – and spun around and stood so that he could press his sex against me from behind while his hands rested on my belly.

'Would you be so kind as to pass the mint sauce, dear

Sylvia,' Ted imitated the elderly banker George with his cracked pensioner's voice. He rocked against me: it was as though we did this in spite of the older, English generation — we were dancing in cahoots. And I broke down laughing so my knees buckled, and Ted had to catch me and give me a kiss, and something in my stomach tensed, as if a contraction were on the way.

I moaned. In spite of everything, it was his crown I carried within me, no matter how many wet gazes girls like Nicola threw his way. No matter how much desire was lodged behind her frontal lobe. It was me he had penetrated and branded. For a lifetime . . . It excited me, Ted's coarse hair against my thighs, his eagerness to bend me open – here and now – tonight. He undressed me completely. Unbuttoned my coal-black tent dress from behind. I so desperately wanted to hold on to that moment. Not jeopardise it with my usual comments, my way of directing and controlling. I would close my eyes. I closed my eyes.

His warm hands. He fell to his knees in front of me and worshipped my large belly. I giggled. He giggled as well. To think that I had not done that earlier today – giggled! I considered the word itself and giggled again and discovered how wonderful it was. Now I didn't want to stop. Giggling – so damn easy, and for me so hellishly hard. How many minutes in one day? An entire day – an entire eternity – a trip around the sun – an entire planet's effort in order for time to travel – and I had only replied with moaning and groaning. I wanted to giggle. I wanted to be caressed to the deepest and most pleasurable pit of the underworld and giggle death in the face. I stuck my tongue out for my Ted and made out right in the face of death.

Was it often like this? I stood naked in the room. Ted circled me and kissed my hips, my shoulders, my bloated upper arms, and lifted my long hair in order to have access to my neck. Was it often like this? I asked myself the question quickly since I didn't want to be distracted by thoughts, when I was here and so close to pleasure . . . But still. Was it often like this? That Ted and I uncovered a black pleasure in making love after the day's activities had been exactly like this, and I had been forced to wrestle with my wolf and my demons? The evil butterfly. Was it often like this? I could not get more turned on, I was at my peak, as if I was about to give birth. Ted kissed the spot where the very tops of my buttocks met. A glowing hot magma flowed from within me. He wanted to enter me. I heard him get up, heard the hasty clink of his belt buckle. His sex against my back, a malleable, warm baton. I needed to stay in place, my belly would be in the way if I turned around, and he pressed against me and kissed me fiercely, his moaning broke against my neck, my ears. I replied with a plaintive groan. I had been so turned on during this final trimester, could I be carrying a son? Was it testosterone I had coursing through me? Was that also why my jealousy took on an entirely different tenor? I could recall none of this from Frieda.

Ted: his darkness finally came, it was his turn, it rode forth. It was when my darkness flowed into him and I stood up like a white angel in the night. It was when Ted consumed my daytime anxiety and transformed it into love-making. It was when he'd had a bit to drink and he accepted that his hands were demanding and pleasurable, that they were hands which belonged to a body, that they were desirous.

It was when he ceased struggling with his weak marble eyes, his poet's gaze, when he no longer saw only fragility everywhere he looked, when Ted no longer judged me for being the anxiety-ridden person I was and measured his distance to me so that we could live together.

It was when I suddenly no longer threatened Ted.

It was then we could make love.

Ted – his name like a yellow teddy bear – his desire bore such a remarkably angelic quality, it was sheer and childish, as if his mother had never marshalled a sexual role model in herself, so had not been able to provide that for him. I had called him *allergic* to intimacy. Patronising, I had scolded him for not being romantic enough. A kind of slackness to his body, a desirelessness. As if the only thing that could spark Ted's curiosity and eagerness to the utmost degree was himself. Such an enormous sorrow in that. Such a tremendous mistake of living . . . an *error*. Inside me, I hated his mother for turning him into this. For not giving her son a libido! No sexuality? There was such gentleness to his touch – and with that gentleness came the fact that when he was turned on, he became horny in such an adolescent way that it was hard to take him seriously – he squeezed his eyes shut, placed a careful hand on your breast and kneaded, as though he were seventeen.

Seventeen and Victorian – an antique teddy bear.

Me! I was made for more expansive heavens! I had been fucked by machismo! I had had all variety of hot-tempered lovers. And how they had taken me . . . How I had made love to them . . . Ted and I had never come close, and at times this thought amused me. I had the upper hand compared to Ted due to how his sexuality lacked any kind of heat.

He was cool like a canned ham.

And, every once in a while, it was all I had, as the one thing to hold against him.

But on nights like these, when I also dared to be completely naked, when I simply made up my mind. When I noticed that something had come undone due to the level of intoxication in his blood and that we had measured ourselves against bigger fools than ourselves – the Tyrers. Perhaps we had even been injected with a dose of passion straight into the flesh by virtue of that sixteen-year-old's wretched heat – whatever it might be.

Here we stood, and there was moonlight, and he would thrust into me. And everything warm would run out of him and out of me, simultaneously, while I rested my elbows against the bed and pressed my large behind against his body.

Afterwards, as I stood before the mirror and regarded myself and my face was aglow with love and sweat, I wished the mirror were a camera so that a photo could be snapped of my smile just now. I wanted to be photographed exactly when the world flowed through me and left its mark on the mirrored glass, how the elasticity of my skin could reach all the way through to the reflection, my tousled hair, how erotic I felt inside. Ted was in the bathroom wiping himself down, rummaging around. I was not afraid that his thumping noises would wake a little Friedagirl, not now, with my senses wide open. What was alive should live. I picked up the comb and ran it through my warm hair. The damp rill left me as I moved, like a small birth. I smiled at my reflection. I should always appear to the world like this: a gorgeous moment pinned in time, nailed to the mirror. My damp skin my softened limbs me. Ted had handled me as if I were royalty. I played the lead, took centre stage, I had a face that babies like the dilettante Nicola Tyrer could only dream of. Lolita, Brigitte Bardot – and me. Sylvia Plath, the poet. My eyes stared right back at me. Small, tiny pupils of light.

Yes, this is how it is, I thought, and smiled yet again, devilishly. I am a hysteric. My husband fucks away my anxiety.

'I will buy a pedestal for you,' Ted comforted me and kissed the tip of my nose in the kitchen. 'I will buy a pedestal for you and place you on it, and I will worship you, kneel at your feet.'

But I was not in the mood.

In one hand I held a carrot, which I glumly took a bite of. I was supposed to laugh, but I scoffed. It was apropos of my writing, because Mrs Jennings had been in touch by mail to inform me that they did not have space to include a short story I had written in the next issue of *The New Yorker*. (I had waddled out and greeted the mailman charged with bringing me the world's most golden fruits in the December frost, but was disappointed and now the rejection letter flopped in my hand.)

It was the American market. And it was when the American market let me down that it felt as if the ground gave way beneath my feet, that I had no place to call home. It was as if all of Great Britain was an illusion, and I stood barefoot in the middle of the ocean where the Atlantic met the North Sea. I was a stranger in this country: they did not receive my poetry very well, but so what, their loss, was my thinking – I still had my America. My ace, my America. My safety in my mind, my glittering flashing paper lanterns, my

America. My way of becoming real before these sluggish Europeans. Perhaps they couldn't make sense of my coarse made-up similes but that was also because I was an American and wrote differently and within a different tradition. And America will publish me, America looks out for me, I had counted on it. As a result, the phrasing in Jennings's letter was so deadly: *It wasn't exactly a writing process I thought I would be reading. You are naturally welcome to submit the complete manuscript when you are done.* (In my arrogance I had thought it would be possible, yes, even welcome, to send material in progress to her, to get a little nudge, to get her comments, but yes, why did I even send her this project? Could I recall? If I asked myself, and I did, in the kitchen in front of Ted, who had simply tried to cheer me up while I cried and ate a carrot all at once – if I asked myself, was it because I needed to be seen validated loved all over again? Was it one of my methods? Was it time again, time to make myself vulnerable in order to then be rejected in order to then throw wide open that greedy hole in me, the one that *ate* rejection? That devoured it like so much food?)

Now I wanted to set her letter on fire.

Ted took the letter from my upset hands that were about to toss it into the flames. 'No, Sivvy,' he said. 'Don't get stuck in your resentment of the editors in this way. Resentment can't save you.'

'But I had counted on being published!'

'In that case, this is about you counting on things.' He was so calm, how could he be so calm when a new life was swirling around in my system demanding my complete attention, and the editor in America didn't even address me with the most basic courtesy? She did not even strike a polite tone.

How could anyone be calm?

'You had built up expectations – please don't do that.'

On these occasions, Ted was supportive, he wanted to help.

He pulled the carrot from my snot-covered hand and placed it on the kitchen counter.

'Do you want a cup of tea?' he asked.

'I tried!' I said. 'I did everything I could do to achieve the tone I know they want. Everything! Don't you get it: I struggled for more than a month, all of October, and now I'm hugely pregnant and don't have the energy to think about it any more. Just this one tiny published puzzle piece and I would be more than happy to sit and knit baby hats on the sofa. Now I can't even do *that* – which I'd been so excited about . . .'

Ted lit the burner beneath the kettle.

'I come along with my big desire and want want want, but I'm the only one who wants!'

At that point, Ted reached out his long arms and held me, offered me the deep thumping of his chest. A steady freight train through the night. I was his. He made my breathing slow down. I could fall asleep in his arms.

This reality was too fatal for me: it wanted to do me harm and I stared at the kitchen cabinets, the brown wallpaper, the faltering firewood turning to a gentle glow in the open hatch of the wood stove. The December light spitting reality back at me. I could never be rid of it. Were I a master of the short story I would be able to use all of it, then the tough, the musty, all the smells of morning lingering in the leftovers from Frieda's breakfast, the grime on the wood floor and this baby – truly, this baby – who ate and ate of my flesh would be of use at some point and earn its keep. All of life's tasks forced upon me, what everything looked like and was and felt like inside me – oh God, if I couldn't describe it and transform it into meaning and dignity for others, then my life would be over.

The editor didn't know that my earthly right to exist was attached to the story I had entrusted her with! For a month, I had dreamt – ever since I sent it in – of how she would laud me in her reply. Finally, a master in depicting the reality we all saw and endured – finally. I had come up with scenarios for what my authorship would look like going forward. When Ted had gone upstairs to the attic to write, I had been consumed by the idea of how wonderful it was that the two of us were working, married, writers. Poet and novelist. The short story would be published and make a name for me in advance of the publication of the novel I had already completed and won praise for – *The Bell Jar* – that would, God willing, take readers by storm. You had to work slowly and methodically. Ted had gone upstairs to the attic and I, I had everything under control, had no reason to feel the evil feeling of jealousy when Ted sat down and wrote the most magical pieces for the BBC, as if his fingers were not merely fingers but magic wands he waved across the typewriter. And voilà, the BBC had exactly the kind of radio material they wanted – never any gaps, never any cause for concern regarding either subject or consequences – and if there had been any, well, then I would have jumped in and patched all the holes, happily spent a night editing his writing.

Ted talked about the cosmos – was there, then, no cosmic justice?

We were in a car headed toward the ocean on the western end. Ted was at the wheel.

Everybody else was a poet except for me.

Adrienne Rich, for example.

Ted Hughes, for example.

Marianne Moore, with her infamous nastiness, which she had doused me with at a cocktail party in New York after I had shown her my trembling poem.

The larger my stomach grew, and it did, the more certain I became that my life was moving backwards while others' lives were rushing forwards.

I sat in the car Ted was driving, a black thing that would take us all the way to the ocean. And I knew from the moment I sat down in the front seat next to him that this was a bad idea: it was December and rainy, and still he insisted on proving to me, in the optimistic Ted manner that sometimes came over him—

That *this is a good idea*.

You need to see the world, Sylvia.

You are not locked up.

The world is here for you.

And as if through a mourning veil, I regarded all of it. The radio informed us that a child had been beaten to death on a beach in northwest England, was that not where we were headed?

'No, Sylvia, we are further south, please, don't worry now.'

The word please said with particular emphasis.

I clicked off the radio.

I huddled in my seat in a foetal position, tried to rest on my side a bit. There was a mountain parked on top of my body and I had a sea beneath it: I already had an ocean, did not need to go look at one.

But in a moment of weakness I had said that I 'needed an ocean' and so Ted decided I should have an ocean.

Valley upon valley of undulating hills in the labyrinth that was Devon and which you constantly wanted to escape from (if you were me), a stern grey light from the heavy sky and then us.

Tucked into a car, quiet, jolted about.

How was I to know whether or not it was the particularly lousy roads as we approached our destination that made me nauseous and gave me heartburn. The baby was already enormous and now it stomped its feet upwards; at each turn juices rose from my stomach and into my throat.

'Stop,' I said. 'I want to throw up.'

Ted turned in by a narrow gravel road. I tumbled out and crouched in a ditch. But only air emerged. Ted looked at me through the windshield. Easy for him to sit there in judgement of someone like me. It was as if he had wanted me to throw up.

'Nothing?' he asked when I returned.

'Stop!' I looked at him sharply. 'I am trying to survive here.'

'Don't you want to go to the beach?'

'Of course I want to go to the beach. Take me there.'

Ted wanted to show me that England also had the ocean, England was also lined with bountiful ocean beaches, where the seals came to rest in the sun, and in the summers you could sink down into the warm gravel and gather special rocks and feel the Atlantic breeze shoot straight into your skin as you swam out.

I so often complained about England: here, you could never see the ocean!

So Ted wanted to do me a favour. It was the romantic side of Ted, the one which occasionally (once a month, when he was inspired by me) wanted to bake a loaf of bread, repair a child's toy, place a catalogue order for seeds. England was actually not a very romantic country, not deep down, if you didn't count that saccharine cute and tea-addicted Beatrix Potter-aesthetic as romantic. So innocent, so benignly Victorian. Not even Victorian with *an edge*. Not even – and this was true, I had witnessed it myself – darkness with *an edge*.

Ted was otherwise fond of me because I was a source of utter darkness! A treasure trove of darkness, an American font of black sludge.

And I was in England merely as a refugee from the darkness and if he had been the least bit interested in me he would have understood that.

'We're there now.' Ted parked the car and turned off the engine.

The rain was even heavier here, the car windows were swimming with water and I could not see the ocean.

'It's down there. Come on. I want to show you the ocean. We're there.'

Ted opened the car door and through the crack I could see the ocean, the one that would carry me all the way home to America if there had been a boat here to take me back: it was a vast, unapologetically raw ocean, which did not adorn itself with white beaches. We stood on a cliff leading straight down into the raw ocean; it was a steep drop and the waves were gigantic.

I felt the tug of vertigo. The thick round baby stomach I bore, the child in there. I carried an entire planet, and Adrienne Rich had started to publish regularly, truly, and here I sat in the front seat of a black car on a cliff near Woolacombe Sands in December.

I didn't want to be me. I felt a responsibility toward the baby to remain in the car and not take any chances, but Ted would have none of it: he would never understand what it was to be shackled, for he was free, free to simply stretch his legs out of the car and walk down across the cliffs to this coarse, crashing ocean.

'I feel too nauseous. I don't want to. The ride made me car sick. I'm sorry.'

Ted's hair blew in the wind. The chilly air gusted through the door into the car, smelling of sex and seaweed and hard, wet, ice-cold rock. He sighed, extended an arm: I would have liked to make him happy by being on board with this trip with him, just the two of us, Frieda with the sitter, stuffed full of juice and cookies – just he and I.

And here I was with my bovine body, withdrawing and tying myself to the back seat. Sitting here, sobbing, and he saw that I was a victim, all he would see was this victim of circumstance who could not manage to throw off her chains and just get up with a chuckle, explore a stretch of the western shore with him.

When he had made his way down the cliff and was no longer visible through the foggy glass, the reflux ceased and words streamed through my head, words.

I could lean back against the seat and feel how the baby stopped kicking me right in the oesophagus, and a calm settled over me, almost like sleep.

I was so at peace when Ted was no longer here, something happened to me. As soon as he removed himself from my life, I was at ease, and this time I marvelled at it. The same thing had happened when we tried to live like two grant-funded authors at Yaddo in Saratoga Springs. Naturally I should be able to think when he was around – but no. His demand that I be a girl who could write and also feel happiness was enough to make me gag. In reality, he constituted the sour juices in my throat. My body was nothing but a reaction.

I sat there in my loneliness and wrote a poem. The space of my mind became sacred. Here, it already felt as though I stood before an ocean and had hurled out an enormous net in order to catch a very particular fish. I already had oceans of sea in my mind, in the store of my memory: I had grown up by the sea, already had the sea in me. I wrote the poem with that feeling and when Ted returned, soaked and with a stern ice-cold furrow between his brows, I attacked him with assistance so he could change clothes and we could return home safely.

'Can't you drive?' he asked while drying off with the blanket I had handed him from the back seat.

Reality came crashing down in me upon being asked that question. He disturbed my peace of mind with his reality. Did he seriously want my hands on the wheel? As pregnant as I was? All the way home?

I only shook my head, and he sighed.

'So fucking beautiful down there,' he said. 'The vast, wild ocean. It was like standing face to face with the universe.'

'Good for you,' I said.

He dried his hair so that it nearly stood up straight like a broom.

'We both have to get out the next time we come here,' Ted said. 'Maybe then you'll have had the baby, and it will be summer.'

He kissed the tip of my nose and drove off.

A pile of knitting lay on the living-room table. I had put it there, and now it stared at me from my place on our red sofa.

I thought that the entire world should revolve around me and my knitting because I had chosen to knit and so of course my story had to do with that, the issue was simply that no one else in this house cared about my story.

I looked out the window, at the father and child.

They had headed out – they saw me seated on the sofa, knitting, and Ted uttered the words, 'How cosy, we'll go out and work in the garden,' while Frieda held up her red little rake. The fifteenth of December, grey, gusty winter in England and I had a bit more than a month of pregnancy left. From the crack beneath the front door, the December winds of Devon snuck in beneath my feet. It was frigid at night but now the sun had returned, it made everything mild for a few hours in the middle of the day.

They headed out and left me on my own. In one fell swoop there was nothing at all pleasurable with the knitting. It vanished, its potential dead. I had something that gave me pleasure, but how could I enjoy it if Ted wasn't there to witness it? I'M KNITTING, I should have said, I thought to myself, and at that moment drawn his attention to me.

Oh, if only he was the one who took *an interest*. It was

so rare for him to be in the mood. Most often, he was far too preoccupied with what he himself was up to. And immediately our roles were cemented. For when he ignored me, my primary interest shifted from what was mine, me, my world, to what was his. Only only his. Ted's. And I could no longer remain in my knitting. I had to go out. I had to go out and be in his definition of what it was to live. Everything true, everything accurate, everything primary. Him.

I took a sip of the cooling tea that stood on the table. Taste of dirt in my mouth. I should be able to help with something out there, even if it was only to scatter bone meal on the bulbs. There was so much to do here in our large lovely house. What was knitting compared to all that? What was I compared to all that was him?

Bone meal.

With great effort, I was able to put on my rubber boots and walked out into the wind with my smile and box of bone meal. They hadn't seen me yet, stood over by the apple tree inspecting branches. Was there something he was going to chop down? Frieda stood on the ground in the gusty wind and had gathered twigs in a pile as if for a fire. Her hat flew off and I could hardly hear how she howled as she ran after it, the wind drowning out her voice.

Everywhere, the grass revealed last year's dead foliage, what had flourished before our eyes last summer when we bought the place. Never before had I been so happy. The house had beamed at us and showed us who we were: it was like standing before a mirror and being validated. All the other houses we had looked at had carried something dark and miserable about them. Nothing but boredom, British ordinariness. We could never see ourselves in a house like that. Ted and I – we needed something rundown that had once been grand and important, which we with our special glow and strength could bring to life. Vicarages were built with pride and from robust materials.

All that was needed now was a young couple to take it upon themselves to carry the past into the future. Ted and I and our children. I cooed like a dove, I was on my way into the ease of the second trimester, had small downy baby rabbits nesting in my chest. I raised my chest toward Sir Arundel, who owned the place, pushed out my belly, showed him how pregnant I was. I wanted him to love us. He should love us for who we were and because I bore a new child into his house and because I was so beautiful and because my entire dream stood there on the kitchen floor dancing before us, and was also exactly what we bought. We bought my dream. The owner smiled half-heartedly but it didn't matter at all, I could overlook it, only because the feeling itself was so full. WE DID IT. We did it! Now we only needed to tend to what we had been given.

'Are you sure?' Ted asked, full of concern, he who had up until this moment been so confident.

'COMPLETELY sure. COMPLETELY sure,' I sang. 'I just need to borrow the phone and call Mother.'

She was the one who would lend us the money. Trembling, I dialled the number to Ted's parents in Yorkshire, where Mother was staying.

'WE DID IT, MOTHER!' I shouted. My eyes teared up from the effort. 'WE DID IT, WE BOUGHT THE HOUSE! WE'VE FOUND THE ONE!'

Mother was as defenceless as any human would be in the face of such forceful intention – to get her to understand my eagerness, my complete joy. Mother with her understanding of my moods, Mother with her suspicion when I exerted myself like that and used up my entire emotional range. Mother who knew my backlash.

Couldn't she at least try to sound happy?

'Oh, how lovely, Sivvy, how exciting, congratulations. So it's a fine house?'

'It's the BEST house, Mother. We couldn't possibly find a better one!'

'Is Ted happy?'

'He's overjoyed.'

'So then maybe I don't even need to come down and inspect it?'

'You can trust us, Mother. We've found our place on earth.'

'How lovely, Sivvy. I'll have to trust you.'

Her cool snottiness, her desire to control, her manner of withholding my own joy even from me.

'Aren't you happy?' I asked.

'I'm curious about the brochure. Please send me the brochure.'

I was quickly dragged down, soon I would be all the way at the bottom, soon she would have severed the tie I had just now felt so strongly within me – the tie to joy. Soon I would fall to the floor, figuratively, and feel dead.

I sighed.

'We'll send you all the brochures in the world, Mother,' I said. 'As long as you understand how grateful I am that you are watching Frieda right now so we could come here and hit the jackpot!'

'There, there, I'm happy to do it!'

'I'm so happy, Mother,' I added. 'I'm so happy!'

Mother gave no reply. We hung up and I stepped back out into the August garden, full of butterfly bushes growing wild with their white spray: such expanses, so many gorgeous wonderful glittering apple trees. So many varieties of fantastic flowers to learn the names of, shockingly red strawberries beneath green little leaves – we could keep bees . . . Bees, like my father's.

I entered the splendour and pulled an apple from the fruit hanging from a tree, and had a thought right then and there: I am in Paradise. Welcome here, Sivvy, welcome to

Paradise! Good thing Ted is taking me from filthy sooty London with post-war convulsions and bombed-out angst and black snot.

I was initially the one who didn't at all want to leave the city since we had everything I could wish for in terms of a literary life – cultural meeting places and conversations, cool writers to get to know and get close to – movie theatres, bookshops, everything. But the more Ted's wish became my command, the more I threw myself headlong into what he demanded and let it become my reality, my language. From having presented all kinds of counter-arguments to him, with the utmost conviction and feeling, I had now completely adopted the other side's argument. Ted's side, his desires, his concepts, his ideas. They were now mine. I had nothing left for city life. This: this was all that mattered!

I took a bite of the fruit and felt its rough sweetness make its way from my teeth into my throat, and suddenly felt like a cliché in the sun.

And now the greenery was dead and transformed into cheap December reality, washed out on the ground. Peat, hay, and cakey mud, it was hard to imagine that this had once been alive.

Ted pulled tools out of the shed – hedge clippers, saw, fork, and a rake – he wanted to cut down branches, make use of his rough hard limbs to *do* things. There was an entire list inside on the kitchen table – a long checklist of repairs to be made, dates for the handyman to visit (oh, couldn't we at least wait until the baby was a few months old, but NO, everything had to happen promptly if it was up to Ted). The gardens needed to be dug up for the spring since we were going to sow as soon as the ground was thawed. Ted wanted us to sell some vegetables in the square. Flowers, as well, in bouquets: we had counted on having an ocean of daffodils and narcissus here by the end of March, if spring came early. Then we could make some extra money. By the summer, our sales would expand with strawberries, and for those, Ted wanted to build planter boxes using old door frames he intended to fill with soil.

He suddenly saw me: he turned around, and his sharp-edged face softened when he realised I was headed toward him.

'We were going to chop off branches and make a fire!' he shouted and pointed at Frieda's pile of twigs.

I smiled.

'I can see that.'

He came toward me, was warm, put an arm around me. I exploded within from the scent of his scent. So particular to me. I loved him.

'I'm not crying, I promise!' I giggled when Ted wiped a tear from the corner of my eye. 'It's just so windy!'

He kissed me on the mouth. Cold, sweet kiss, his thin lips hit me just right.

'How's the knitting? Weren't you going to knit?'

'I'll do it later. Should I scatter the bone meal?'

I held up the box.

Ted shrugged, not particularly impressed.

'Sure.'

It was as subtly swift – again – as when I lost interest in my knitting.

Ted left me with my box of bone meal.

I stood there and felt the tingling sensation fade and disappear. I came to him – I came to him and Frieda and wanted to be a part of it. I'd had a dream, a vision, I stood here as a result of that dream and then, just as I approached, the dream died.

I'd had a dream of scattering bone meal. I had thought, inspired by Ted's progress in the garden, with the trees and his parenting of Frieda, that I wanted to be a part of it. I also wanted to be in the dream! I didn't want to sit alone in there, knitting.

Ted sawed down one of the large, overgrown tree branches while I looked on, the ones we had talked about for months, how they needed to come down before the spring. He wrestled loose from one of the branches that had gotten caught in his clothing, turned around to me and shouted through the wind:

'It's the bulbs you should pour the bone meal on. It's probably a good idea! Take the plot of narcissus and daffodils, do you know which one I mean?'

He waved his hand.

Yes, I knew which one he meant.

It was with tears in my throat that I walked around like a farmgirl in the wind, scattering bone meal across the plot where hundreds of narcissus bulbs were buried, waiting for spring, covered with heavy, winding peat.

Frieda only cared about her father and her game.

Small, ridiculous grains of ground bone. Poor animals. Poor innocent animals ground down in a mill at the factory so that I could have nice bulbs to sell in the square. Fucking awful, really, awful.

I looked at the tiny grains caught in the wind, falling stupidly to the ground. So ridiculously simple, so unintellectual to go on like this. It *pained* me to do things. I did not like the doing itself, the doing was about sealing things and moving on, about letting go and no longer dreaming of doing. The doing never became perfect to me. Then I would rather remain in the dream: it was an illness. But to scatter bone meal over bulbs along with my daughter and husband had been so much lovelier in the dream. I had seen it before me . . . It was tied to a strong feeling . . . Where was that feeling now? In reality everything just felt ugly and shame tore through me for feeling that way. Ungrateful brat, I heard my mother's words in me. Ungrateful brat!

And Ted called: 'Great, Sylvia, looks good!'

I threw the empty box to the ground in an exaggeratedly dramatic gesture, but it couldn't be controlled, my limbs moved as if on their own. The box gained speed in the wind. Frieda ran after to try to catch it.

I went back inside to my knitting.

I had read somewhere that the final thing someone does in life is call for their mother. That was the moment of death: nearing death, the usual struggle to not be too attached to one's mother ceased. All effort to move away from her vanished. And the human essence shone through: this, that a human being extends her hand and calls, 'Mother.'

'Mother, where are you.'

'Mother, come.'

Ted, in my life, time and again did just that: made me want to: 1. write, and: 2. call for my mother.

We had argued. What was it that felt so completely dead in my chest? As if I was about to go under?

After an argument, I could never look him in the eye, and it could go on all evening. I looked into Frieda's instead. The glimmering light from her gaze as she pulled off her wool socks in front of the fire where it was warm.

The diaper. The pony tail. She had a little stuffed elephant whose one ear was gnawed-at. She put it to her mouth now. She would brush her teeth with Ted, but I wanted to sit with her for a while, smile at her, feel the fight I'd had with her father fade away.

I could write about this, I thought (but I never managed to bring the fights with me into the writing, would never manage to depict them). Frieda was still a small child, she wasn't yet harmed by our fighting. And as long as it fed the writing and made me look around for alternatives to life with him – gasps of air – for example, lifting my gaze and looking around for my mother – it was fine. Refreshing.

It had only been half an hour since I had uttered the words, in the kitchen: 'I forgot that one must never insult Ted Hughes.'

The tall man, the tall lanky poet with so much muscle and sense, the glittering intellect behind his eyes. Could he not afford to be generous with me? Could he not remain calm?

He *hissed*, as if we were animals. He frightened Frieda. He frightened me because he had frightened my daughter. My first impulse was to keep her clean of the pain, clean as a bone licked dry, white and porous. Keep her away from the weight of her past (the two of us), clean of fear.

My heart pecked away on the sofa.

But that would not have worked and I thought: I'll write about this later.

Ted gave Frieda an enormous hug as if to show me: this hug was intended for you but now you can't have it, because you are in trouble, but I still want to show you that it exists, so now I will give my love to our daughter. Because I am a good father.

What had I done?

I raised the little charm from my beating chest and placed the antelope I wore around my neck to my lips. The silver tasted of metal. I would write about it when Ted and Frieda had gone to bed: it was the only way to free myself from the pain. I would use it. He is good for my composure, I thought. He mortifies my writing soul, he keeps me above the surface in frigid English water.

What had I said to him?

He hadn't wiped out the kitchen drawers before putting back the cutlery and the measuring cups and the serving spoons and knives. We had cleaned out the kitchen after the renovation that had unfolded during the fall and now he thought everything was done, but the tendency I'd seen in him to do things halfway, to, plainly speaking, be sloppy: I couldn't bear it. I was of a mind to clean out that quality; it was an artefact of his mother, the filthy pans she left in her kitchen in Yorkshire, the sour smell of the poorly wrung-out dish rag. All I had seen in her kitchen was ugliness and how bacteria spread while we ate, I could even see how she had them on her hands. That Ted's mother could even be joyful in such a kitchen, that she could fill others' stomachs and be content with the end result! She and Ted and Olwyn laughed in a kitchen like that even though everything was unclean and things hung sloppily and askew and unaesthetically along the walls, and the floor was covered in crumbs no one had bothered to sweep up. It was a worker's kitchen. Ted Hughes reminded me of everything my mother had taught me to despise and which I now wanted to punish him with. I worshipped my mother for everything she had taught me about my fastidious housewifely ideal. I summoned her in my chest. Ted would make me call for her. Time and time and time again.

Mother.

I had that charm against my face, traced it across my nose. It was an antelope from the savannah; my father gave it to me when I turned seven. *For your gaze, my Sylvia, for your flashing gazelle-gaze.* I sucked on it for a while. Frieda bounded into my lap to say goodnight. I inhaled the scent of her hair and wished I could stop time: the smell of honeysmooth hair and cream. Her face was completely open. If everything else came coursing at me, streaming and tugging, then she was an inhale, a point in time where everything hung in the balance.

Each and every minute, I chose to be her mother. I would kiss her hair so many nights when Ted and I had fought or made love. For that was life. 'Night, Mommy,' she said and clung to my neck so that I nearly choked from her awkward movements. 'Goodnight, honeybee,' I replied.

And then – in the argument – I had said to him, for I could not bear sloppiness in the kitchen, could not bear his simple worker heritage and would like to beat that shit out of him one day – and yes, I would – I said: 'YOU FLUNKED THAT ONE, TED.'

And it was the word, the word flunk, the word flunk he couldn't handle. It was as if I had spit out the grime he bore within him, and placed it right in front of his nose. As if I had suggested that it was HIS dirt there inside our drawer. His dirt he had not bothered to wipe off. As if it was about us – was about him. Flunk. And no sooner had I uttered the word there in the kitchen than I heard how horrible it sounded to him. In his ears: awful. Loathsome. His eyes narrowed. Ted's crystalline sly little mint lozenge eyes. Narrow foxish. Thin hard. His eyes, so embittered.

'Say something nice instead,' he had said. 'I've cleaned the entire kitchen. What have you done? You're welcome to clean, as well.'

'I've had Frieda.'

'But you've always had Frieda. Oddly enough it happens that I've had Frieda and *still* cleaned. It makes me sad. Can't you see what I've done?'

'You aren't sad at all – you're offended.'

'No, I'm sad.'

'The most easily offended human in the history of the world,' I said.

And it was as if all the air in the entire kitchen had been transformed, become radioactive, full of fumes, and I thanked Frieda, thanked her for not yet having a proper language.

'Don't come here and tell me I've fucking flunked. Say something nice!'

'Come on, I said it with a sense of humour?'

'What humour? Your sense of humour is fucking awful!'

'I said it with love!' Here I could sense my defeat in that my voice cracked: it was the voice of pregnancy, it could not hold, it was at a disadvantage.

'You didn't say anything with any kind of fucking love.'

'Don't swear!'

'I can swear however fucking much I want!'

We spoke these words as the shrieking from Frieda's mouth rose in volume. The more we shouted, the more she fought with us. She wiggled in the high chair, her body impossible to fix with my gaze. I gave her kernels of corn – they kept her calm.

Washed-out fish soup for dinner that he had cooked – I thought it wasn't salty enough but dared not add salt since I felt the risk of humiliating him even further was too great. We ate dinner in silence and did not look at each other.

Food is good, I thought. It's good to eat. Then the feeling of family will return.

But then came the next wave of recriminations, and it was the final one which injured me the most. Ted knew it and I knew it: it was his prerogative to strike the death blow, it was his to distribute. For I had hurt him and therefore I should suffer even more hellishly for it (it was yet another defect from his childhood, I thought, he had so much baggage from it, so much simpleton in him, so much warped rotten anger living in there).

He said:

'You can flunk your students. You could flunk your students if you had any, but that's right: you don't *have* any students any more.'

Silence. Him again:

'You gave that job up because you were going to be a full-time writer.'

It had happened hundreds of times and it would happen hundreds of times again: that my anxiety and panic ratcheted up because it was my fault, I used the word flunk – I insulted him, everything was my fault and I had ruined dinner, but since my husband carried much heavier artillery when he humiliated me regarding my writing, the deepest plunge of the knife, the bloodiest wound – I could never ask for his forgiveness. It was my pride, I knew that, but it was also my husband's power over me. I hated him. Yes, still now, as I sat on the red sofa and observed how he showered his bed-bound daughter with love: I hated him. Another child with him – I was even worried about how that would go.

And here I fumbled for some kind of salvation: spring. Writing. I will sit outside in the garden and write, I thought. I searched for the ultimate salvation from the sudden humiliation that had just struck.

Mother.

Mother would come. She suddenly appeared as a possibility. My mother, whom I loathed and whom I needed to be separated from by a vast ocean. The entire Atlantic.

My mother, her cool splendour, her crackling perfection, unspoken and constant. Her demands of me, which never aligned with any kind of tenderness, any kind of love. Only demands, only demands so she could feel splendid, to allay her anxiety.

I should be good – I should be educated – I should have a degree – I should at the same time become the free woman that she, hostage to her generation, could never fully be. I should be famous (just enough), I should travel far away and realise this professional skill – the writing – that she herself had never had the glory of, she who had only learned shorthand, that hieroglyphic gobbledygook designed to help someone else catch the essence of a thing.

Mother, who could not get enough of instilling in me anguish and ideals and housewifeliness and itsy-bitsy little secrets you needed to know to be a woman in this world. She was so anxious that I be liberated but could not help but raise me rigidly so that I could welcome my freedom. She saw my fragility and could not bear it, could not bear the wound it opened up in her. How could I ever stand strong and free in the world, with that fragility? Woman never hysterical. Woman never hysterical. Woman never fragile. Woman only decent, respectable. How could she ever dare set me free? It had become sport to fool my mother. Fool her into thinking I was happy. Fool her into thinking I could fend for myself. Fool her into believing that I loved my life. Fool her into thinking that I was truly free. Fool her into thinking that it was possible to be free and at the same time deeply involved in a relationship with a man. Fool her into thinking it was easy to be a writer. Fool her into thinking that I believed in myself, never had any doubt.

To be loved by her, I had to fool her.

I had done nothing but fool her, my entire life.

Now I fooled myself into thinking that it was my mother who would save me.

So I fetched an envelope and stationery and began to write a letter.

It's time for Mother dear to come visit us now, I wrote. We've decorated the house for Christmas: the blood-red corduroy curtains I sewed myself and the red ribbons I tie around them.

I wrote about the practical: every day, we light a fire in the fireplace, I am sitting in front of the glow of the fire right now, and we have had to order an electric heater which will arrive after the new year and in time for the baby's arrival (even if I despise all things electrical). The midwife who visited us really felt that we needed to keep a warmer house. It's heavy for me to carry firewood, I have enough to carry, but you should see how Ted works for me! Anything I cannot manage, he handles.

Frieda is in her prime, so blindingly adorable, and she charms all the neighbours. They want to hand off all their old toys the minute they see her. I tie your light-blue silk ribbon around her hair each and every morning, then she's as beautiful as a bow. I'm so happy about the issues of *Ladies' Home Journal* you sent. You can't imagine how happy they make an American! To get letters and greetings from you is the highlight of my week. I feel so at home then. I miss the American recipes, all the food here is so dull and English. Is it the pregnancy that makes me so uninterested in English food? In any case, I've developed some kind of aversion to it.

Ted is so good to me, he massages my feet every night, and if there's something I'm calm and confident about, it is that our child will have the finest parents in the world. I am so eager for you to come here! The house is as perfect as could be for a little family like ours, we have really made it our own. This spring/summer when you visit (I've already begun to prepare your trip!) I'm sure all the wonderful bulbs waiting underground will have reached out their leaves and buds and will bloom in the sun. We have so many daffodils and narcissus in the ground that Ted thinks we can sell them in the square and make money. Well, any and all funds are welcome, now that our expenses for the house and repairs have skyrocketed. I can hardly wait for you to come visit and provide us with some stability and security.

Frieda misses you, she says, she started to talk about you the minute she saw the framed photos you sent, which we placed on the dresser. 'Gramma!' she says then. 'Gramma!' and it makes me furiously happy inside. This little baby tumbling about inside me, I am certain you will become so attached to it . . . A new little life. Who would have thought? Sylvia, mother of two by age thirty. I want four, so we have come up with names for four children, it's a fun pastime to imagine our large family. Megan, Nicholas, Frieda, and Gregor. I think we will have another girl.

Now we are wondering how things are with our Gramma, and with Warren? Sending you both a big hug across the chilly waters of the Atlantic. Hope you have a lovely and peaceful Christmas together. My heart breaks from not getting to be with you. It's best to hold tight, as waiting for the great miracle is the most important. You should know that I have let go of all writing, for now, and derive all my pleasure from Ted's successes on the radio as well as my knitting projects. I really just lie on the sofa, rising like a dough, as I should! And if I feel like reading something I always have those mindless magazines like *Ladies' Home Journal*. The magazines competing to refuse my short stories I am putting on the fire, I can't bring myself to care about them. Right now they really can't cause me any pain.

Yesterday I poured bone meal over all our tulip bulbs, daffodils, and narcissus while Ted and Frieda played in the wind. It was wonderful to walk around and imagine how the little bulbs absorb the bone meal from those poor animals and will greedily shoot even higher into the spring air when you arrive. It's so palpable here in the countryside how all living things are part of a large cycle. As are we! With this closing thought (and with hopes for a rosy spring charged with cherry blossoms) your Sivvy sends you a big kiss.

Merry Christmas!

When Ted came shuffling back like a tired animal after putting Frieda to bed, heavy and conquered and mighty, phlegmatic this time – then I felt full of courage and hope again. A fire within me, tall flames of pride that made me subdued, calm, able to live. I said to him, triumphant from the red sofa, so the war could go on:

'I forgot that one must never insult Ted Hughes.'

The war was back on in one second – it was our war, I couldn't live without it. It was something that sustained us both.

Ted snarled at me for a long while in the hallway, which made me more convinced than ever of my own superiority – it was my inheritance which was superior, it was my mother who was the healthiest of our two mothers, therefore also I – and he swore and said:

'So keep going, then, dig up all the shit you can find, go fuck yourself, you fucking cunt.'

There! So I had won. He went as low as one could go. Ted was always the one to fall. I triumphantly licked shut the envelope to my mother, while Ted pulled on his rain clothes and went out to dig in the December night.

It was our first Christmas at Court Green, and life was absolutely wonderful. I had conquered the arguments, conquered the despondence – that was what I had set about to do all my life: conquer, emerge on the other end. Pregnancy had dulled the flavour of coffee for a few months, now it was delicious yet again. Holidays – what good were holidays if not to put the greyness of the everyday behind, and finally let oneself celebrate? I was, in a way, cut out for parties – to tie on a pair of red silk shoes and follow a recipe for a yummy cake and finally put my smile on display to the world.

Well, we weren't going to have quite that much fun this Christmas – we had decided, Ted and I, to be on our own. I had longed to finally get close to him, or, rather: to have him just to myself, but would not say so. It was just a feeling. The candles had been purchased, I had ironed foot upon foot of table cloths on our new ironing board, had decorated with hyacinth and the amaryllis would soon bloom grandly from its hard, thick buds. I had asked for my grandmother's recipe for carrot cake and had already baked three of them (no frosting) that I would keep in the freezer. Christmas Day our shared Christmas traditions would become one, a single unit, but I had a feeling the emphasis would be on my traditions, since Ted came from a home which did not quite sit right with me, not yet.

It was the morning of Christmas Day. I was wearing my red dress. Even though my stomach protruded like a basketball beneath the fabric, I squeezed myself into the red, and it still felt wonderful – to get to be a human being, a real living woman, Ted's woman, his wife, in a dress he also had other memories of me in.

Me. Who was I? Who was I, today?

Who was I, who would cook the morning oatmeal just as my mother and grandmother always had on Christmas Day? Who was I, in my pearl earrings?

Who was I, in my apron, in the kisses which tasted of honey this morning, when I gave them to Ted?

Who was he?

My lanky youngster, whom I loved most of all, who kept death and my mother at a safe distance. Who was he who had the power to realise everything I had ever imagined about life? Who was he, the tall dark man who this particular morning did not, for our sake, write?

He was someone who wiped his mouth with his shirt sleeve after eating his morning oatmeal.

The flavour was not at all like at home when Mother cooked it, and our kitchen was quiet: no one had put on Christmas music.

'It tasted better when I was little,' I said.

Someone else might have laughed at the oatmeal debacle but instead I turned the shame inward, like a shard of cracked plastic as sharp as glass.

'At least Frieda likes it,' I said nervously.

'It's good, Sylvia, it's good.'

I looked out at our living room that I had decorated in

red, and it struck me that I had no idea what visions Ted actually had about our Christmas.

The nuts he would have liked to have in a bowl on the table.

I had gone for hazelnuts.

I worried about what *he* thought about my choice of colour: that it was so desperate, all the red – as if I had built a cave of blood for us, the interior of a heart; as if I so desperately needed to push us into something that pulsed of warm blood, otherwise I would lose myself in panic and anxiety attacks all winter long. England was so cold, I often complained, so cold and grey in that evil, dull way – nothing ever opens up here, even the people are marked by it – so reserved, damp and worn and grey – they never give off any crackles or sparks and they never feel as stable and broad and expansive as back home. They live as if in a box! And I did not know what Ted thought of me then, when I said such things – perhaps I was the one living in a box, who tried to force life onto a polished surface. I who was prim, formal – not at all the English people, as I made it out to be. Perhaps I was the one who held back, and I was the one who would explode. Ted sometimes tried, in our nightly conversations, to be wise enough to let me hear it:

'What you judge in others is actually what you judge in yourself,' he would say, but the penny didn't quite drop for me, not yet – that what he was really talking about was me.

What did I know of Ted's deepest thoughts about me, he who would probably never let me understand (it was too risky) that my colour wasn't red at all: it was blue, like the ocean.

What did I know of Ted since I did not let him stand before me in his full force?

Was I afraid of it?

Did I need to keep it in check?

What did I actually know about Ted?

That I loved him?

So how would I then manage the fact that perhaps he was unhappy in my Christmas?

In my story about our Christmas.

I was full on carrot cake when, toward the afternoon, I sat down to write a letter (another one) to Mother. The fire crackled in the stove and Ted sat reading his Christmas book – yes, he actually read it for the first time – Aldous Huxley's *Brave New World*. He had his hand on my foot.

When I was this happy – when it was this blissful, to live – then I grew afraid, since I knew from experience that this was when catastrophe would strike. And I tried to turn back the sense of terror, but felt it clearly like a slowly rising fluttering feeling in my throat. As if someone was in there with a feather. I tried to gather myself and just write the letter, and perhaps it was the letter which would calm me down, but just the same it was present: the ticking toward a darker demise than I had gotten used to thus far.

I sucked at the tip of my pen.

Was it the child who would die? I thought. (Such things happened.) Was I the one who would pass when I gave birth? Was it my husband who would lose himself on one of his many trips to London, break a leg so that it took too long for him to return home, and he would miss the birth? Would we have a power outage, would my mother have a stroke far away in Boston? Well, what was it pressing against my chest, tearing at my spine?

I tried to breathe normally. It was Christmas! It was a perfect still-life if life could just consist of still-lifes: it was the crackling fire and it was Ted's hand on my foot on the sofa. It was my pretty red dress. It was his writing upstairs, waiting to become radio. It was my novel, also waiting, fantastic.

It was Christmas, our first Christmas together to celebrate

without the interference of family and friends (such a damn relief). It was my beloved.

Now he leaned forward and told me that it was a Swedish writer, 'What's her name, Karen something, Karen Blixen . . . No, that's the Danish one, but I'm pretty sure there's a B in her last name . . . Anyhow.' Her name was Karin, a Swedish writer, Lucas had read her dystopian novel, *Kallocain*:

'I'll bet it came out before George Orwell's *Nineteen Eighty-Four*,' Ted said, 'but it's a damn sight better. Orwell should get credit where credit is due, of course, but those damn Brits, they hog all the fame and glory for everything, even things other people create.'

His grip on my foot was very firm. Could he let go?

'But Karin who wrote *Kallocain* maybe took all her inspiration from Aldous Huxley, in turn, and you don't mention him at all . . .'

Ted shrugged.

'Regular intertextuality.'

'It's also because he's a man,' I said obstinately and wiggled my toes so the grip would loosen. 'Don't you realise that?'

'Of course,' Ted said. 'In a way . . .' He let his gaze linger on the fire. 'In a way I think it's as godawful for all writers, regardless of sex.'

I gave a laugh.

'Godawful?'

'The slog is the same. It takes ages to get a grasp on your motive, and once you do, you have to sit down and write and rewrite, and write and rewrite . . .'

'What is your motive?' I asked, as if it was the first time we were having this conversation.

Ted smiled.

'What's yours . . .?' he countered and pressed both hands around my foot. This wasn't a massage, this was something else. Acupressure? What was he up to?

I looked up and around the room, searched for an opening, for a movement somewhere where everything felt full of life and teeming as if on a movie screen. But it was as if the silent rooms of the everyday were paralysed, even if it was Christmas Day. I disliked the mechanics of thinking, the cramp of repetition, this emptiness when nothing new gained speed and expanded. As a woman, I thought I would be this new thing for my entire family. I would be the circus and the lottery and the fair and the bright glow of the new moon, I would be the lipstick, the lay and the tenderness afterwards. The open embrace. The food on the table, the warm and irresistible pussy. The thighs in the darkness. A kind of goddess-like component of raw material, which life could never manage without. I would be what guaranteed eternal rebirth in our home. What relieved Ted's emotional cramps when he had them (oh yes, he had those).

But then he posed a literary question to me and it was as if my mouth were completely barren of words. It was as if someone had passed over me with asphalt.

I did not want to stand before him empty and with no reply. Everything had to remain in motion, as did I. I could not bear stagnation – so do not be stagnation! On Christmas Day.

He will lose interest in me, I thought. The great authorship I imagined, KNEW I had before me, would diminish in dignity once it was eyed closely, and as a writer I needed to put myself on display. That's how fragile it is, I thought. That's how fragile being a writer is. I can't even stand being asked a question.

I cleared my throat.

Frieda was scooting around on the floor with her doll, on its belly like she was. They appeared to be engaged in some kind of game.

'My poems stem from joy, I've come to see,' I said in the

end, and heard how idiotic it sounded. Ted's furrowed brow grew smooth. He seemed genuinely interested.

'Fascinating,' he said. 'Go on.'

'But regarding the dystopian, and regarding scenarios for the future and big feelings.'

'Keep going.'

'I'm not the type of writer who wants to dig around in darkness and despair. I feel it so strongly – my poems come out of light, joy. Out of being uplifted. I feel good when I write them. I want them to meet someone else's inner light . . . Sort of. You know?'

Ted nodded.

'Of course. I've seen it in you,' he said. 'That's why you will write best-selling novels.'

I laughed – see, an opening. Breathing was suddenly easy.

'You're a novelist or a painter, that's what I've always said. Prose. Prose is your thing. Poets are mad, you're not mad.'

Here I moved Ted's hand away, kept it from squeezing my foot, and grabbed a hold of his enormous foot instead.

'Give it up. YOU aren't mad, in any case.'

I became so worried that he was fishing for something.

'How do you know?'

I chuckled nervously. Looked at Frieda on the floor. Never would I let her hear this. A father who himself claimed to be mad, no, my God.

I laughed to smooth things over.

'My Ted . . . My darling . . . You can say whatever you want. You're still the most stable, strong, and patient human I have ever been with!'

And there the conversation was over, for me. But not for Ted.

'Don't think you know things about me, things I haven't told you.'

I was impatient, he needed to stop. His voice was spiteful.

'Do you need to do this on Christmas Day?'

He got up, followed me as I went searching for the nutcracker in the kitchen. Stood there behind me with his book, which he waved in the air.

'I think you should read some dystopias. Read this – read *Nineteen Eighty-Four*. Read *Kallocain*, try it in German. I think you need, for your poems, to realise that everything you write can't stem from joy. It's an impossibility . . .'

He had caught me with the German. I knew that Ted spoke in riddles – he wanted to be married to a woman who spoke German, true, and with my German background I shouldn't be able to deny him that – but I did. Living fucking breathing paradoxical me!

Was this Christmas Day?

Did he need to talk about dystopias this very minute? Everything was so peaceful and quiet, I didn't want to have to think about writerly ambitions and momentum, above all not dystopian scenarios for the future. Why didn't he just leave me alone? Why was it Ted who set the stone in motion . . . Why did I appear to be the one at a stand-still?

I ate a rancid nut and had a hard time swallowing. Ted threw the nutshells in the sink with a clatter.

'Oh well,' he said bitterly, and went upstairs. 'We'll have to finish this some other time.'

That's how irresponsible my husband was. So unthinking, when it came to caring for other people's feelings. Now he had put my body on high alert, when it needed most to remain calm. This baby I was carrying, tumbling around in there, just now it had lain still, sleeping! It was his fault . . . Ted couldn't stand that I was someone who wrote and was *happy*. He tried to make me become this perfect razor-sharp black-and-white poet with a veil across her face who spoke German. Who dug around in the impossible, in the past and in the future. But what if that wasn't me! What if I was technicolour and glossy like the pages of a magazine, modern and bold, imagine – God help him – if I was *happy*!

I held out my hand with four cracked nuts for little Frieda, then adjusted the enormous harvest of Christmas cards lined up on the mantel. They gave me a sense of good cheer. Here we had greetings from every corner of the world – greetings to be happy about, for what was life for if not good cheer and joy in the face of beautiful successes? One day perhaps Ted would permit me to uncover his gloomy, priggish, repressed despondency and resurface out of the mud like the bright, positive athlete I knew he was.

My completely unattainable Adam.

No, it was too hopelessly snug in the back – I unlaced the red dress and put on the Christmas nightgown Mother had given me.

New Year's Eve had come and gone. A freezing northerly wind came in from the coast and it was terribly grey and dull outside. Ted had taken the double-decker to Exeter at dawn. I had kissed him farewell and gnawed at my wrist afterwards, the thick part, while my other hand held Frieda in a firm grip. The house was freezing. I had been forced to put the hot water bottle in my waistband. Now it was ten o'clock and the hours had already mouldered been pulverised vapourised without me writing a word.

This awful pathological emptiness when Ted wasn't home. I could have shot a duck and placed it guts a-splay in the garden as testimony, or why not a child? Ted must understand, Ted must truly understand what he did when he left me alone like this. That cosy glow from the fire that used to fill me with equanimity and something like . . . comfort? was just a deathly glow when he was away. The glow of death. I stared into my own eyes, my own brain when he was gone, which no one who truly knew me should ever let me do. It ought to be forbidden to leave Sylvia Plath alone with herself.

How I contorted myself in order for my husband to understand! Had he not made some sort of vow to always stay at home when times were tough, in sickness and in health, etc.? I would like to remind him of this fact but a telegram would take three damn days to reach him. Everything was slow, only my brain was quick as a lizard. God forbid that this should happen . . . with only two weeks left!

I moaned when Frieda tugged at my hand and said, 'Um, Mommy, um.' She wanted to get me out of the sofa, didn't think I should lay here.

'Mommy tired,' I said, and felt a deep burning shame – 'Mommy tired': children shouldn't have to hear such things. I slowly pulled myself up and turned on the radio in the kitchen. It was playing jazz and New Year's greetings, which fortunately distracted her. I could lie down beneath the blanket with the hot water bottle in my waistband again.

I wanted the martial law of my pregnancy to spill over onto the man as well. Ted. Such a terrible injustice I was forced to live with. The pregnancy spun itself around me like a thick fog of suffocating spider web, layer upon layer until I could hardly breathe and even less recognise myself in the mirror. I had the body of another, the face of another. My thoughts were expected to still be mine but I mistrusted them nonetheless, knew that the thoughts were not my own. The thoughts were freakish, they were invitations to the most banal images that an enlightened consciousness can conjure: a perfect tea set in a shop window. Sundae glasses brimming with banana splits. Marilyn Monroe's nightgown and mussed sexy hair. Key lime pie, Mother's recipe. A large bouquet of bone-white cut flowers. Save me from myself and my mental demise, I begged Ted. Be here to protect my body from being shrouded in this bitter bunkum. To lie large and fat on the sofa and even consider thinking about baby booties! Knitted by Gramma! I was sick.

I'm sick, Ted, you've made me sick and I have fallen to pieces so the least you can do is be here to keep this madness at bay, this sneaky pregnancy that dumbs me down and makes me slow when I want to be quick, ugly when I want to be God's most beautiful girl on this earth.

(I didn't believe in God but as a simile for the highest of the high, the word made sense.)

This is what I did, in my state of abandonment, while Frieda complained and pulled at my arms:

I clawed at my own insides with long nails honed by my mind . . . I beheaded myself in my mind's eye with a big, fat axe. I jumped up and stomped on my own body. I tore little Frieda to pieces. I would not be here for Ted when he returned, no, I would destroy it all – then he would see how to manage the ruins left behind by his life choices. Sylvia Plath in ruins. I would shatter all the mirrors. I would burn all the rejection letters, my diaries as well, everything would be tossed in one fell swoop. I would get rid of it all, including myself. When Ted returned from his trip to London tomorrow morning at nine, when he was done chatting with the BBC ladies on the radio, who pecked him on the cheek and laughed their asses off, inflating his ego – then I'd lie here, dead. Then the man I loved would be filled with bitter regret.

I lay immobile on the sofa while Frieda sat on the crimson living-room rug and played with the doll Gramma had given her for Christmas. Was she babbling, humming, was she silent? I had no idea. Perhaps she was quiet out of consideration for me, perhaps she had already mastered the rules governing her mother's psyche.

As if in slow motion I watched how the girl placed the doll in the crib Ted had made for her before Christmas and which I in December had painted white and decorated with red hearts and blue stars. It already felt as if we had done that in another lifetime, when everything was still hopeful and real, now that everything was lost.

Ted had travelled to London even though I had begged

and pleaded for several days for him to stay home. It's just this one radio play, he said, it's just this final recording for the BBC before the baby arrives, it's just this final confirmation that our tenants in the London apartment are managing. I had wanted to vomit the pregnancy all over him and let him take care of it himself.

Was I now supposed to cook for Frieda, was I now supposed to assist her in her games, were we supposed to go for walks together to buy eggs and bread? I had no inspiration whatsoever. Work, work was my saviour, but now there was no fucking work to be had.

Only the breakfast dishes on the table and Frieda's patience with the game would soon expire and then she'd bounce up at me and demand, Where's Daddy? Where's Daddy? And I would be tempted to reply: He's dead, Frieda, he is dead to me.

Why was loneliness crueller to me than it was to anybody else? My greatest fear was this loneliness, this complete stuckness in myself, even though Frieda walked alongside me, her hand in mine – the mitten with its hole (tippy-toeing to be able to reach me, and sobbing, since I had already scolded her once), and even though I had greeted the mailman kindly (no mail today!) along with an idiot neighbour, I would be pickled in my jar of loneliness. It was this fear that paralysed me, which paradoxically made me incapable of reaching out to friends. I imagined that friendship provided for a richer life and I knew that I had *had* friends, people in my life who had loved me. The original scene would be the spring when I met Ted, 1956, my red ballet flats like two candy apples to coast on through life. Wherever I went there was someone who wanted to see me, kiss me, stop and talk with me.

I chose Ted. I had reached a perfectly calibrated status in

the world. I had studied my way to the wisdom of life and science. I was so educated that I had begun to apply my theories to life itself and forget where I had found them; somewhat deceptively it was possible to believe that they had emerged out of my brain, that the thoughts were mine, the memories mine, the philosophy entirely my own.

But it could also be that this was the case since my young body, my young gaze – I, the modern, beautiful, young educated woman, was also the first of my kind to own and articulate this, so when I went out into the world and rendered it, it was an epochal event, something as remarkable as the fact of the Earth's rotation.

I had just had it all in my cupped hand, like a fistful of sand fetched from the sea, and what did I do? Yes, I sold myself to Ted, I married him in June of that year, only three months after we had met. It would all happen so quickly that life would cease to have an effect, at such high a speed that life glommed on to me and could not throw me off. Blindly, almost: love felt most delicious then. (From my diary that spring: oh, good God, there's no time, everything must happen now.)

I wrote nothing then, when Ted came into my life. Up until those weeks I had gotten exactly where I wanted to in my writing, been on top, almost touching the sun, the most beautiful girl in the world of beautiful American girls, I had exhaustive images of where I was headed, what everything looked like, how it felt. (London, Paris, Nice.)

And then I had to die, or at least be reinvented, reappear in a new edition.

Me. I had *had* a me – I knew it. I had just become someone again. Cambridge – Richard Sassoon (my anaemic, strait-laced boyfriend whom I loved), my friends there. I *had* me. And then I handed myself over. I let myself fall in this strange gentleman's hands.

How I doubted in that spring of 1956. And now, in hind-sight, when lone strolls with Frieda were all I had, I could even imagine that the guy who lived in the room across from Ted, the big fat Boddy who saw me and whom I was afraid would spread rumours about me (he did): HIM . . . that he was of course placed there to stop me, I should have let him stop me!

Why didn't I? Why did I hand myself over? Because I needed a father? Because I needed a mother? Because I needed someone to be everything at the same time: father, lover, and son? Because I needed to greet life with laundry and apple blossoms, dirty dishes and macaroni, if only to avoid the feeling of dying at some claustrophobic moment each and every day? Because I needed a lover who measured out the distance to my horrible here-and-now, who encapsulated it in a possible future? My heavy-footed stomping into the world, like a general: oughtn't I be *stopped*?

I needed a chest to breathe against and a heart (not my own) beating beneath it. I needed another. I needed more than just myself. I never thought I could lose myself, once I let go and let him enter. Like life in London in 1960 and 1961: I thought I could never lose it, when we moved here, to Court Green. I thought I could never lose myself in Ted.

And how I was lost . . .

Frieda cried over her frozen hands, she held up her fists red and hard so that I had to blow warm breath upon them.

How did I dare call myself a mother, I, who could not even keep track of her mittens?

This is what I ought to do, instead of walking a lonely miserable walk with Frieda while I felt in my pounding head that there was something in here that was awry – something was chemically wrong with my substances: I ought to get new friends. I should write a letter . . .

As soon as this walk was over and we had milk and butter to bring back to the kitchen for a pound cake, I would have to sit down and: 1. paint my nails red (I needed to be reminded of life, of being alive, my God, if no one saw me in real life I needed to pretend to have an audience and red nail polish inevitably brought me closer to the sensation of the red carpet, besides, it smelled so good) and: 2. wipe off the kitchen table so that I could write a letter to good old Marty in the US. Perhaps she could come for a visit, after my mother came this summer? It would be so refreshing: in my mind's eye I could see a tall glass of bubbling soda, served with a straw at a round table on a beach not far from Winthrop on a hot summer day. We were wearing bikinis.

The woman in the shop was very young, that much I could see through the shop window the closer we got. It began a few hundred yards before we reached our destination – cheeks receded, the soft face regained its plastic form and my mouth could once again smile, the corners of my mouth rise.

So. I would smile at her in the store and I would sink into her image of me: very pregnant woman, tired and heavy but happy, holding the hand of her first little girl. It would be impossible to suspect me of ill will, self-satisfied American narrow-mindedness, or even that I for God's sake should have murderous intentions.

'Hello, madam. What can I do for you today?'

'We'd like bread, and butter, and eggs for a pound cake, and naturally some candy,' came hurtling out of me as I saw the tall glass jars filled with colourful candy, the only thing in Devon to crackle and shine, and behind which I could glimpse the shop assistant. 'I'm in my ninth month,' I explained. I pointed at my belly, as if it could save me.

She stared at me blankly. Stupid young blonde. I knew

that I ought to sympathise with her, so young and so listless, so pristine – but *fuck*. Who the hell was she to stare at me?

When I had spent ten minutes writing, the feeling which had begun like a rising, a leap beyond a blue eternity, a diving board onto the glittering ocean, had yet again been reset and I had nothing left to write: my head was dark. Who was I again? What time was it? What day was it? Where was Ted?

Frieda had gotten up and started to peel off pieces of wallpaper, and a fierce anger rose up inside me.

'Stop!' I screamed, got up from the sofa, and Frieda was scared, started. Still, she kept pulling.

'Don't do that again!'

Frieda began to cry, and I had her in my arms even though I would have loved to kick her away from me. Between us lay a nest of wallpaper shreds, white striped with red.

'You rascal!' I said and tickled her, for what else could I do, I had to let go of my anger and regain her cheer.

What was some wallpaper?

What was a novel compared to a small child?

I kissed her dirty hair, which I knew all too well that I tonight needed to wash clean in the tub, to make her presentable to Ted. Kiss and wash. Care for and feed. And now the girl needed food, of course that was what this was all about. While I with great effort remained on the floor with my mountainous stomach beneath a wigglingly adorable one-and-a-half-year-old girl child, the words on the page in the typewriter over there decomposed. Or no, they affixed themselves even firmer, and their futility screamed at me.

But I was so happy, like a kitten, when Ted came home. This was his return, I was not Penelope, but this was his return, of the proud variety. I was a proud woman, his woman (not 'wife'!) with an apron. There was a golden pound cake in the kitchen. The entire house smelled of Home. He tossed his suitcase in the hallway and attacked Frieda with hugs. My entire interior glowed: there were little electric shocks everywhere. I waited for my turn.

He came over and kissed me – not as I had imagined, but still fine. He smelled of city and smoke and the unknown. London our London, I had sent a representative there – a spy, someone who maintained relationships with the rest of the world.

'Have things been all right?' I asked. Stupid question – he could barely tear his eyes away from his daughter.

I swallowed cold saliva.

I wished he could barely tear his eyes away from my belly – that he would run a hand across it, perhaps kiss it, ask how we were doing. The baby and I. That we also were living elements of his life, just as he was highly alive and illuminated to me.

I listened to the response, as boring as the question.

'The train was fine.'

Then I was there again, steering and directing since I was suddenly struck by a violent desire to tell, tell him everything even though he had not asked me, but so the joy crashing inside me had some kind of release and the emptiness revealed by his laconic response did not take root in the room:

'We went for a walk, puttered around the house, and wrote letters and I just began to write a new, long poem that I plan to send to the BBC to be recorded, it's inspired by Bergman,' I said far too quickly but right there Ted's interest faltered and what I had said was devalued, retained nothing of worth once I had said it.

Was he not interested? Was it not fantastic that I also could write for the radio?

Ted followed Frieda's movements with his gaze, attacked her with hugs yet again and dug up picture books he had brought for her out of his suitcase, and a large plastic horse, which Frieda welcomed with little meowing noises. I still stood hovering over all of it like a bird over its prey, but I was unsteady, no longer knew when to attack.

'Well, shouldn't we get up and have some pound cake?'

That night I wanted to fuck Ted press my nose into his soft completely perfect and sweet-smelling hair, cut last week and now so elegant. But he moved further and further away in the bed.

'Don't you want to?' I asked, wounded and proud. I felt wet and warm in my white Christmas nightgown from Mother.

'I don't know,' he replied gloomily. 'You're so heavy.'

'Come on,' I said.

Ted's chest was bare. I was dripping with lust and desire for his strong, hairy chest. Those arms that could manage to carry everything.

'Take me from behind, then, if I'm so heavy.'

He glanced at me and it was as if he saw through it all, was about to blow my cover. He could see through my joy, my relief upon his return, he could see through my pregnancy, our temporary kingdom, the clouds upon which everything was constructed. For a moment as we let our differently brown eyes rest in each other, he could see its fragility. His coolness and my burning fire, how would we ever reconcile them?

On the evening of January seventeenth, as I had early contrac-
tions, Ted lay in bed caressing my large belly, balancing a hot
cup of tea in his other hand. He was exhilarated, I was focused.
Frieda was asleep in the nursery. He whispered things like:
'You know, Sylvia, how it's possible to know that outer space
has a beginning and an end?' 'No,' I whimpered – I had dived
deep into the contraction. His voice could fill a cathedral. He
said: 'You know because the sky is black at night.'

He grabbed my sweaty palm and kneaded it while I sank
away from my body and time and tried to just be at the centre
of the universe. I hated this, hated the pain but still I loved
what would come tonight, the planets rotating around me.
The pink and white curtains kept the dark night out and our
red heat-lamp hummed in the corner, cast my arms in the
same red hue as the blood beneath my skin.

'I think it's time to call the midwife,' I breathed.

Ted crawled down off the bedspread, where I knelt on
all fours, eyes closed, and disappeared down the stairs. He
suddenly sounded like a boy calling his grandmother, asking
if he can come by and play the following weekend, and I
felt a sense of irritation: *If he wasn't so damn meek and hard
at the same time, if he wasn't so tacky and at the same time proper,
my English poet, if he wasn't so working-class and still so cool*

and power-hungry like a suited-up boss in downtown London; if I could nail him somehow, fucking Ted, but I can't, to bear his children is my only way to surround him, tame him as he has tamed me.

The midwife Winifred Davies cooed like a dove when she arrived in her blue car and I was proud, for the electric heater had been on all day as she had instructed me, and Ted carried her heavy midwifery equipment inside.

She remained standing in the kitchen for a bit, asked Ted to move the bulky seeds he had bought in London, the ones he used to sort with a rustle into the proper compartment in the seed box he had made himself. I heard her slam the midwife bag down and start pulling things out: the funnel, the nitrous tank, rubber gloves, towels, Vaseline, and of course the hot water bottle.

I contentedly eavesdropped on their activities in the kitchen: she bossed over Ted, asked him to boil water for the warm towels. Her steps were heavy kind mother-steps and this was what we needed, someone to dominate Ted, to cancel him out, I thought.

Ted did as he was told, he came upstairs to me.

Winifred Davies gently walked up the steps behind him, my noble midwife with robust morals, and she wore a blue apron over her stiff white hospital uniform. She tied the scarf over her hair, placed her hand against my forehead and beamed at me as if I were her very own child.

'And how is our dear Sylvia?' the midwife enquired, in just the right way. This is how you treat royalty: look and learn, Ted, I thought.

'I've had pains since this afternoon and I would like to use the nitrous.'

'Here you go.'

I took some of the gas, began to laugh. I felt so wonderfully free inside.

A toast to my honour – finally, as the blood rushed through me like a brook in spring, clear and fresh.

Oh, how grand it was to give birth! To for once be completely at the centre of things! Birth, I had noticed, had become a thoroughly wonderful event for me, ever since Frieda arrived in London and Ted marvelled at what a good warrior I was, made to give birth to his children not in the British modernist fashion by lying half-paralysed in a hospital bed stuffed full of medication. No, I came alive! I lived like the European–American oxygenated blast I was.

Suddenly I knew it was a boy, something in me communicated that fact to me. I heaved out a moan, in Ted's arms; he was strong, could handle it.

If the midwife was happy or concerned or felt rushed in that very moment was unclear to me – still, I knew.

I closed my eyes and felt the most minute movements she made, where she stood, what she was thinking, what she did at that very moment. She held the glass of juice in her hand and let the straw rest against my lip. Here it came, the contraction, and it rolled and played against me, drove a ball straight into my mouth so that I needed to scream a muted scream which rumbled out from my deepest insides.

I tumbled down from the struggle caught my breath was conquered in Ted's arms conquered. I was a small piece of conquered flesh held by him. My face so wet and warm, and I thought of everything we had been through, all the memories blazed by. Ted had me etched into his heart in all manner of ways. He had our first kiss, the bite in his cheek, all my battles, my struggles since I was a child, an unkissed sweet-brier from the sea outside Boston before death had infected me with my father's condition and farewell. He had all of the ecstasy at the fact of us, the Cambridge struggle, my entire interior battle of being a human alongside his human. So it was such a relief to be completely knocked out by this mudwrestling with another – oh! – there was a contraction again, it was on the rise! – another human being who would pass through me. He was tough as taffy in there, he was a burning orb who would disappear out of me quickly and right away! Please!

'What's happening with the laughing gas?' I puffed. 'What the hell isn't working?' I glanced at Ted's half-afraid, half-comforting face and his gaze was dark. What my look told him I did not know, I only knew what it was like to look into him then, as if our universes met, two different solar systems.

Oh God. I could smell marshy blood already, and there was the midwife with a horribly harried and grim expression. What was she tinkering with? The nitrous tank.

'It's empty,' she said, turning around.

'What?' Ted gasped, and I was happy he reacted.

'Empty,' she replied in the same flat tone.

'My God, what are you saying?' rushed out of me. What had just been a dance with God was now a dance with the Devil, for here came the contraction again, here it came, now it rushed across me like a deathly moaning and my Gooooooooood how I burned in what was no longer my vagina no longer my body but a large house on fire that I needed to remain inside to struggle against the Devil.

'It's too big!' I screamed. 'It's too big!'

And so the final push, the final warbling screams from my mouth and the final trembling aid of Ted's supporting hands from behind – I felt his fear now, equal parts fear and ecstasy. And the midwife, yes, the midwife, she stood there, cheering us on.

And so the slippery splash as he stole out of me and turned the bed to a beach. As he liberated me from the pain. And I saw him lie there, blue and attempting to wiggle. The white umbilical cord lay coiled and fat and sticky around belly and throat.

He was in my arms. A tiny wrestler with a compressed forehead.

'I gave you a son!' I laughed and looked at Ted. 'He looks just like you! A Hughes!'

And Ted's eyes were filled with tears.

'I'll leave you for a moment,' the midwife whispered and walked out of the swampy dark room that smelled of freshly cut hay.

Actually, it smelled of the sea. Ocean and seaweed, and my son was sticky as if fetched from the sea. I looked into his eyes. Black and with a gaze of iron. Who was he? Where did he come from? Why did he also smell of freshly baked bread?

So many questions and no answers. He was here now, and it was still January seventeenth, for another five minutes. I wanted to hold on to the moment even longer.

The boy lay crashed like a rose in my arms – healthy and slippery like the dew. It was only I who was a seal with sticky blood between my thighs. And now I had a temperature of 39.5.

Ted emptied the chamber pot Ted came with the thermometer Ted forgot that I also wanted a kiss on the cheek.

The midwife cancelled her follow-up visit. Her father had taken ill in some respiratory condition, and I couldn't muster the energy to rehearse a performance before anybody else. Then I'd rather be alone with my husband, even if everything healthy in our life – Frieda's smell of wild strawberries! The little boy's downy hair! The midwife's manner of saving the world, with all her female knowledge! Ted's jaw that softened when she was here! – seemed to freeze as soon as we were alone together.

I sat up in bed, leaning against the headboard. My head throbbed. The boy I put down to sleep on his stomach at the foot of the bed, dressed in white.

Mastitis.

This was the entire problem:

I was struck by hubris.

I had been struck by the completely commonplace I've-had-a-kid-and-my-freezer-is-fully-stocked-with-pound-cake-and-a-dreamlife kind of hubris. That kind of ecstasy. Completely wonderful, once you have a taste of it. So it felt as if my coat was made of American wedding cake and my son's cheeks were a pair of candied cherries. I strolled about like a wonder woman in white, with my new wonder child (my second). If not even my own mother and grandmother could see him, surely I should show him off to the entire neighbourhood around Court Green! So I strolled and showed him off and put on my panting smile which I always knew ran out of gas in mere minutes. Stepped about like a prima donna with her hand on a pram. And forgot to remember that I wasn't at all made of sugar and not wrapped in cellophane – I was animal, I was cow, I could moo, I was woman. I had blood that rushed out between my legs (such things were called lochia). I was chock-full of hormones and had milk in my boobs. And just as I reported to a woman in a very grey coat and a fox around her neck, who lit up and wanted to pinch both of Nicholas's cheeks – just then, I sweated a lake *while* my milk came down (it must have been when she pinched his cheeks. My body's impulse may have come out of my protective instinct when she did that). And it was as if the milk became a plaster cast in my breasts.

Idiotic vanity! I, who was now animal, thought I could put on an old minimal coat I'd had when I was young and gorgeous in London. And what did I have for it: FEVER. MASTITIS.

'Cabbage,' the midwife said when I called her, out of breath. 'Cabbage, do you have a head of cabbage at home?'

'I don't know, I can ask Ted to look in the fridge, I'll see, it's possible.'

I covered the receiver so she wouldn't hear how I hiss-screamed at Ted, who was tinkering with his seeds in the kitchen: 'DO WE HAVE ANY CABBAGE?'

'What?' he hollered.

'DO WE HAVE CABBAGE?'

'PACKAGE?'

'What the hell, do we have cabbage, goddammit! White cabbage, do we have cabbage in the fridge?'

A pause.

'Yes.'

'Yes,' I answered the midwife. 'We have cabbage at home, why?'

'Then you can remove a cabbage leaf and lay it against your breast. Yes, dress the entire breast in cabbage.'

I felt like laughing.

'In cabbage . . .' It was the vain, happy, young Sylvia who wanted to laugh. 'It just sounds so hilarious. But fine. Cabbage. I'll do it.'

'Try it and call me back in a few hours. I feel for you: mastitis is not fun. It can be particularly tricky in this cold weather.'

'Frieda was born in April, and it was so different, spring had already arrived that year.'

'Cold is also good.'

'I thought you were supposed to keep the breast warm?'

'You can try a towel with a few ice cubes in it.'

'Thank you so much for your attention.'

'It's my job.'

'You're priceless, Winifred.'

'I'll come by tomorrow. One more thing!'

'Yes, what?'

A part of me wanted the conversation with her to never end. Such a large hole in me, this lack of intimate conversations with an older female friend. They were like the hard American boys in college: they made me believe that life was in fact a completely normal thing and not either a gallows hill or a heavenly paradise.

'You have to make sure to nurse as much as possible on the affected breast. Nurse, nurse, nurse. Little Prince Nicholas should suck and suck and not go hungry for a minute.'

'I'll make sure of it, little Prince Nicholas will suck and not go hungry for a minute!' I repeated with a gentle voice, a voice I would like to use when I spoke to Ted, or when I turned to myself. But then the voice was another, usually so stern, a voice I would myself grow fearful of, but in this phone conversation, with this woman, with other people I did not have a deep relationship to: velvet.

Ted gave me cabbage and at that point the fever had risen even higher and his hand felt so steady and cool as he placed it against my forehead.

'Poor Sylvia,' he said, for he knew that I softened when he used that word, 'poor.'

'Poor Sylvia.'

He kissed my forehead and I went and decorated my white hardened flushed breast with large cabbage leaves.

The cabbage leaves squeaked and had an acrid odour and were soon soft and sweaty from my fever, and I fell asleep clad in cabbage. I was like a flower, a warm living flower in the sun that my little boy wanted to suck the nectar from.

Ted stuck his head into my fever room, making noise about going on the first fishing trip of the year.

'Fishing! I'd so love to go fishing,' was how he phrased it. 'Is it okay if I go to the Taw with Andy for a bit?'

Andy, the variable that would prevent me from saying no.

I smiled a weak fever smile, 'Okay go, honey,' my clothes stuck to the pillows I had fluffed up, then he was gone with his fishing rod.

The stickiness between my legs was palpable when I got up, shuffled to the toilet and pulled the brown-red pad from my underwear. It smelled rancid. In with a new one – and Nick had already started to scream from the bed. Someone needed to take care of Frieda, I couldn't manage her now, and still, then: *fishing*.

Fishing, as if it were the right time of year.

Fishing, as if the river really awaited him just now.

Fishing, as if what the family needed was fish.

I already reeked plenty of rotten fish I ALREADY REEKED PLENTY OF ROTTEN FISH, I had time to think, before I was back in bed (my temple my castle my mountain my ocean my fish pond prison life) and Nick and Frieda both lay curled like seals of different sizes at my feet.

At my pillow: old cabbage. Two pale bows of cabbage,

softened by the warmth of my body and like pieces of a corpse next to me. Frieda, actually a lamb, had hardened and now she struck at my newborn with her fist, right into his stomach. An entirely unexpected rage rose up inside me: could you even become so furious with a child? I threw my hand around hers so she would not do it again, for that was what she was set upon. Her mouth in a sly grimace.

'Stop, Frieda! I don't want you to hit him like that!'

All the while I heard Ted's background voice, in my head: Fishing. Is it okay if I disappear for a bit? I want to fish!

The fever in me rose, what the hell could I do, when it rose?

All I could do was deliver myself to the panic.

'Frieda,' I said in what I imagined was a steady voice which cracked like a glass bowl against the floor. I wanted to sound like the authoritative one.

'So Daddy is away and I have a fever.' As if a nearly two-year-old knew. As if she knew what fever was. She wiggled like a robot toy in bed. It was as if she was wound up with a key in her back as soon as Ted got it into his head to leave.

'Right, and then you have to be still, you understand? Still.'

When Ted came back home I lay apathetic and immobile against the pillow. The hours had run into me like rubbery slime. I was no longer responsible for children or a house or anything. Nick slept like a changeling who had fallen asleep because there was no other option. Frieda slumbered some-where, the house was silent.

I saw his shadow move in the bedroom but did not want to focus my gaze: it would be empty and helpless in that way where he, with his sense, strength, and manliness, would come to in order to understand how close to catastrophe we were when he left me feverish and just out of childbirth.

Couldn't he go fishing some other time? My God! What could now be more important than the health of his wife and children? If I had been in better spirits I would have written everything down on a slip of paper, in bullets, so he would understand. I had read in a book on Buddhism, *to love is to understand, and to love is to be understood*. Did he not show me, then, time and again, that he in fact no longer loved me? He did not understand me.

'Ted,' I whimpered.

It was the umpteenth in a series of breakdowns signed yours truly. Would he assign this particular one meaning? Would he accuse me of acting out, in order to not be capable of being alone with our little ones? Or would he capitulate in the face of my sorrow, submit, and shower my feet with kisses until his saliva ran dry?

'Sylvia,' came from Ted, silken-voiced. 'How are you, my beloved? My Pussy.'

'Stop – don't call me that.'

'Is it February bringing its darkness to you.'

'Cut it out.'

'You always get sick in February.'

He snaked over to me in bed. He looked healthy, ripe and full of ideas; the fishing trip glittering in his eyes as if he had emptied his eyes of tears.

'Broke your leg in February, sinus infection, in the psych ward all the way until February, miscarriage and appendicitis at the same time – in February . . .'

'Stop!'

'February is your month, my love,' Ted said and kissed my shoulder where the gown had slid down. He was filled with his fishing trip, his freedom, that was for sure.

'Easy, easy, we'll survive February,' he said and I suddenly felt I could soften and hand it to him, actually receive his voice.

In my silence his voice grew stronger.

'And I can keep going for ever. Mastitis in February . . .' he said.

He had my head in his arms.

'Met Ted Hughes in February . . .'

I snorted so that a flake of snot flew out and hit his lap. I was soft now – soft. I laughed at his vanity, the egotism we all lived with as if it were a third invisible child.

'Yes, perhaps that wasn't the best of ideas?'

Our gazes met. Ted mussed my hair then he picked up our sleeping son, carried him to the cradle and fixed his hair in the mirror. Stood with his hands in his pockets and looked at me.

'We didn't catch any fish.'

'Sorry to hear that.'

'Sometime I want to go to the ocean with you again. We'll go to Woolacombe.'

'Don't you understand that I'm sick?'

'I want to bring you to Woolacombe. And I want to go to Australia with you.'

Ted had dreams in his eyes, as if a madness had surfaced there. Australia! Who could even think about Australia – now?

'My head is killing me, go fetch some aspirin.'

Ted lifted his gaze from the floor. It was if he had been speaking to someone imaginary, not me.

But his reference to February made me spend the night thinking. I lay in the light of the candles I could not bear to put out when I nursed. I sweated out the fever, fresh air rose inside me and made it possible for me to feel hope.

There was something about February. Something about the frozen stillness. Something about the rebirth that had to occur in February, as with the purification of the year which had passed. Something about the fact that I was surely

CONCEIVED in February, I who was born late in October. It was my fate, February. I had been in the hospital in February – me. Me – February. I was so ecstatically terrified that time, that my leg had been damaged, as my father's leg had been damaged that time when I was seven and the toe turned blue and he had to amputate. At that moment I saw my father's leg in my own. I lay in the night in the white hospital room and imagined how the leg beneath the cast turned blue while I slept. And when the cast was taken off – how afraid I was of my own leg, which had taken the form of a dead person. I stared straight into my horror. My father's leg in my leg. The skin was pale and mushy as if on a corpse, the hairs straight and thick, and the flesh had shrivelled behind the dead skin, as if the leg had no intention of living any more. So shrivelled and disgusting and all this belonged also to me.

Me, the luminous young hungry loving laughing beautiful good attractive blonde. I who had never thought I could die – die for real, not even a single piece of me die. I had to eat crow that time. I had to laugh in the face of my own invincibility.

Now the son started with his sugary whimpering and I pulled him against my tender breast and it was so intoxicatingly wonderful as he grabbed at and sucked on me. His weight in gold, completely heavy and sweet-smelling.

It's such good luck that I have you, I whispered and kissed his newborn downy forehead.

Of course I have my wretched Ted, but it's fortunate that I have your love, I whispered a bit louder. Ted was asleep anyway.

And I continued to think about February while I nursed the boy.

It was last February, when I had felt so intensely purified.

I had had a miscarriage and appendicitis, at the same time.

I had to once again lie in a hospital room and be quiet and not get involved in any family matters.

Each and every woman deserved such a thing. To lie like that – quiet and cut-off and without any demands. I did not need to show myself to anyone.

I lay there and could become – again. Be born – again. Be created – again. Ted came walking along the infinite endless empty hallways just like the man he was when he met me. Tall (six foot three) and hawk-eyed beneath his bangs and full of admiration for me and my intellect. To have me at a distance – yes. That was how he could best manage to live with me. Perhaps that really was the case. In order to live with me such as we both would like to, he needed me at an aircraft carrier's distance. There needed to be a hallway for him to meet me in. The realisation saddened me. But perhaps it was the same for me, that I needed the empty other side, the place and the space and the room of my own, far away from him, in order to live.

I cupped my hand around Nicholas's crown – so soft and unspoiled, there was nothing evil in him, no deceit, no disappointment. His eyelids two sheer lilac leaves in the wind. May he remain just that.

I returned to the thought of Ted and I in the hospital in February of 1961. He walked there with Frieda in his hand, the tiny toddler whom it was so remarkably easy for him to care for on his own. Incredible. I had thought I was indispensable. But it was just fine. The girl loved being with her father. At the hospital I did not have to deal with all the clinging – the girl who clung at my body like a baby chimp – and all the logistics I was beset with. I did not have to deal with anything. And it had arrived as a blessing because all my power was gone, I had just used it all up, there was nothing left of me after a year of nursing, nurturing, carrying – my arms, my forces had turned to dust.

And the cosmos took care of it by giving me a miscarriage and appendicitis.

Ted's seed in me a mistake, the recalcitrance of nature, to be cleared out of me. Bleed to end.

The nurses paced back and forth between the rooms in their anonymous clothing and I was sure as hell happy not to have to be one of them.

I was the one who should be waited upon.

I was the one who should lie in her own room.

I was the one who had an author husband to be visited by.

I was the one who should write books.

I was the one who should be paid attention to.

I was the one who should receive care and affection.

That was the contract. This was what I was worth. The National Health Service money and my body. That was it. That was all I needed to be hurled out into my own voice again and begin writing anew. Such was the starting gun. February, the illnesses, blood, and my own convalescence and the red tulips on the table. Here was the story, the pages seemed to say to me. Here was the voice. *A book is not a book, but two is a tradition*, as Ted's friend Luke had sourly pointed out to me, after the wait for book number two following the debut had been a touch protracted. (My God, what kind of rush were these people in, anyway?) I would show him. I would show him again.

For then – then! I began to write. I came home, over-flowing with new oxygen, new empty pages upon which to attach the experiences of memory. I had energy, I had desire, I had fire in my belly and I had been given time to breathe. Then I started to write *The Bell Jar*. What happened now? What would happen next? What kind of writing would this month of February – its heavy mastitis and convalescence in the bedroom on Court Green – supply me with?

What novelty awaited me?

I fell asleep that night completely drained from all this thinking, ruminating, the insights which arrived to me clear and damp as dew drops. Nick lay fully fed and ballooning like a Buddha on the blanket. I wrapped it around him, then kissed Ted on his stubbly cheek – he was so sound asleep that he did not wake.

I had slept on Frieda's plastic horse. I threw it to the floor. It was Friday, I was healthy, the spring sun had emerged, I was expecting company. Tomorrow the children would be christened.

I hoisted Nick in his blanket up onto my shoulder and stood on the threshold of the terrace door and inhaled the garden, gazed out at our future and inhaled fresh air and thought: Yes, now I have overcome childbirth, Yes, now I have stopped bleeding, Yes, now I am a proper lady, Yes, now I am in the middle of my dreamlife. And I was seized with the desire to summon a photographer.

Then I caught sight of Ted walking like a dark horse in the garden, pouring the spring dose of snail poison across the paths. He stuck his hand into a bag of chicken manure, which he scattered across the beds he was preparing for our strawberries. Ted had devoted the spring to these preparations, placing seeds in large garden beds filled with black soil; he had spent the spring dedicated exclusively to books about gardening. I had not kept up. Ted was far ahead of me in that regard. I had barely been out of this large, white house; I had been the house itself.

He did not see us. I wished for a tool to extend out into the garden and haul him in with – a grip of some sort – imagine if there was a whistling call he would answer to, which meant 'It's your dear wife Sylvia calling!', imagine if he wanted to turn around in love each time he heard the whistle.

I tried with my voice.

'Ted?'

He did not hear, or else he ignored me. I did not want to disturb the neighbours, it could not become a habit that I called for my better half as if he were my property or one of my children. Ted had truly come much further than I had: he was transfixed by the garden. To him it was urgent that our dream house should become just as beautiful as we had imagined – lavender in rows, clematis clinging to the wall and navigating the worn ivy, new, crisp raspberry plants to compete with those terrible vines. Had Sir and Lady Arundel really not done a thing to the decayed garden when they lived here?

Ted was meant for living. So skilled with soil and animals and everything that kept us rooted to the earth, to what was constant, he was so skilled with tools, it was in his power to ground us, we who had flitted about with our youth, our beauty, our literary abilities criss-crossing life in London. Here, in North Tawton, vanity meant nothing!

I stepped through the terrace door and put on some lipstick – apricot, for spring.

Nick lay snoozing in the carriage and I rolled it back and forth on the rough gravel, wishing that Ted would come and observe us, drink in me and his son as I drank in the vision of him, that we could somehow be equals, that we would share an equal interest in each other.

I looked down at the little bundle in the carriage. It was as if reality slipped away from me; time and life wasn't really worth anything as I stood here alone and unobserved. Two months since the birth and I was ready to be looked at now, to feel like a woman in the eyes of my husband, to be kissed on lips soft from lipstick.

I stood here pushing the carriage to and fro for naught.

I would like to find a way to tell Ted that my loneliness was painful. That my loneliness when I was not permitted to be alone together with him made me a despicable piece of humanity — a kind of half-being, someone you could use as a character in a dystopian novel about ogres. Unliving. Half-dead.

I needed to be reassured that I was alive, that I stood at the centre of the story and was worth lipstick and a greeting.

Suddenly Ted approached us; heavy boots made tracks in the mud. He threw off the gloves and reached his arms down to Nick.

'Have you been up long?' he asked. I regretted my lipstick, regretted the feeling of wanting to be photographed. I jealously watched Ted assume control of our two-month-old little marionette, kiss his stomach and carefully hold him up to the skies. Suppressed the urge to object: no, dammit, his neck isn't steady yet.

'Why aren't you answering?' Ted asked.

'I'm just watching you,' I responded. It was my only reply this morning: *I'm just watching you.* Then we discussed snail poison.

'Say, do you want to marry me?' Ted asked when we had lain down to bed late at night. He nuzzled against my face, still smelled of garden, sea and sheep. 'Will you go steady with me? Will you marry a no-good, an unknown English poet who doesn't stand a chance?'

'Come on, you stand a chance.'

'Not against you. Against you I've got nothing. You're my genius author queen.'

His statement grew like a little bean sprout on its way up to the light and within me grew this desire to write. I walked with firm steps away from breakfast the next morning, handed him his son, said with a bite to my words that I needed to write now, even though it was today the children were to be christened. That wasn't so strange, was it? Ted didn't care for ceremonies, anyway.

So although I had an enormous longing attached to today, a light within me that crashed across the Atlantic and illuminated my mother over there and told her that, *Yes, today your two grandchildren are to be christened, today we are realising this business of morals and propriety*; in spite of this notion I had gone along with Ted's idea the entire time – a SIMPLE ceremony, just like when we got married, a simple event in the church while some other local children also were christened – yes, our children were to be christened today almost as if in passing.

Ted's way.

So then there was nothing strange about Mother Sylvia extricating herself from breakfast, nearly going up in smoke and turning to dust before her family when announcing:

'I'm going to go write now. You can clean up – the christening clothes are next to the bed, make sure to brush Frieda's hair.'

A deep silence hung in the kitchen after I had spoken. Ted chewed his breakfast as if it were animal feed and I knew that I had already lost the crucial morning hours we always struggled over – him fishing, or me writing – but now I could no longer be responsible for Ted's feelings. Now I simply had to go.

Go, with the peculiar feeling of having robbed my family of peace and routine because of this pull in me: to go up in smoke, become air, alight from the floor and become spirit and word and no longer Mother.

Exhale on the desk chair, lower shoulders, convince yourself that you have not committed a crime.

I went through my papers that had been beset by dust,

these pages, these sheets which consisted of me, my cramped flesh, my horrendous ideas.

They made me feel so good!

They lay there and became material in my hand as it moved across the pages, turning the blackened paper thin as silk. There. First glance at them, then look yet again and see that it was no lie: the chapters were there, the proper titles, the story of the first defeat and collapse of my life.

It had taken two raw months to write it, like opening a boarded-up door, the contents behind which had lain in preparation and ripened to pure perfection. I had only needed to lead the material out and it took shape. Now I had dedicated the remaining six months to sifting, rewriting, altering pages which to me had been lost and were just too *much*. I had directed the writing, changed names and feared for my mother's eyes on it. I had considered burning the lot of it but then the writing had throbbed in me like a heart in the night. And who tears out a heart and places it on the fire?

It was this writing that supported us, it was this writing which de facto gave my family, Ted, Nick, and Frieda, more life; it had started to also be about us. For we still had one dose left of the grant money *The Bell Jar* provided for us. The grant foundation wanted to reward a project written *while the funds were distributed*, one year in all, and I had been ashamed of my sly manoeuvre of fooling them and that was why no one could say a word. Every time I had sent already-written material to the foundation I had felt like a notorious criminal who tries to make up for their crime while committing a new one.

I polished it a bit, that was what I did this morning. I needed to glance at it and polish and see that it was enough. I needed to wake a few pages to life in me so that I knew that this writing breathed and lived, Esther Greenwood was alive, her temperament her gaze in the world her ideas all her deep longing. She had not fallen to pieces simply because I had not touched her in a few days. To judge from everything, Esther was my creation and no matter my feelings of love toward her – perhaps I did not actually love her, perhaps I carried a sting of sorrow within me regarding how the writing actually turned out, that it became so amateurish and entertaining. She had a right to live, she lived, and therefore a piece of me, a piece of oh-so-important flesh had more life, it lived on these pages completely independently of me, so if someone picked up a page and began to read, something would happen to the person reading: Esther – I – would change something in the world for ever. And that brought a shiver down my spine as good as anything.

My children would be purified before God. I just wanted to get it over with. A young boy from the village performed Haydn's piano sonata like a death fugue in church, and the rector poured water over my children's heads as robotically as if they were melons. I stood in my hat weeping and thought: what have I done? Who am I, agreeing to make this so simple? I had naturally imagined a colourful, sunny day followed by pavlova with guests from far away arriving with the most delightful gifts and my mother, who would peck everyone on the cheek in a slightly continental fashion and thereby represent *me*; tell the guests who I was, show them what I came from.

Who was I, who had let everything become a compromise between Ted's Celtic chill and my grandiose American bluster?

Now Nicholas had been christened at the hand of the rector. At his monotonous summons, little Frieda rushed to the baptismal font, reached for the water and began splashing her own head. Comedy struck: even Ted laughed, that was something to be happy about. But overall it was a day of disappointments that passed with a gasp. No wolf in me, no movement, no comfort even though our children were radiantly angelic and did not whine a bit – only the neighbouring children did that, the others christened today. All of it was austere and Ted had not bothered to iron his shirt.

'We hear *everything* that happens at Court Green,' our neighbour Rose exclaimed as we exited the church and gravel crunched beneath our shoes. Frieda ran across the graves, she criss-crossed the headstones askew on the grass, she thought this was her garden. 'We can hear everything! And now the best season is here.'

I did not know how to reply to this peculiar announcement from my neighbour. Was there something in particular she was trying to tell me? It made me forget all at once about the christening.

'We have nothing to hide!' I chirped in return, and then I grabbed Ted's arm, commanded him: 'Will you run after Frieda, I'm so afraid a headstone will fall on her.'

Ted was at Frieda's side in a split second. He stopped by a tall tree and lifted her up to the first branch, where there was a squirrel he animatedly pointed to. That thing with animals, I thought, what is it about my husband's fondness for animals? Rose had vanished: the entire group had dissolved without any proper goodbyes. I wanted to go home to my writing. Across the cemetery and our garden, the same birds flew.

April was here and it was the most gorgeous of seasons in England, manifest in our garden where hundreds of narcissus and daffodils in bloom made it something of a dream. People went out en masse to look at our garden: it was apparently a North Tawton tradition since the others' houses and gardens were so dull. And, naturally, this was what we had talked about all winter, exactly this, so now we would be forced to offer up our fecundity. *Be careful what you wish for*, my anxious mother had said to me in a subdued voice back in America and since they were my mother's words I only listened with half an ear.

My chicken with powdered ginger and honey stood in the oven and potatoes were ready and peeled in a bowl. I carried out coffee and two pieces of chocolate on a tray to my husband. He looked up from behind his shovel, fixed his hair and loudly announced, 'Oh, Sylvia, you're a genius! An afternoon should be named after you.'

Hardly had the words left his mouth than I felt the familiar, proud heat inside me flutter by, before there was a knock at the door inside the house and he was gone for a long while, until the coffee had turned cold and I stepped inside to see who it was.

The little girl, Lolita, what was her name, Charlotte? Scarlett? I couldn't name her. Her name was Nicola, that's right, the neighbour's daughter. Her.

She was on leave from school in Oxford and here she stood, on our steps. Ted held up a book and a couple of records it looked like he was about to lend to her. When I approached from behind him, she stepped back and looked helplessly into my eyes.

'Should I go?' she asked. 'Is this a bad time?'

'My God,' I replied. 'Am I that frightening? I was only going to ask if you wanted some coffee? I just made some.'

'Nicola wants to read my books,' Ted said in a low voice, 'so I thought I could give them to her.' He looked into my eyes for permission. That's absurd, I thought, why should I care who you give your books to?

We walked through the kitchen, where it smelled of ginger chicken and where Ted grabbed a pen. We walked out into the sun. I refilled the coffee.

He signed his books for her, an inscription in each. She smiled and crossed one leg over the other and somehow pressed it against her groin. She didn't think I noticed. There I was and got to listen to their conversation, which oddly enough grew more and more intimate the longer we sat there, and somehow deepened, and I knew that Ted was a ladies' man, I knew. I saw that he did something with his bangs and eyes that made him impossible to resist. And he was a poet. Grew more and more famous for every day in this place. I needed to get used to it.

This was what it was to be the wife of a beloved poet.

And a few days later the same scene played itself out in our garden: it was a Swedish journalist who suddenly got in touch, even if the visit concerned me. She came to interview me. We had been corresponding with each other, she had read my work in the anthology *New American Poets*, she wanted to translate my poems into Swedish. And yet, still, it was between her and Ted that something was set in motion.

She tossed her hair, blonde and cut short but still possible to toss, and looked curious with her crooked nose. Nodded eagerly, asked follow-up questions, politely urged Ted to explain what he meant by the way something in particular had been phrased. And then she asked us: what is it like for two poets to live together?

The longer she sat there in our garden and I was forced to show her my boob (she was Swedish, didn't care), the more it hit me that this was what I in fact was not capable of: I could not live like a poet, it was a phantasm, pure delusion. A faint taste of iron in my throat, as if I was bleeding some-where. I spoke up and loudly stated that it was great, we wrote in shifts, Ted first and me a bit later in the morning – Ted is such an early bird! I caressed his cheek and he turned away from my touch since Siv Arb witnessed it, which he did not want, for before Siv Arb and any other woman who entered our home he should appear a virgin.

It was then and there that I realised my hands were dirty: baby goop, mother's milk. I was repulsive.

'Things are going very well for Ted right now. He writes plays for the stage and radio plays for the BBC, and I am going to begin reviewing children's literature for *The Observer.*'

Siv Arb took notes in her little book, even though nothing I said was of any value; she already knew everything.

All the while, Nick squirmed on my stomach. I saw in Ted's entire being that he wanted to unhitch himself from me and our children. He was fidgeting in his seat. It must have to do with the fact that we had not made love in a long time, mustn't it? And then Siv Arb gestured toward our garden and made a tart comment that it must be a super-human task to care for such a large garden on your own.

Do you have a gardener? And so I thought: Watch out, watch out you sensible Scandinavian woman who does not understand what it means to live in the real world. This is England, this is Sylvia Plath and Ted Hughes, don't you get it? And it struck me that I wanted to grab a shovel from our garden to chase her off. And it struck me that I wanted to be alone with Ted, if not now, then when? And if not now, now when we had a tiny newborn to watch over, when our love should be in its fullest bloom . . . If not now, then when? But I only swallowed the imaginary blood that ran and ran down my throat. I showed her the difference between cherry blossoms and nectarine blossoms while Ted gathered the china and then I took her stiff bony hand in mine and said goodbye.

As if it wasn't enough to have strange women running around in our garden, the neighbours also took it upon themselves to visit, and I was the one who had to manage them. Neighbours! If you are a human in this world, neighbours are a fact of life! And a body, and a bank account, and a car – indeed, there were certain practical details you simply couldn't escape, as a human being in the world. Not even if you were a poet.

We had dressed all in white to have our photos taken in the spring light among all the daffodils and narcissus. Have our family portrait taken to send home to Mother, Aunt Dotty, and to Edith et al. in Yorkshire. To Olwyn, as well. Ted and I, alone behind the towering ivy and the trees which had begun to shelter us from public view with their budding branches. For that was how I wanted us to be: free, and still walled-off. I wanted my beloved to myself, and it was such a heady moment, this, for him to stand there with the camera trained on me and regard me in a heightened light, with a doubly powerful gaze aimed at me through the lens. Exposed. The most forceful gaze in North Tawton.

Just as I was sitting there among the spring flowers with Nick on my arm and Frieda by my side and he was photographing us, Rose shrieked like a bird over the wall wanting to tell us that Percy was on his deathbed, he had fallen ill, some sort of heart attack. Naturally, I had to get up and invite her in, ask her to come inside and help herself to the hot tea. And all I could think about as I listened to her speak were the luscious scenes that had just unfolded in our sea of narcissus: white and yellow, they were now captured in the photo and I wondered just what expressions of mine had been made immortal, what my smile had looked like.

To be photographed was virtually erotic. A sharp sense of being turned on sprung up in me for the first time since I had given birth to Nick. And then Rose's endless stream of information came to an end and she awaited my reply.

'Yes, of course, we'll help you with whatever you need,' I wrapped up with a bang.

I walked back out into the garden and watched Ted adjust Frieda's pose in the grass. She held a daffodil that she had picked: he quickly snapped a few before she was up and running about again.

'Well, then, please send our hellos to Percy, you poor things,' I said and cued Rose to leave. Then my energy was gone, I couldn't manage to be polite to the entire world, and then to Ted as well. Nick wanted to be fed again because that's what he wanted all the time. This was the thing, though: I couldn't BEAR it.

I told Ted later, as we ate leftovers from the previous day's chicken dinner.

'I can't bear it,' I said. 'I can manage ten minutes, then it's as if . . .'

I couldn't manage to eat, just cry, and it was as if my skin was gone and there was just a path that cut straight into my blood.

My skeleton was charred wood.

'But then don't bear it,' Ted said. 'Don't bear it. I can bear it.'

'But I have to bear it,' I said. 'I have to bear it!'

'You can bear what you can bear, no?'

I was priming him for a fight: I raised the point that it's an impossible equation when he takes off for London all the time and I'm the one who has to entertain Frieda with tales of what the cows on the farm sound like and feed Nick food food food from my own flesh. I'm the one who needs a bottle of nutrients, the kind you pour on your plants, but no one ever gives me any! Don't you understand?

Ted gnawed at his chicken and remained silent: so let me think, his body seemed to signal, I'm thinking so be quiet, all right?

Acres of soil to till and plenty of repairs to the house and two miniature humans. My God, Ted, I was about to exclaim, let's surrender to all of this before it's too late!

But I couldn't force any voice up into my mouth. It was as if all I had down there was black soil, silent black soil.

We chewed and swallowed, couldn't muster the energy to fight.

'Can you watch out for my breasts?'

Ted lay with his hand on my boob in the moonlight. I didn't want to lose him, but it was still something I needed to tell him, that now my breasts were Nick's, they were no longer an erogenous zone. He had come climbing up onto me just as I was about to fall asleep. His kisses were quick and intense and I made an effort to feel taken with him, tried to recall our interactions from before, when we made love often, in all kinds of ways, in different positions. I moved Nick. 'You lie there in the crib instead,' I whispered and caressed his downy forehead. Then I made up my mind to give myself over. I needed to want to make love, too.

Outside, the moon was full of a glow and aimed its flood-light all the way in here. Were we not also merely animals, wasn't Ted right after all, with his equals sign between humans and animals? Were we not simply flesh and hunger?

It was the first time since my son had journeyed through my body out into life, the first time I spread my legs for someone else. This first time seemed incredibly pleasurable for Ted, while it was trying and uncertain for me. My sex was stretched out and I tensed my legs to force the area that held him to become tight, pleasurable tissue. But it was still too large, distended and sensitive: he was overcome by an intense desire that was out of alignment with mine and then he came, a spasm of his heavy limbs as the pleasure released its hold on him and he gave in to a raw bellow. He emptied himself in me, he roared up toward the ceiling, and I glanced at Nick, who flinched but did not wake. So, he had come, inside me, without waiting for me, without my sounds, my gaze.

He kissed me desperately on the mouth.

'You feel so fucking good, Sylvia,' he said. 'Ah. I needed that. That's the best thing that's happened in a long time. Wow, Pussy. You're back.'

I scoffed, and pulled on my nightgown. I still looked good, was just a bit soft in the middle; my sex was soft, but it would contract again, I knew it would, in a short while I would be completely restored.

Nick woke up, I fed him and while the milk came down and Ted's snores rumbled through the house, I lay and consid-ered the fact that I had been Siv Arb, or the little neighbour girl Nicola; they were the ones he had fucked tonight, they were the ones who had aroused my husband's desire. Crooked journalist noses from Sweden and tacky Lolita-tights beneath a short skirt. Instinct summoned an urge between my legs, an urge distinguished by a muddle of deep erotic feeling and sheer disgust.

May in England was truly everything I had been told: it seethed with eroticism and creativity! Ted cut the grass, Frieda following him with her plastic toy lawn mower. The air was intoxicating with the scent of all the little flowers rupturing and promptly blooming in our large garden. I sat for a while in the easy chair by the window and offered Nicholas my breast until he settled down, watched Ted walk bent over his machine, deeply absorbed – as always – in thought. I followed my own thought past the finish line: men, and their machines! If he knew how sick I grew of *one* way to sit here and nurse and nurture and shush and plan lunches. How much easier it would be just to follow a machine. But when I did that in the fall, made a big deal out of trading responsibilities and saw it as my opportunity to shine, to be a 'modern woman', walk with the power mower and slaughter the tall fall grass just like that, it had suddenly become so heavy, far too heavy for my arms, my expectant body – I couldn't manage it. 'I can't manage it,' I had to tell Ted and he sighed and muttered, 'But I told you so,' and had gone out into the nascent dampness of dusk to finish what I had left behind. Ted despised unfinished projects: they frightened him. Unfinished projects made him think that he alone was responsible for every crack in existence that required repair.

Men, and their machines. And then they wanted food, and Ted was no better than anybody else. I sat there and got worked up about his unshaven cheeks. The way he kept on about tending to the lawn and keeping it smooth, he ought to make more of an effort to shave his face. I wanted to ask him to shave, but if I did there would be all kinds of trouble: Ted hated it when I bothered him about his habits. And then I became so afraid of his indignation, I, who had intended to shower his smooth, shaved cheeks with love . . . Stubble *was* unpleasant, like poison ivy, weeds, and besides, I loved how good Ted was in the garden! Wasn't it fantastic to have a man who cared so deeply about delicate things like vegetation and nature and animals?

Nick spit up on my shoulder.

Ted stomped in on the linoleum floor that we had finally managed to get the boorish carpenters to glue on top of the rotting wooden planks in the hallway. He wiped the sweat off his forehead with a handkerchief.

'I want to write,' he breathed heavily. 'I'm dried up, can't get any air.'

'Have a glass of water.'

'I need to write.'

Ted downed the glass of water I gave him in three quick gulps, slammed it against the table. A few drops dribbled from his lip.

'I'll finish the grass later.'

I walked up to the window, Nick asleep on my arm. He was starting to get heavy: I would put him down in a minute.

'You didn't finish the grass?'

My heart beat faster.

Ted shook his head.

'I'm going to go write.'

'But the grass . . . You don't usually leave it unmowed . . . I can take a walk with Nick while you finish. He just fell asleep, then we can have lunch?'

Ted shook his head. He looked empty, his gaze hollow.

'I'm going to wash up in the sink, then take a walk, then sit in the office for a while. I need . . . Sylvia. I don't know. I need something.'

'Are you not feeling well?'

Frieda was still out among the berry bushes, digging at the dirt with a spoon.

'Sylvia, I'm a man with ideas. I need to think. That's all there's to it. I need some solitude. That's it.'

I looked back out at the garden, where Frieda turned around, searching for somebody's gaze. Her mouth was ringed with black, as if she had gorged herself on dirt.

'She's eating dirt!' I shouted and ran out around the corner in my stocking feet, catching her by the arm.

When Ted was back I phoned Winifred Davies, the midwife. At that moment she was the only one, the only person who could offer an escape and salvation. The phone, heavy with promise, hung in my hand. Ted was up in the attic like an elusive shadow. He had gotten the children to sleep: wasn't it magical? After ten rings my midwife answered, her voice cloudy. It cleared when she heard me on the other end.

'Sylvia . . . oh, Sylvia! How are you? How's our little Nick?'

'Our . . .'

I was crushed by her warmth when she said it – so *that's* how a good-hearted human, a practical and life-affirming human, lives, YES! *Our Nick* – and I was reminded of the crazy January night when he was born and I had been furious with Winifred Davies for forgetting that I was someone who required A LOT of nitrous oxide. But by now I had forgiven her for all that.

'He's wonderful, Winnie, utterly wonderful. He's peaceful and poetic, like his father, still colossal, he empties all of my reserves.'

'Make sure you're eating plenty, that Ted cooks for you, that you get all your vitamins and minerals – you're going to need it when you start bleeding again.'

'Well . . .'

'Have you started bleeding yet?'

'No menstruation yet, thankfully.'

'And marital relations?'

I wound the cord around my finger, looked up the stairs toward the studio where Ted was sitting.

'It's had to wait. Ted has so much going on. We have a whole garden to fertilise and tend to . . .' I laughed, and when I laughed Frieda could hear that something was up: something playful and merry was afoot when she heard her mother's laughter. And she woke up and called for me.

'Mommy! Mommy!'

'I have to get Frieda now . . . There's just that, about the garden,' I said.

'Yes? What?'

'We have an idea – we'd so love to keep bees. Naturally, it's a gamble . . .'

'How wonderful!' my midwife exclaimed and, as if her fingers were inside me, a heavy and strange sensation welled forth in my sex, a warmth, as if from sisterhood. Could she be the sister, the warm mother I never had?

I felt myself smile.

'Yes, that's the plan . . . Bees. I want to do something special for us. I also feel that it's a kind of obligation . . . To nature. I don't know. Ted will be happy, I think.'

'You're on the right track. There's nothing as thrilling as keeping bees. Do you have a beehive?'

'We haven't gotten that far.'

Frieda was up, tugged and yanked at me.

Couldn't he be done writing soon? Couldn't he come alive soon?

'Come with me to the beekeeping club's meeting in June. It's sooner than you think! Oh, and how is the garden turning out?'

'I've got to run . . . Duty calls.'

'Then I'll see you at the beekeeping meeting. Oh, and by the way . . .'

There was something Winifred Davies wanted to tell me, she didn't want to stop talking, couldn't see how Frieda was pulling at me. 'Oh, I have to go now,' I shouted, since the receiver was no longer pressed to my ear.

Outside in the spring air, the heat simmered and Frieda showed me how to plant rhubarb: all you had to do was dig your silver spoon as deep down into the dirt as possible, then you dropped the plant in, that's what Daddy had done.

All I saw was greasy pans left on the garden table, Nick sleeping peacefully beneath the laburnum tree but he would wake up in a minute, and then Ted should be back – but he would of course have to finish cutting the grass so I would be the one who would have to take Nick, regardless. I could feel how the impending baby howl grabbed a hold of me, as if our bodies were symbiotic: once the baby felt my body hover nearby he wanted to evaporate out of what held him now – sleep, his own sleep – and become me, become a pendant at my breast – he wanted to *merge*. I whispered to Frieda, 'So lovely, my darling. So lovely.'

Frieda was two years old; she didn't understand whispering:

'YOU do, Mommy!'

My head buzzed with bees, with chores, with swarms of hives to be put out to generate sweet honey, with the books Ted had read too many of and which I would one day aim at his head. (COME DOWN TO EARTH! WASN'T THAT WHY WE MOVED HERE? WHY DO YOU READ SO MUCH – DO SOMETHING, THEN! MOTHER WILL BE HERE SOON! And he would say: 'Aha, so *that's* the rub. You want everything to be taken care of for your mother. So you don't actually want the grass to be cut – it's because your mother's coming in June that you need to decorate and get everything in order, make it perfect. You know what, Sylvia? Kiss my ass.')

All this and much more took root and shot up in my head while Frieda screamed and chucked her black dirt onto the rhubarb. I shook a pair of earwigs off a tablecloth that had been mussed in the wind: earwigs and big daddy longlegs and greasy pans were my lot. And boom, the baby howl, boom, my conversation with Winifred was over, the delicious plan to keep bees, my idea to maybe take a walk: it was as though everything had been blown away. Nick was awake and, like a straggler to our life, Ted stepped out onto the porch and rubbed his eyes as if he had just woken from a deep sleep.

'Welcome back to reality!' I remarked acidly. Now I could care less if the neighbours heard.

Ted roared up the lawnmower without a reply, began to steer it across the grass at a desperate speed, his gestures bullish. And yesterday the two of us made love! Pah! *Fucking bitch, idiotic pain-in-the-ass wife!* – I *knew* that was what he was thinking, I *knew* it.

'I'm going upstairs to write!' I shouted.

★

I sat with the manuscript; it lay scattered across the bedspread and my body.

Ted was right: I had felt my mother's breath in each and every bud that burst open this early summer in our garden. She'd been there in each and every stark yellow daffodil I'd cut and trimmed the stem of so that it would look nice. She'd been there in every bouquet I'd wound twine around and wrapped in a veil of white sandwich paper. She'd been there in each and every bunch of ten tucked away for sales at the square; she'd been there in each and every preparation the earth made to thrive alongside the sun. Aurelia.

Now I thought of her with every step I took.

But really – why should I concern myself? Nothing could touch us now. We had our dreamlife, I had an entire family between myself and my mother – my own family, of my own flesh and blood and of my own capacity and intellect and will. All of it had bestowed joy upon us – all of it – everything *I* had stood for and created – not her. I was free of her, I was not my mother's lackey, not her headache, either, not her solution, she knew nothing about me.

I had my own garden now, I had my own tall, lustful husband who at night lay in my marital bed like a plank cut from the most beautiful slab of walnut. I had a handy husband, a musically inclined husband, a cosmopolitan and interested-in-cooking husband, a poet husband, a good-looking husband, a best-father-in-the-world husband, no matter what Aurelia Plath thought of Ted in June of 1956 when we were married and she unfortunately was our only witness. Whatever she thought of her new son-in-law, her first son-in-law, whatever reproach I could see then in her gaze; whatever acid remarks that throbbed behind her pious indifference, whatever martyr material I could detect when we left for our honeymoon – it could no longer hold me back, it could no longer claim any standing.

And if I only took a deep breath and truly showed my mother how delightful life in North Tawton was, then we would never get close to any kind of danger. She would see that the dream was for real, I had not cobbled it out of a poem, it was not written in a happy letter sent to America.

It began to grow bright outside, a fluorescent yellow Atlantic light. I sat leaned against the edge of the bed and it was as if all of me was illuminated, the light radiated straight into my heart. On my arm a bright lump of rising dough entirely warm. It was the May sun, Ted would say, but I knew what was May sun and what was the Difference in my life. So now Ted had gone out to the mailbox this morning and fished up what would make the difference in my life.

I needed to sit here and slow down, needed to sit here and not make too big a fuss, needed to sit here and moisten my lips and neutralise; besides, I needed to sit here and nurse, keep my dough rising.

IT READ THAT THEY WANTED TO PUBLISH IT IN JANUARY, it finally said that they wanted to publish it in January, and I had gone out, been greeted by Ted's mail harvest, grabbed the envelope, read the telegram sitting on the steps with my knees against my chest and then the tears had rolled the way tears of acceptance do, authortears, when all the toiling with what you had wanted to portray and make peace with steps out into the world and states: Let us reconcile, the war is over.

(From Ted's book on Buddhism: *He suffers, who must be listened to.*) Now it was clear: I would be listened to. They had finished reading my American garbage at Heinemann's and finally approved it. These snippy English girls at the publishers who sat with heaps of manuscripts overflowing in their laps and issued verdicts against anonymous wretches like me! They had captured my text like a swelling jellyfish out of the ocean, brushed away the sand and said: Here we have potential! Here we have something to wrangle! Finally – poems were impossible to place, but the art of the novel, prose, the highest of the high, that's where you could count on action!

And besides, I had crammed a fair amount of lyrical poetry into my book.

Oh . . . Esther G . . . I loved her . . . I saw her before me . . . If only she knew . . . I also loved myself . . . After all, I was the one who had created her . . .

Nick interrupted my thinking with a burp that sounded like vomiting and I expected an ocean on my shoulder but there was nothing, only my petrified fear of all that was white and sour, excrement.

Ted had pulled me up from the steps and embraced me in a bony hug and wanted to drag me out on the floor, have a spin. 'You queen, you genius! I knew it!' Lion's fire in his eyes. (I wasn't ready for it.) Now I sat here in bed again, sweating and biting my thin fingers and wondering how I could minimise the damage, the harm:

How was I actually about to publish a novel like *The Bell Jar*? How would I be able to mask it? Send it out into the world without having to be held personally responsible for the contents . . . It was going to become reality, and I thought I had been seated safely behind my typewriter!

I looked down at Nicholas, who lay in my palms, on my thighs. Just like a child . . . The feeling of publishing a book was just like bearing a child into the world: may this child not cause any harm, may he walk away with no care for me and my faults, I, who am so wrong and inadequate, God help my son to manage without me! May they not see in him that he has my darkness, that he has my soul!

Let him be pure . . .

The Bell Jar . . .

How would Ted now be spared from being set off by my success? How would Ted manage it? May the world hold its breath . . . A mosquito dove down into my flesh. I didn't want to wake Nick so sat there and watched how the little mosquito body filled with blood, before I skilfully laid my palm over the animal and let the blood spread onto my thigh. My blood, mine. Nick of course woke from the movement and I had reason to remain seated to finish sorting through my thoughts, since he needed to be put down again, nursed, carried . . .

Ted's poached salmon lay on the serving platter among radishes and spring onion. He stabbed a serving fork into the pink fillet. It sank as if into mud. Pink silt smeared the fork. I studied the worry and shame in his face.

'What is this?'

As if the salmon had offended him.

I smashed an ant headed up my leg.

I unfolded my napkin and spread it across my lap. 'There, now. I'm sure it's fine.' I grabbed Frieda's plate. 'Frieda? Shall I serve you some?'

'Yuck!' she shouted. 'No!'

We helped ourselves to the salmon in silence, Ted from his end and I from mine. Expectation had hung in the air: now it was strangely quiet. I did not dare say that it smelled rancid and sour. I now had the competitive edge, Ted was in lower standing in our house of writers.

'Now let's celebrate Mommy,' he had said.

Poached salmon or not – what was it inside me that could not let itself be celebrated? That boasted and at the same time racked me with anxiety for boasting and longed for yesterday when there had not been any letters that had hurled me out of my days as a struggling author queen, diligently trying, plodding, the fighting queen – across to the other side, among the soon-to-be-established.

That was where I would now be:

Established.

I tossed my hair and thought it was fine and good that the poached salmon turned out the way it did, that Ted sat there sullen and ugly on his wooden chair in our filthy kitchen, our old farming kitchen which we were in the process of transporting into the future, into sixties modernity, picking at his disgusting chunk of fish.

'It should have been in the oven longer,' he whined. 'Damn recipe. Fucking disgusting fish. Norwegian salmon!' He groaned. 'You can't trust Norwegians. I should have fished it myself. It's the produce that's bad: poached salmon shouldn't turn out like this. Irritating – when you've put so much work into it.' Ted described the brine the fish had marinated in for a long while: dill seed, carrot slices, fennel seeds, white pepper, and dill.

How could it then not turn out well?

I wasn't the least bit hungry: I was full of large white clouds, my insides were completely soft.

Frieda picked at her potato and got a hold of a lump of butter with her index finger, which she licked.

'I'll write to Al Alvarez right away and tell him.'

I wiped my mouth with the napkin, slammed it against the table and then I was gone. This was too much, this was too grand to let myself be dragged down by a vile piece of poached salmon. He could sit there, my husband, let his mouth sour and munch on spring onion. I left the dinner table and it nearly felt like a triumph and, equally, as an assault on the family.

'I'll invite him here!' I called from where I sat hunched

over my sudden letter at the coffee table. 'I'll invite our beloved critic, sometime in June. Won't that be fun, Ted: that's fine, right?'

I didn't sleep that night. Thoughts rumbled through my head like gravel: wherever my thoughts turned, there was a crunching and I had no peace. It was as if someone had switched on one of the newly purchased strip lights laying in the kitchen waiting to be mounted beneath the kitchen lamp – of course someone had surgically inserted them into my brain and here I was, a cephalopod, bodiless, and it was as if someone had chopped me in two.

Me, and my body.

Was I not the one who had willingly hacked myself free of it, so that I in the end would no longer have to put up with it, so that the only thing that would bind me to this earth and this time and this present and these hours would be this tremendous brain, this vast light which from now on was inside my mind? There was a symphony inside my mind: everything else was extinguished. *The Bell Jar* and within me I held the words from its introductory page: I alternately edited it in my mind and was blinded by the words' magnificence, myself. How. Fantastic. I. Was! Had written this! Mother wouldn't believe her eyes.

And in the next thwarted thought I wanted to curl up in a foetal position and so I did: folded my knees up from where they lay flat against the sheet in the rough bed, pulled them to my stomach and rocked over to my side and held myself there. (Nick still like a pig in his crib.) Mother, hold me, I'm going to publish a book, I thought. Mother, give birth to me again, I'm going to publish a book, I thought. Mother, spare me, spare me from this awkward hardship that is life and which I can never understand, help me, make me rest, put me to sleep.

A rain arrived in the middle of that thought, a pattering against our panes and I, in my mountain of legs and limbs and flesh and skin, was the only one who heard it, registered it and had the thought, the word: *rain*.

How could I be such a genius that I in a single sentence – a single one, merely one – in the same breath could evoke a consciousness, a place, a time, a season, a self, a feeling, and a political dilemma? As well as intrigue?

It was amazing, in the grand scheme.

Astonishing.

I was astonished, and with this thought I illuminated myself: the gravel no longer crunched, I thought I heard this rain, merely this rain breaking against the straw roof and the panes of our house. I heard the birds' wings beneath the tiles at the edge of the roof, how they closed themselves off from the rain as I closed myself off from time and the universe where I lay, liberated, rocked to sleep by my own words, my own perfection which I through some mysterious coincidence and chance had somehow created, like a rose that blooms in summer: it just arrives, when the right temperature has been achieved, when the soil has received rain, when the sun has pushed through and people are on vacation and ready to stick their noses into blooming roses and inhale their scent. My genius had arrived in the same way. I had worked hard to refine my qualities, I had grafted them, cross-bred them, culti-vated them, watered them, trimmed and struggled with them, and then one day, as the sun rose over an interior summer, hot like the one when the Rosenbergs were executed, I came up with the idea of writing the entire story and now it would soon belong to the world. I knew it – it would be the world's. The world would be touched by it. I fell asleep, I slept . . .

Without looking at each other, we made love like animals in heat on top of the bedspread in Frieda's room. Ted talked about the importance of having a fuck-you attitude: you need to have a fuck-you attitude, Sylvia, you're going to need it once the book is out, because I couldn't stop complaining that since everything in the novel was personal experience, what would happen with Mother? With Prouty? With Dick? With my reputation?

Ted lay resting on my arm.

'Heinemann's make my head spin,' I complained but what I said was absolutely true. 'One day they write that the coast is clear, the next I get a call from an anxious editor who yet again says they need to "clear it with an attorney" whether I am the responsible publisher of all contents, or if the publisher will claim some responsibility.'

'But take that pseudonym, then.'

'Victoria Lucas?'

'Your last main character's first name.'

'Sure, of course I could do that. But it's just the feeling of wanting to continue being Sylvia.'

'You will anyway.' He dragged himself up and kissed my forehead. 'You'll still always be Sylvia Plath. An authorship takes time, it cannot always be controlled.'

He put one foot in his trousers and then the other; the clinking sound as he buckled his belt was familiar. I slowly pulled myself up to sit and went and rinsed myself off in the sink after his carrying on inside me.

'I invited Assia and David Wevill too,' I said and paused in my step. 'The couple.'

I held a tray with dirty dishes. Ted lay on the couch reading a book.

'You said you did what?'

'I took the liberty. I asked if they wanted to come visit.'

Ted carefully put the book down on our coffee table, open midway, and struggled to sit up.

He said:

'But you didn't want any more intruders.'

Looked at me for a long and lonely while.

I felt an itching all over, it was the mosquito bites, and I held the tray in my hands, couldn't remedy the sensation.

I shrugged.

'The thought has sort of occurred to me before and now I made it happen.'

He slid back down onto the sofa.

'I don't understand you,' Ted said. He raised one hand's fingers into the air to count. 'We have Olwyn and Edith and the gang coming in June, God help me, we have your mother – your MOTHER, Sylvia – and we have Al Alvarez, whom you "took the liberty" of inviting as recently as yesterday.'

I put my weight on my other foot, felt how I expanded inside.

'Well, now we are expecting two more guests.'

My voice held a new pressure; it sounded convincing as I spoke.

I approached the coffee table and put down the tray. The glasses were greasy and slid into each other.

'Assia and David are writers,' I said, my arms crossed. 'They've wanted to come here for a while. We've talked about wanting to show them our house. So what's the problem?'

Ted sighed audibly.

'No, I suppose there's no problem at all.' He paused, stared into the wall, ran a finger across the wallpaper. 'Just don't come crawling to me afterward asking for mercy. Don't come crawling to me when the guests have gone home, don't complain, don't exhaust yourself with the food, don't make a big fuss with the cookies and for God's sake just make it all simple. Okay?'

I couldn't stop myself, I was already hypnotised. It was the feeling of wanting to invite the entire world that compelled me to speak. I said:

'I'm sure they'll be able to help us with some weeding. The scaffold you want to build, maybe David can take that on? We'll ask them for help. That's what you do in life, you ask for help with things you cannot manage on your own.'

I picked up the tray and walked out.

He was in London and I could fill the freezer. He wouldn't notice that I had arranged everything in advance. He wouldn't have a hold on me and be able to trace my anxiety. I adored cooking and baking because – and someone ought to write this simple quote on a label someday, so I had it saved for a future cookbook authored by *moi* – 'FOOD: Because the preparations are poetry, the cooking meditation, and the eating – sex.'

My cuticles were stained red from cherries.

Frieda was asleep for the night and Nick lay sweet and doughy in his pram before me on the kitchen floor, so wasn't it then fantastic that I could whip up a cheese pie, set a dough for a slow-rising loaf of white bread to have in the fridge overnight, and as icing on the cake and in deep secret, in my innermost circle of loneliness, pit two pounds of cherries from the market in Crediton and pour them with a smatter into a wide pie dish?

All while Nick lay gazing at the ceiling.

I licked pie dough from a finger, grabbed the rolling pin and leaned my body into the rhythmic movements over the pie dough, which smeared out across the counter and grew round and wonderful, and then I picked up Ted's loupe, which lay on the window sill, also round and wonderful but in a small way, and placed it against the dough and cut out little rounds.

I would have everything ready in the freezer. Assia and David wouldn't believe their eyes – cherry blossoms in bloom and cherry pie, *already?* – they would think they'd gone to heaven, and I would laugh, generously amused and uproarious.

I had so many recipes for everything in my head.

This was how Ted's desire for improvisation could be circumvented – his insistent way of making do with what was in the fridge.

It would be a perfect weekend.

Ted's loupe – occasionally placed against a preserved butterfly or Frieda's foot when she had a splinter that needed to be removed – became sticky with dough and there was something delicious about it. Carefully, without ruining anything, I laid the pie lid across the cherries. And as the pie cooked, sweet little cherries oozed out of the circles with their brightest red, and I sat for a while in front of the oven and watched the pie take shape.

It was so lonely to be home without him and no matter which angle I looked at in the mirror I couldn't find one that accurately reflected who I was. I would be an author, soon it would be the novelist Sylvia Plath with whom people would be in dialogue. It was possible to grow, expand your repertoire, be both poet and novelist – I didn't need to limit myself. I carried Nick and pushed Frieda in the pram onto the bus toward Crediton and there, in the little ladies' shop, I found a pair of white sandals adorned with gold chains. I hesitated for a moment and looked at the price tag several times while I kept a tight grip on Frieda's wrists to keep her from destroying the entire shop. Were all other living beings as subject to temperature shifts as I was? Outside I was freezing but as soon as I entered the shop sweat started pouring. Forty pounds – they were expensive sandals – but I would buy them to celebrate myself: I would soon be a published writer. A book was on its way. And perhaps I would attend a launch party not far from downtown London this spring, toast with sparkling bubbles and be kissed on the neck. Of course a writer should have sandals with gold chains.

Sometimes I wished that shop assistants would see that you were a particular kind of important person, but I couldn't very well explain it to her as I paid: This winter I am having a novel published.

I carried the shoes during the long journey home and could not look Frieda in the eye even though she did all she could to get my attention.

Sweaty like an animal I threw the shoe box down on the hall floor at home and caught my breath. Carrying children on buses and taking them to ladies' shops was really not for me! So why, then, did I do it? Well! Because I was a writer, and a writer must have sandals with gold chains. Frieda tugged at my hand, she wanted green peas from the refrigerator, and now what, now what? I asked the mirror, couldn't the mirror now reflect my true self?

I kicked the shoes into the closet when Ted came home and gave him an honest answer when he asked, *What have you been up to, then, while Daddy was in London?* but I left out the sandals, didn't want to tell him about them. They lay in the dark of the closet and waited for the right day.

I have written about her, I thought.

Just as she stood on my porch, I saw it: but it's her, from my poem *Three Women*, with the marble uterus. I had forgotten the nature of her beauty. Now here she was. And it was I who had invited her.

The husband David behind her, sour and grey.

Her hand was cold when I held it in mine, just as I had thought. We had met before but then the bell had not tolled for our union. That time we met in London, in my beloved apartment, Primrose Hill, she and her author husband David were to rent our flat and we had spoken of slight matters, of no significance. Now she was here again, in our new house, our new life, our existence which had been rearticulated since we last saw each other. The noose had been drawn tighter, especially around Ted. I could see it in his face now as he looked at her, as he took her shawl. It was as if he would have liked to press his snout against the silk and inhale its scent. But I looked at him. With a burn.

I saw how she freed herself from our gazes upon her in the misty summer. Entered our home and became the main character, threw herself at some book tossed on the dining-room table, rocked her hip. Sent an arrow of love into what was ours and had been so closed off to the world until now.

And then in a gust of air I also glimpsed myself: I had thought I was battling the winter and motherhood, and that I loathed the subsequent isolation. But in truth I was complicit with it, I sought it out and loved standing there in the frigid air full of bitterness and tears, abandoned. Loved blaming anything and everything. Loved the smokescreens, the blurriness of not being able to see clearly, of using my writing as my only redemption.

Wrong: I had done everything so fucking wrong!

Now it was May, the early summer month I had longed for. From the outside, everything was as it should be, as usual. But now she had arrived. She the black-haired one, she the childless one, she with a uterus like a marble hall. She who could not bear any children. And she was beautiful like a disgusting Frenchwoman. Like all the dark-haired ones on the continent I had not been able to compare myself to.

Assia Wevill.

Oh, how could it have eluded me that she was the witch! The fatal one, the one I should be careful not to let into our home. How could I have been blind the first time I saw her last year, when we were renting out the flat in London? My jealousy knew no limits now as she set herself free in our home. She was liberated, she was the fiery flame. Ted followed her, he wanted to show Assia the house.

She laughed, she had a cracked, sexy, airy voice. I had children in my arms and at my fingertips. I followed with tears in my throat, I suppressed them with every muscle in my body.

Assia had the light of summer in her legs, in her veins, she was carried by a kind of levity.

She looked at Ted. Not at me.

It was poisonous.

Ted showed Assia my studio. She casually walked around the room, fingering my things, sent out long thin tentacles and I lost a hold on the manner with which I usually presented myself. Her nails, painted in tiger stripes; she stuck her claws into my notebook.

'Yes, that's my book,' I squeaked. 'Yes, that's my new manuscript.'

'T-h-e B-e-l-l J-a-r,' she spelled it out slowly. Looked up at Ted. 'What does that mean?'

At that point I tore myself away from my post by Frieda, was right there and slammed the stack of papers together just as she was about to leaf through it.

'Watch yourself!' I hissed.

And my rudeness rang through the room, erupted with its clarity and stink. Fucking me, fucking inferior creature to these squirrels, these love birds, whose activities aimed to move them closer to one another and leave me standing on the outside.

'Well, sorry,' Assia snipped. 'Sorry. I won't go through your papers.'

'I'm sorry,' I said, since I interpreted Ted's look to mean that I ought to explain myself so that my out-of-control behaviour could be rationalised. 'Sorry, I guess I'm a bit touchy when it comes to my manuscripts.'

Ted kept going. He hunched his way out of the room with the low door frame. He had a hole in his back, a pitch-black oblong hole that drew Assia in. It was as though she would fit there in his hole, as though he would become pregnant with her. A new couple. A new love being constituted.

I stood there with my pens and my paper and of course Nick on my arm, and I thought: Sylvia. I grasped for my name. Sylvia, it means spirit of the forest. Forest, fresh air, fragile damp leaves and trees, trees, trees. That was me. I would be someone to hold on to. I would be Ted's forest, and he would be all the animals. Such was our bond. My growth, his life. My soil, his capriciousness. My pillars, his desire and impulsivity.

'Ted,' which meant God's gift. I didn't believe in God, but I believed in Ted. That was it.

How it had always been.

And now there she was, already guarding him.

He was already hers.

I saw it.

And I had written about her.

Assia!

This fickle temptress that already grabbed him like a flame, the flame I lacked, and let him be inspired, make his way to his desires, yes, say yes, orgasm from some movement she made, see how the nights were illuminated and sparkling and not at all dark and silent as they were in the forest. Assia, the modern woman! London and the life we had left! Assia, skyscrapers and white marble cheek! Assia, in his gaze he had already given himself! He was giving himself, I saw it now in Ted. They had climbed up to the attic and his studio, his arms waved about as he explained. I hadn't heard Ted's voice say so much in months. He gave her his time and his voice and his gaze, everything I had wanted but had failed so miserably at earning.

Oh, madness – failure! Failure was my lot and the air I breathed! Here was misery, failure and misery! Here we were. And I had his children.

Down in the shallows in the large house that was our paradise, our Court Green, I tried to restabilise myself, take out the china, set out the coffee and tea. I was off kilter, as if someone had snuck me a sedative. David had already read half of my *New American Poets*, was so kind and interested in it.

Sylvia, I thought, just remember that I am Sylvia I have borne his children this is just a regular visit.

Ted reared himself like an animal against Assia as she came stepping down the stairs in her heels. He had to take her hand on that final step; he was vain and ran one of his hands through his hair at the same time. Oh, let me have him for another life, I thought, let me live at least one more of my nine with him.

Full moon in Scorpio. My sign. But the conversation belonged to them, completely. Even though there were four of us around the table, Ted turned only to her and said, straight out into the clear moon night while she let a column of smoke rise from her fingers:

'If there's one thing I miss it's the people in London, to just gaze in any direction and be taken in by anybody at all, not having to search for what you want to get out of people, like here – they pop up everywhere anyway and surprise you. I felt at home in London, with the eclectic and the unpredictable, I didn't realise it before I moved here. I thought of myself as someone other than who I've now discovered that I am.'

She laughed.

'So, how do you actually like it in the countryside?'

'*So-so*, to be honest. Truth be told,' he looked at me with an oddly grim expression, 'I'm quite bored. I think people here are strange in a boring way, they don't amuse me, and I think the entire village has something unintelligent about it. You die inside a little bit, aren't challenged.'

Assia laughed again.

'You'll have to come back to London and be our neighbours,' she said with her voice – thin, brittle, hoarse, witchy.

I gathered the plates and walked into the kitchen. It was May, my mother would arrive in a few weeks. My brother was to get married on the other side of the Atlantic, and in my mind, everything had been ready to go, our children would have cousins, and Grandmother was on the way. And everything would be like a postcard, finally, a fixed image. And then it was ruined – in one fell swoop, swift as a flame. I had her spit on our spoons, our plates. I smeared off the grease, rinsed and rinsed again with warm water. Cherrystain, cherrymouth and forevermoon and conversations about war. What she wrote about – she was also a 'poet'. Oh, dear God, let the night sprain her leg, send her out of my home and let her take that animal David with her, as well. Out of my house!

Saturday morning. Through the kitchen window I saw Ted and Assia sit and talk in the sun between the laburnum and the lilacs. Little cups of coffee they forgot to drink from. He held his cup ridiculously high in the air. He laughed; she made him laugh. It struck me that I hadn't seen his teeth in so long. I had been turned on by his ugliness, had missed everything else he was capable of. Stood here with a cold in our kingdom and complained. Now, when we were near the finish line and summer was here, that's when he was prepared to betray me! And the children were drawn to me like magnets, naturally. I would pry them loose and pass straight through the garden and place them in his lap. Assia could think whatever she wanted.

David – he wasn't capable of making sense of the drama unfolding, anyway – stood and read the spines on our shelves, complimented us on our exquisite wallpaper and the elmwood table Ted and my brother had built. Oh, nonsense, I said: that's nothing.

'Ted!'

And I wanted to hand him the children, fat, heavy Frieda and little sparrow Nick. He extracted himself from the conversation, stared worriedly in my direction. Busy – he was busy.

'What?' he asked.

I could see how Assia took a sly interest in my response. In a way that would make me want to be sent away. I didn't intend to stand before Ted and gorgeous Assia and explain myself. How the children were magnets to me like those two had just become magnets to one another. This warm early summer evening in May, in our garden. It went without saying that an attraction would sneak up on them: it was less about her than about Ted's non-existent love for me.

'Do I even need to explain?' I asked. 'It's just that as soon as I do anything, even put a cake in the oven, she's on top of me.' I nudged Frieda's little shoe with my foot. 'And this guy, little crab, wakes up in the pram as soon as I think I have a minute free. And are you there to pick him up then? No.'

So I had to defend myself anyway.

Huh – I sighed.

Assia tilted her head.

'What's it like having two little children?' she asked, gently pressing her lips together to moisten them.

'I thought I just told you?'

Ted looked at me uncomfortably.

'My God, Sylvia – I'll take her.' Ted reached for our little girl. It was as if she suddenly carried the weight of being a pawn in a game. 'Come, Frieda.' She sank down into Daddy's arms. Ted turned around, picking up where he had left off with Assia.

I hurried away from them, felt the winds of fate in my legs that carried me through the garden, the lawn I'd nagged him about mowing, these roses which made me anxious when I'd seen the black aphids and how the weeds had eaten at them. And Ted had stood there in front of his roses and instead inhaled their scent and said, 'Stop it, Sylvia. They're roses. Roses are always hardy. Don't you see, roses have survived war, roses grow through drought and cold and rain. We can see roses far into the autumn, my friend. You don't need to worry about the roses. Save your worry for something else, my love!'

Now he turned around, shot his voice out through the laburnum tree behind me.

'Sylvia, Sylvia!'

I stood in a cloud of white, the white house, my white clothes, the icy white apple blossoms in the tree crowns.

All of it such a failure. I wished it had been my mother coming to visit us during the bloom of apple blossoms. That she could see how beautiful it all was. I swallowed the taste of blood.

'What?'

Ted approached me with Frieda in his arms. Assia stood up and sauntered after him, entered our circle.

So tired of intruders, so tired of visitors, must the entire world come visit us just because it's summer and the sun cracks its light open? Must they come here just because we had a new baby? Nothing I needed more than peace and quiet, and I wondered if these thoughts were apparent in my face.

Ted tossed out:

'We were thinking if David and I should go out on the heath, so you and Assia can be on your own and get acquainted for a bit.'

My eyes on her, how she curtsied behind him, nearly, while smiling at me.

'Will you take Nicholas, then?'

Ted glanced at the pram, said: 'He has to sleep anyway, it's better if you take him so Frieda can get out and run around.'

I looked at Assia again. Plump, pouting lips.

'We can do some weeding,' I said firmly.

'Good idea,' Ted said.

'Are you joking?' Assia laughed.

She walked after me into the shed where we kept the tools.

She was older than I was, still, she was remarkably beautiful. She was beautiful in a worrisome way, since I used to be able to dismiss people by saying that they were talented, of course, but that they were so terribly boring from an aesthetic point of view: beauty and genius so rarely accompanied each other. But the brutality of Assia Wevill was that she was intelligent and beautiful all at once. And what was even worse – she was gorgeous in a different way than I was. Nor was she a mother – she had never brought a child into this world – which made men hunger for and want to mount her. Maidens like that could not walk around on earth unfertilised: someone had to empty their seed into them and impregnate them. Such was the design of woman and man, it was nothing I had any say in.

She stood behind me and breathed her silly breaths, pulled on gloves, and I placed a shovel and rake in her hands, making her completely asymmetrical with those objects, incompatible. I laughed.

'You're not used to weeding, are you?'

'I may live in the city, but I'm not afraid of rolling up my sleeves,' she replied.

I walked ahead of her and pointed to the rows where mounds of onion skin already lay sodden on the ground, and from beneath them radiated a mish-mash of daffodil leaves, chickweed and thistle.

'It all has to go,' I said. 'We've got stinging nettles, too: watch out.'

Assia pointed at her dress, her knees.

'I'll get dirty,' she said.

'Welcome to the countryside.'

Assia sat down, her bare knees in the soil, and I realised I couldn't subject her to this – I had to show some mercy. So I said, sweetly:

'Would you rather borrow Ted's overalls? They're on a hook in the shed. You can just pull them over your skirt.'

She left, and I took the opportunity to look at her, how her hips swayed from side to side, composing a swing in them while she walked. She returned with Ted's enormous pants on: now her limbs and his were already triumphant, I thought. Now she had his imaginary crotch against hers.

Fucking awful.

We lay in the rows and pulled up thistle and daffodil roots. Assia was spectacularly bad at weeding and I felt both offended and angry at such a dull protocol which dictated that the men go to the heath and fly a kite with the older child, and the two of us should sit here and make nice over girl things, now that we didn't have anything else in common.

'Who is David? How did the two of you meet?' I asked.

'Oh, we met on a boat . . .' Assia paused, looking up at the sky. 'It was probably nowhere near as romantic as it was for you and Ted.'

'Boats are romantic.'

'I don't think so. I was stuck there, on a ship crossing the Atlantic from Canada, so I guess I was bored, in a way, and then I met this wonderful European man. That's what I thought then.'

'You don't think so any more?'

'David,' Assia said, smiling as a long white root leapt out of the ground. She simply threw it aside. 'David's best years are behind him, poor thing,' she said. 'Even men have expiration dates, believe me.'

I fell silent for a bit. There was dirt on my apron – I would swap it out for a clean one before lunch – and there was a pungent scent of onion in the air, since we were seated in the middle of the onion patch. We sat among the little onions that had fallen from my, Ted and Frieda's hands early in the spring, when Nick was just a month or so old, and which had now turned into large white balls with green stalks. Little brown-white marbles into the cold earth. I recalled that moment – something could exist on earth for a single instant – then the growth had taken over, drifts of thistles and nettles, and the onion had to struggle in order to appear out of its thorny hell. How long could something beautiful get to exist? Why were there weeds – why could the earth never be pure?

'How out of breath can weeding actually make you?' I asked.

'I'm not out of breath at all,' Assia said.

This is what I would later tell Ted: how she was impossible to be friends with. I would present my argument as directly and politely as possible so that he would have no choice but to understand me. We would circle the bed in our bedroom and put on pyjamas and nightgown and he would reply, 'My God. What a pain.' And it would be grist to my mill and I would continue, just keep going on about how horrible this woman was, so dull and dry, not the least bit spiritual. And Ted would understand me, he always understood me, it was his stellar quality, always so understanding, and how he listened.

I was cheerful for a moment again.

Then Nicholas woke up, and while I ran to him and lifted my child out of the pram Assia also let the shovel and rake fall to the ground and tossed the gloves on top. She sat down with me by the lilacs and the laburnum. It was embarrassing that she should glimpse my nipple on the breast I was feeding Nicholas. But Nick sucked and clucked, and the peace within me – the peace.

Unbeatable!

Now I looked up at her, I saw her as if anew, since everything that happened while I nursed had its own immaculate glow, and all was forgiven as if for the first time.

'What were we talking about?' I asked.

And Assia took the opportunity to talk, for she saw that I was listening. She told me about the war in Europe, which

I – monstrous – had not been a part of, since I had been safe behind an ocean.

Nick clucked and sucked, sucked and clucked, and the breast was emptied. The more the breast emptied, the more alert I grew and saw life clearly again.

A furrow on her brow as she talked about how wounded she had felt during her childhood, how lost she was. Jewish . . . but not. Assia, it was Arabic, she said, did you know it means 'the one who protects'?

'So what do you protect, then?' I asked.

'Maybe my identity,' she said. 'I have no integrity . . . So I protect myself, build a wall so that no one gets to hurt me and ram right through my defences . . .'

Nonsense, I thought. She's full of nonsense.

'It seems to have required many men to arrive at that hard-earned insight,' I replied. 'Who is he, in that order?'

'David is my third husband,' Assia replied.

'Gosh,' I answered.

'It's not as dramatic as you think. Of course, you think I'm a man-eater. Well, I've wanted to do the right thing and so I've also married.'

She looked right through me. Her gaze travelled all the way to the cemetery.

She giggled, as if thinking of something, and pulled a cigarette out of a case.

'May I . . .?'

'Of course.'

Assia smoked and I regarded her thick, pink lips that held that elegant thin stick between them and let the flame hiss, and then I had the smoke in my lungs and it was as if she had just been fucked, just kissed, as she exhaled in my direction.

And then the gentlemen returned. They came walking across the grass with their pink cheeks and had the entire world's lighthearted joy on their faces. Frieda ran at their heels to keep up with the brisk pace.

'Are you sitting here smoking?' Ted asked. 'Weren't you going to weed?'

'We're talking about you,' Assia said and let the ashes fall onto the grass.

'Besides, I was just going to tell Sylvia about when I nearly murdered my first husband,' she went on, and I was stunned and receded into my physical solitude because Ted had just lifted Nick off me.

Ted's eyes widened in a smile at Assia: wasn't she wonderful, there was something wild and mysterious about her, something altogether different from what I had to offer him; I could see that he felt that way, for I knew my Ted.

David gave a dry laugh.

'That . . . That . . .' he said.

'But go on,' Ted said. 'Tell us.'

'What would you do, Sylvia, if you suspected your husband of being unfaithful?'

Ted looked at me. Our eyes the tips of two swords meeting in one strike.

'I certainly wouldn't try to murder him,' I replied.

Ted turned his gaze back to Assia.

'You didn't want to kill him, did you?' he asked.

'I wanted to threaten him,' Assia said. 'I wanted to be the one with agency. I wanted to show him who had power over their life.'

'I don't think it's particularly independent to threaten someone's life with a knife. I'm a pacifist,' I said.

'Sure, Sylvia, sure,' Ted said. 'I don't know . . .'

'You don't know what?'

'You're not exactly an angel,' Ted said.

Assia chuckled, looked down at her glass.

How could he betray me like that?

How could that betrayal surface right before my eyes, in the middle of an early summer day?

We had it all. Paradise lay before us. And now this snake! I knew I shouldn't have agreed to sell our paradise to the whims of others' souls. Why the hell did I invite them here?

'Well, at least I'm no murderer,' I said.

Ted stuck out his lower lip, mocked me, insinuated that I was a martyr.

So I left. I walked away, empty-handed, without children, hastened into the kitchen to prepare dinner.

Dazed, I pulled the pie out of the fridge and tore off the foil, stuck a meat thermometer into a large raw roast that someone should have put in the oven several hours ago. All I could do now was stand in the kitchen and be consumed by those pieces of me that were suffocating. I would stand here in the kitchen and look out at them through our window. I would stand here and melt and feel what it was like to be betrayed in real time.

Did they not see that I also wanted to be loved, as they sat there and began to love each other?

Is there no true love, is there only tenderness? The time that paused as my son – so perfect now, Buddha as he sat in his puddle of sun on the floor – and my daughter gazed into each other's eyes and she danced around him where he sat, and I was the cheering onlooker, their only audience.

Ted's gaze was evasive; I was indispensable.

It was as if my core was at the centre of the room – if I snuck away from them, they went insane. My flesh for their flesh, my presence for their sanity. So I betrayed my own flesh day after day that early summer, betrayed my own sanity.

The radishes lay yanked from the soil on the kitchen table, the bunch of spinach next to them wilting in a pile. Ted was up in the room and I sat on the floor, as if stopped by time. My white clothes, my dirty hair, the opus I offered him; I was the motivation as I sat there, what he wrote about. Ted and the time that had stopped: my children and I.

But I had no love for eternity. I wanted to get up, I wanted to remain standing; in this strange calm before the storm, I wanted to stand up and fold my sheets that had finished drying in the attic, book a riding course, I wanted to call the midwife and make sure that she would come with me to the bee meeting.

My face was like an unfired lump of clay; someone had entered our bedroom at night and resculpted me.

I did not like it.

I had no love for eternity, I had no desire to be a part of Ted's chapter about me. His way of getting to the essence of what was me, extracting eternity from me. I just wanted to live. That was it: I wanted to live and share the life I had been given with him. I had struggled to live, that was true. Couldn't he see that struggle, couldn't he give it to me? I avoided going upstairs and bothering him, I didn't want to ask him to focus on me, be a bother. Didn't want to take up his time and look into his dead face – it was dead to me, dead to Ted-and-Sylvia, dead to our family.

Couldn't Ted, my husband, also see the joy in our son's face? How his teeth invaded his gums? How his sister tore off her clothes and wanted to dance and take her brother's hand, nude in the sunlight?

They were my children and his. They were eternity, they would survive us all. They were our debt, they were our responsibility. So live with it, then, I thought.

I thought: Ted, you talk about having to become the person you are intended to become. You're always going on about it. But can't you see: here is concentration. Here is focus! Here is our dailiness, here is where the trees' branches shoot out their leaves. I cannot afford the luxury of striving to 'find myself' and becoming 'whole' – I must be theirs. I must belong to my children, be the green wall of chlorophyll they are surrounded by, their sun.

He could sit up there in the shade and be a full-time author, above all.

I would belong to the children. I had no choice.

I was tired. I lay down with Nick on the floor, in the white beam of light. I held my son's index finger. It was June: my debut book had been released in the US.

And nowhere could I find peace except in the circle of Nick's little finger.

He was my eternity.

And I had to love Ted for it.

I had to, I had no choice.

I cried a chilling tear at that thought. Frieda stacked her dolls on the floor, wanted them to sit in each other's laps. I yawned, soon fell asleep . . . Only his little finger in mine.

A soft June light lay over North Tawton, the air humid and this sweet stink of flowers. Ted was over by the car door waiting for me to gather all of myself and our children and get out of the house sometime. My husband. My short dress. I had both children in my arms, dumped Frieda in the back seat and liked how Ted looked at me when I stuck my ass in the air.

Maybe he could see, maybe he couldn't. It was not my business to decide but since a few days back I had given up my fire, my storminess, had grown calm and receptive. He should take note.

I had stopped storming, now I was all about punctuality and being alert and pure. To undress the very innermost, abandon myself to what remained.

Women and children first, and here was an emergency. There was nothing left to puncture, the air had gone out of what had been inflated, out of our castle in the sky, the air was gone.

My shoulders bare, I sat down with the lump Nicholas our son in the front seat next to Ted and he nodded, my husband's long nose his steady chin, and then Ted put the car in reverse, snaked his limbs over the wheel and dashed out across the back street, out and away in our black car.

I was silent and happy. I had remembered to rinse the children's mouths clean and I was enveloped by the little one's pressure upon me, his weight that forced away my worries, there in my lap. Sniffed his hair, scent of milk and forehead.

Ted was a bad liar: he had scheduled several trips to London this summer, more than usual, and he was terrible at lying, so I suppose I have to lie on his behalf, I thought.

Sit here and be calm and strong.

Ted stopped the car and I carried the children over to Elizabeth Compton's little plot where her single-storey house extended from a flowering hawthorn bush to another with white lilacs. The scent was intoxicating, and a little pond swelled in the middle of her garden.

'Keep Frieda away from it, not to mention the little one,' I asked Elizabeth, and she spread her arms wide to show how happy she was to watch our children. 'Of course, Sylvia,' she said with her lovely high voice. 'Don't worry, dear.'

Her softness, her friendship – her, of all people, I liked. She suddenly patted my cheek, when I had kissed Frieda and the little one goodbye.

'What?' I asked.

'Is everything all right?' she asked in response.

I smiled a rusty smile.

'Of course. Or . . . It's a bit stressful that Mother is coming, but otherwise we're fine.'

'Are you keeping well?'

'Knock on wood, no more urinary tract infections, and the most important thing is that the little one is healthy! Now I'm going to see Winifred – the midwife!'

She smiled. We smiled. Me in my pretty white dress. So happy that I had friends here, so glad to be a woman with friends, proper blond friends. One day I would invite Elizabeth over for glazed cherry cake, really show Mother who my friends were. I walked across the driveway and opened the car door to Ted, who I knew had watched me.

I tried to turn on music, but the radio had no reception.

We drove to the beekeepers' meeting in silence. There was nothing to say, only a melody to hum, and I hummed it. I couldn't tell if it bothered Ted: he mostly cleared his throat and remained silent. I wanted to know what business Ted had in London, but did not ask for I knew what his reply would be: I need to get out, he would say, I need to go to readings, I need theatre visits in my life again, Sylvia, experiences, I need to mingle with the right people.

And here I was, the right person, in fact.

'Oh – I have milk on my dress!'

I saw it trickle out of my breast: a large, circular stain that grew as we observed it. There it was – the milk, Nicholas's milk, he would have wanted to eat right about now – or was it a feeling I had inside me that made the milk come down, a strange feeling of being frightened in Ted's company, my husband who was suddenly so quiet?

I pulled out a napkin and placed it against my breast, squeezed it.

'Why are you so quiet?' I asked. 'Why won't you say something?'

'Dear, I'm driving,' Ted replied. 'I'm driving and I can tell that I'm getting a cold.'

I replied nothing more than, 'Oh, poor thing.'

And then we stepped out together, walked over the hill to the circle of beekeepers who had gathered this evening, the seventh of June before the Pentecost.

I looked around for the midwife – she hadn't arrived yet, my trusty knight, she who had helped me birth my prince Nicholas like royalty.

A sweet heavy scent from some sweet pea vine somewhere, and a hedge of white cow parsley, hawthorn in bloom that smelled absolutely insane. A sky far too blue.

I walked on my own up the hill. Ted did not want to touch me. So here were the beekeepers, then. This was my escapade. The breeze grazed my shoulders and made me realise how my skin was showing. Here in England. They all turned around and looked at me at the same time, the village beekeepers in their white outfits. Ted turned inward with his hands in his pockets a ways away. And someone descended on the hive and I noticed some whirling animals in the air who had the power to attack me.

When the sun passed behind the clouds – did it not suddenly turn quite cold? Wasn't it odd how I suddenly felt so naked? I didn't know that beekeepers used so much protective gear – or had I as usual been naive and banal, romantic in my conception even of this, that beekeeping could be like any summer adventure, any adventure at all?

Oh, to transport yourself out into the world, childless – there was an emptiness that spread like an infection in the body – to be empty! Contentless! For your bare shoulders to echo. The children's skin used to cover my body like a kind of religious vestment and here I was, my shoulders bare in the wind while the others wore protective gear.

Protective gear!

I tried to laugh at Ted where he stood handsome and sexy like James Dean, but I couldn't do that, either. Bloody hell, I thought, we should have gone to the ocean.

Beekeeping had been my idea and I had nagged Ted, coaxed Ted, who had been a lovesick teen who would rather think of something else: oh, but please, let's do it, for my sake. I wanted him to get excited about me and my ideas the same way he did about his own ideas, the strawberries and all the animals. But then this deadly insight rushed toward me: the more I imitate him, the less he loves me.

The more I tried to show an interest in animals and nature, the more he looked away!

The more I made an effort to write naturalistic poetry and poems teeming with animals the way he did, the less he showed an interest in me! Why couldn't he see how I tried? Who did he then want me to become?

Now I wanted to go home – in an instant – I wanted to go home and listen to Beethoven and write poetry and nurse Nicholas.

But see, I was here. Now I needed to stand it.

I walked over to Ted, wanted to ask him if I could borrow his blazer.

'Can I borrow your blazer?' I asked. 'I'm cold.'

Never had he been so handsome. He shrugged. He looked like he wanted to listen to the speaker.

'Go get it, then. It's in the back seat.'

He handed me the car key; said the words without even looking at me. So I chose not to.

I gazed in fascination down into the hive of crawling bees. There should be a queen, a lone queen whom the hundreds of workers sacrificed their lives for, but the queen was gone that night, and all the local beekeepers laughed.

'Madam, you who don't have much on, maybe you should watch out so you're not stung,' said an old man with a sharp blue gaze that cut through his black hood. He looked at me with sincere concern.

Oh Father, I thought. Oh Father, suddenly the thought consumed me like fire – oh Father, help me.

Father, help me persevere in a sea of wholesomeness, your soul, help me, to persevere in the world. I'm standing here with my bare shoulders because I thought beekeeping would be like a summer adventure, something festive and fun, something that would also bring Ted and I closer to each other. And, as usual, it was boring and brain-dead, not elegant and subtle like when you dedicated yourself to it. Nothing that would take you by storm. Dammit, Father's spirit. Dammit, Father. The gusty air is from the ocean. Dammit, Father, blow me away with it. Let me lift into the air. Am I not too finely dressed for them? And if I am now so chock-full with your force, then why does life never ascend? Why am I still chained to this place? Set here to be bored to death and yawn and want to go home.

The only things that afford me a sense of life and pleasure right now are Nick and Frieda. They do something to me – they *create* me. They make me creative as well. They don't amputate me, like everyone else dear to me does. If you only knew, Father. If you only knew who Ted is. His dark shadow, the rotten garbage at his core. Now it surfaces. Now I have to manage it – now. Now it is clear that everything I built our love on was air. It was never durable . . . I, who thought I had built it on fruit pulp and sweet strawberries, cherry blossoms and carnal walks in the fortifying sunshine. It was air the entire time, Father, *air*. And I have to stand it and breathe in this exhausted air – the air that is spilled for me, when our castle in the sky shatters. I am suffocating.

I'm so sad, Father. Help me!

I saw the little blue car belonging to our midwife drive up the hill, lowered my shoulders and exhaled. Who I wanted to be: if held together only by a smile, a kind soul who had been dear to me, who had placed her fingers inside me. She had seen me struggle! She knew I was a fighter.

'Hello, Sylvia,' she said, 'now let's look at some bees.'

As soon as she stood there in all her maternal glory, I could breathe a sigh of relief. There was something about the queen that thoroughly fascinated me, that the queen bee was gone. The bee society's central bee. I laughed at the midwife: 'She must've gotten tired of having babies!'

But the midwife was focused on the hive.

'Aren't you experts at this kind of thing?' I asked straight into the air. 'I thought you beekeepers knew what you were talking about.' I wanted to get someone to laugh with me, but no one laughed.

An old man approached me with a protective hat and net,

drowned me in white fabric and I was suddenly veiled, suddenly one of them. Through the black mesh of the protective hood I saw Ted, who of course would never think of blending in, still in the background further away.

'Come on!' I waved. 'Come take a look at a queen!'

And the only ones who were stung that June evening were the rector and Ted, and I laughed at that, but the queen was nowhere to be seen, she had gone up in smoke: what a diva, I thought, what a fucking diva.

I wanted to say something as we drove home in silence and Ted scratched at his bee sting.

I promised him that I would rub ointment on it once we got home.

His profile with the English landscape rushing past behind him. I wanted to tell him that I loved him. I had a feeling he no longer saw me, that whatever I said it would pass right through the car window, through him and out into nothing. In truth I could care less about bees. I cared as much about adult arrangements and glorious plans as he did. I also wanted to fuck around on a hotel bed in London, or whatever it was he saw before him when he imagined summer. I didn't care either about children and possible greenhouses, I also wanted to suck on glowing cigarettes and be a wild, dreamy spirit first and foremost, loved and desired in his arms, my neck covered in marks from his kisses.

'Did you get a taste for bees?' was all I said.

He briefly looked away from the road and glanced at me.

'Maybe a bit much work? We have to have time for something else this summer too.'

Of course. It was my project. Absolutely.

'Why can't you take as much of an interest in my projects as I have all spring in yours?'

Ted cleared his throat. 'What was that?'

'Oh, nothing.'

He placed a hand on my thigh, let it inch up toward the skirt. Each and every touch these days made me tremble as if it were the first time he touched me. I was in love. So hopelessly, madly in love, even though it was already too late.

Sorry for the children, I wanted to say, sorry for one thing and then another and for who I am.

He interrupted my thoughts. Caressed me all the way up between my legs; it was almost as if he was going too far.

'My little dreamer,' he said. 'Daddy's girl, Sylvia Plath. The beekeeper!'

We turned into Elizabeth Compton's garden, where she was already standing with the children.

'I'm proud of you,' Ted said, and I got out and took them back.

I walked around with a weight in my heart. He was my first and final reader, always, he had given me assignments, encouraged me, but from now on I would never again show him my writing.

Ted knew it. He eyed me in the evenings as I walked around and drew hearts on anything I came across, even scratch paper on the coffee table. A magic spell.

Suddenly so quiet in our home – quiet and in preparation for the impending storm, the storm that was my mother. So suddenly quiet and creaky, the wind blew straight through the house and whisked the curtains with it since both doors stood open – out with the old, out with the cold spring, out with the dirt, out with the childbirth that took place here.

Out with the novel – out with the goddamn novel that was accepted by the English publisher I had sent it to, and which I had decided – it grew clearer and clearer the closer the date came to when my mother would arrive – would be published pseudonymously. Somehow, the contents had to be masked. I had gone too far, been too bold.

Out with the novel into the chilly air, away!

And in with the new, in with love again.

At dusk, Ted came in with a bouquet of roses he had cut with a knife, the scent enough to make you insane. He came in and sat down on the bedspread, folded up a section so the bed below was visible.

'Here, lie down here,' he said. We had not touched each other for a while. I removed a necklace in front of the mirror, paused, held on to the chain before I let it drop down on the nightstand with a jangle.

'Come here, Sylvia,' he said.

'I saw how you were looking at me before.'

Ted, in his smile. His million-dollar smile. I wanted to kiss him but only if his intentions were pure. Did Ted have pure intentions? I was afraid of everything I had filled our relationship with up until that point – anguish, demands and doubts, wretchedness. For days, I had accused him of being an amoral womaniser. In my head I had already played out the scenes . . . In my head he had already slept with that woman. Oh, what kind of instigator was I?

'What are you ruminating on, my love?' he asked.

'I'm not ruminating . . . I'm thinking of Frieda.'

'What are you thinking about Frieda?'

'If she'll remember my mother, when she comes. If Grandmother is grandmother to her. I'm trying to figure out what it'll be like.'

He reached his hand out to me.

'Stop thinking so much. Come here instead.'

He patted a spot on his lap.

The scent of the roses was intoxicating.

I loved him. I loved him, he was my Ted. I love you, I thought. I want to just love you and I want to know that I get to love you.

In a moment of weakness I sat down on his lap. His strong, earnest lap. And it felt like all the animals outside paused by our window just then as if to listen to a story. All the squirrels, the fox that snuck around on the lookout for chickens, all the nightingales and blackbirds and swallows we had in abundance and the deer and roe deer. The rabbits, of course the rabbits. They huddled along our wall at the same moment that I melted onto Ted's lap. Melted, and was caught by him. A little girl for a moment, in her father's lap. Inhaled the scent of him. Wool and work. Wished that I could be given a second chance. Wept a bit in Ted's lap, then he put his arms around me even tighter.

'Don't cry . . . Sylvia. Don't think you can control everything anyway. Frieda and your mother will love each other, that's how it is. I know it. You have no reason to worry . . . none at all.'

I looked into his face. I was red from crying, he was tired. This was how I wanted to rest with him for ever. When he was sensitive and sleepy as well. When the roses were fragrant.

Ted got up, he carried me like a bow, like a heavy child, and laid me on the bed.

He closed the window, pulled a curtain. He unbuttoned his shirt. Then I knew what awaited. He always loved me so much when I wept.

A frightened woman is a beautiful woman, I had read this in some ladies' magazine once. *A frightened woman can so much more easily make a man want her . . . Sadness makes her desirable, according to research. A sad woman emits hormones that make her more beautiful. This is why a husband is happy to put the fear of God in his beloved spouse . . .*

It was June, the twelfth, the house was asleep save for us, the neighbourhood asleep, the cows asleep; the mosquitoes and birds awake.

I was terrified when he mounted me, when he climbed on top of me and pulled off my clothes. So now it suits you, I thought, now it suits you to kiss me. Now I hunger for her, I thought, and was back inside Ted's head, now I want her, now I am ready.

And when he pushed himself into me and closed his eyes,

eeled all the way deep inside me and uttered the words, 'You're so hot, Sylvia, so fucking warm,' I wondered if it really was me he desired. Something had scratched up his gaze and everything was far away. He had barged into something as fragile as our love-making and begun using it for his own personal gains . . . I turned my head away when it was time for him to come.

'I'm going to come soon, darling, I want to come with you,' he said, and I also wanted to forget about the world and cheer. I wanted to dethrone that other woman as well. But there was something about Ted's movements that was so silly, was all an act. He kissed my neck and sucked at it with his lips. 'I'll get a mark from that,' I said, 'be a dear and stop.'

'I'm a fucking dear, for sure,' Ted suddenly said and pressed himself into me. He was so quick to accelerate into me, this was not how I had expected him. When we hadn't made love in such a long time I'd like it if we could do it more calmly, especially with Nicholas there, mute in his crib.

'Stop it, Ted. Stop.'

He paused, pulled out of me but he was not listening. He wanted me on my side, to get me on all fours like a dog again, like we used to, again.

A long time ago.

His ten fingers bent me.

But this was another body, I had this body now, I had this large Madonna-like protective body now, I had triumph in my body, I had a son to care for with my body, I was a lady, was no longer some meek girl.

Couldn't he tell?

'Ted, Ted, please, take me sincerely,' I whispered, afraid that he would misunderstand me.

He had in any case paused. Sat upright and stared into a painting.

Sighed.

'What kind of a fucking thing is that to say?' he said, sourly. 'Why can't you ever . . . ever . . . let go?'

He looked at me with the usual accusatory expression in his eyes.

'Let fucking go, please.'

I wanted to change my mind again. If I could I would always change what was me, my actions, what I did, how I appeared to the world.

'I'm sorry.'

The day my mother arrived, the air was fragrant with fruit and all the flowers were in full bloom. Exeter lay bathing in sun and the streets were warm. She stepped off the boiling London train like a tiny paper doll. There was something alien about our love and the embrace we gave each other was stiff: it jutted out sharply from my end. I aimed carelessly and regretted it later.

'Mother,' I sang and shed sentimental crocodile tears against her neck. Ted six feet behind us. 'Mother.'

Later, when it was Ted's turn to hug Aurelia, the air dried up and became difficult to breathe. I was reminded of that summer, our first summer together, what had been Ted's and my first summer, 1956, which we had spent part of with Aurelia on a silly honeymoon to Spain, a complete fiasco. I felt like a murderer: it was such a luxury to murder your mother without needing to actually murder her – I simply denied her a role in our marriage, played the part of the just-fucked daughter who doesn't give a rat's ass about anything. Ted and Aurelia didn't get along at all and that was the revenge: revenge for everything she had done to me, her betrayal when she became a widow and had been cheated by death and had sacrificed herself for a man who just died, how she had then used me for her own purposes, when she made me the *exception*, the *exceptional* human being, who would remedy her own insignificance.

Aurelia entered straight into what I had written in the letter dated June 7th: *This is the most magical life I have lived. The children are little magnets of love . . .*

She bent down, took Frieda in her arms and together they looked at little Nick, who sat on my hip. A human monkey, penetrated by her gaze. She looked at him so carefully, tentatively, it was as if she thought her very looking brought him into being.

My son.

'Here he is, little Nick,' I said hastily and emotionally as I handed my son to my mother for the first time. Mother pretended to wipe a tear from the corner of her eye and everyone in the group smiled. Ted had carried up her bag to the car and regarded us from a distance with his hand in his dirty pants pocket. James Dean. Was he really that cute? Was he such a prime specimen?

I grew suspicious. I thought: My sin. For I have sinned. Here he was, the golden boy who had turned everything upside down. As soon as I saw my son in my mother's arms, I understood that he was the one who had turned everything upside down.

And I looked at Ted, gorgeous but who could no longer make my heart tremble. Stood there like a telephone pole. Not even the scent of summer and nectar from flowers in the park did anything for me.

We had been a couple with one child in London: cheery Frieda, blonde and stubborn but who still let me maintain my autonomy. When my mother kissed my son on the cheek I saw that I was the one who had been born, who on the seventeenth of January that year was birthed on Court Green by Winifred Davies.

I was born and became cow again and lost my direction.

That hard-won direction.

That luminous independence, a triumph after years of freedom and education.

I was born on January seventeenth and became the new Aurelia Plath.

Let her love the house, I thought during the car ride home. Let our marital love be clear and glowing like dew. Let her love the garden. The children. Me. Let me be able to receive her. Let my old fears not rear their heads. Let her grow happy from inhabiting our world for a while. Let this be for real. Let my words from the letters be true. *This is the most magical life I have lived. The children are little magnets of love . . .* Let her want to settle near us. Let everything go well and for her to enjoy England. Let me be new − be light.

Ted, the baby and I sat in silence while Mother listened to Frieda's adorable chatter in the back seat. We stepped out on the driveway and it was like an entirely new house, our tremendous white Court Green, when Mother came. I saw it through her eyes.

She inspected the thatched roof, the cobble stones − and I looked at Mother. She had aged. I knew how she set her curlers in her hair at night in order for it to curl just right in the morning. I knew the scent of her perfume, exactly where the tube of hand cream was set on her nightstand and how her hands wrapped around each other as she covered them in cream. I knew how she had chosen to be a mother. But I knew nothing about her innermost feelings, even less about what she actually thought of me. I had spent my entire life guessing, had wanted to extract a reaction from her, had forced her to be shocked by my acceleration through life. If not love, I at least wanted a reaction.

Mother set down her bags in the entryway and adjusted a painting on the wall. I was already at the door to the garden so that the curtains would flutter in the breeze and the scent of flowers from the garden would find its way in. Nothing was allowed to be the least bit musty.

I wanted it all to be overwhelming.

'Here, Mother, here you go, here's your room, this is where we've set you up!' my voice chattered on. Frieda trailing me like a tail, it was as if we were dancing across the floor. As long as my mother's mouth was shaped like an O. As long as she was amazed, as long as she was polite in her amazement, as long as it was a theatrical moment and we were in the trance of arrival. The moment when everything lay before us like a letter. My mother was pure as she shaped her O. She was surprised that it was all so nice! She ran her hand along my back, across the light-blue dress, the small of my back. My mouth was a red heart. I was the motif, I was the archetype, I was the dutiful actor. I was daughter, mother and wife. I played all the parts.

I had always known how the parts were played.

For example, how a smile eats its way up your face, disappears sorrows and uncomfortable memories. How it rises up like two flower stalks out of a stem. Open, desirous, contorting. I put everything I had in that smile, and then some. Wide smile. Wide and authentic. Wide and wonderful.

I struck the little garland we had hung in the doorframe to the guest room so that it would flutter when mother walked in. *Welcome, Mother, to Court Green!*

'I love it,' Aurelia said. 'I love it!'

I could already hear Ted listening to such hyperbole; I could just hear how American it sounded. I had acquired his ears, his British gaze, as well. It was like Christmas for me. For Frieda, too. It was a game. And Santa Claus was my mother, her grandmother, who sat down on the bedspread, the white one, ran a hand across everything to smooth it all out. Said:

'Are you good little children, then? Do you listen to your mother, you and your little brother?'

'Yeeees, Gramma!' Frieda shouted, and led Mother out into the garden, to the rhubarb. I followed them, for I knew there were piles of thistles everywhere in the grass. Wilted nettles give off a sharp scent, hay and toad, and I didn't want Mother to comment on it.

The house when I saw it through her eyes, the garden as she moved through it – everything was exposed and in hopeless need of renovation. The nagging sensation along my spine and taste of blood in my mouth informed me that Mother, in fact, was an intruder. Ted followed and there was an obvious collision in the air, how she walked and dragged her gaze along everything, it drove me mad! Picked up a glove tossed in the grass and placed it in her pocket, ran her fingers through the laburnum and discovered bunches of goutweed beneath it. She pulled them out of the ground without even asking.

Mother stood there holding the goutweed, the chlorophyll-rich plant that invaded my garden in the same way that she did. How to describe it? Racing pulse, dry throat, oxygen-depleted blood in my frozen muscles: I needed a bottle of wine to straighten myself out. I needed the protective gear the crazy beekeepers wore.

'You need to keep an eye on these, Sylvia,' Aurelia said with her brusque voice, the one that became brusque when she had to do with me. She held up the tiny plant. 'This is a particular kind of weed that can become *permanent*. You can't get rid of it if you don't put in some effort.'

My mother – she never stopped! I gasped. It was insane. I turned my head to be met by Ted's gaze, a look of shared understanding, but he just gave me a quick glance, HE KNEW MY MOTHER BECAME LIKE THIS.

'You need to make sure you get each and every little seed leaf,' Aurelia said, on her knees by the laburnum tree.

And I, what did I say?

'Okay!'

I lay down on the grass with my ass in the air and did exactly as she said.

I looked at everything else that actually grew just fine. The rhubarb, two feet high, couldn't she see it? The little wild strawberry, and the strawberry plants with their white petals in the planters . . . I had bragged repeatedly about the apple blossoms in my most recent letter. Now the little pink petals lay on the ground. But the lilacs! The digitalis about to bloom! There was so much eroticism here, so much beauty in our garden but all my mother could see was the goutweed!

I suppressed my sadness, jumped at the sight of Ted stepping out onto the porch and into our kingdom, he, the highest most gorgeous bloom of them all, still in fact mine, still, he was.

'Here, here are refreshments!' I said to Mother, who looked up.

I gave my boy the breast while we sat down at the table and my mother continued going on about killing weeds – in America there was a particularly effective chemical – and Ted hummed and occasionally glanced at me.

I can't trust anyone, I thought to myself as I looked into Ted and Aurelia's faces: strangers, strangers all around.

No one can give me my love.

And then I looked down at the boy, my soft-skinned tender boy with his full lips. He was content and regarded me with his oblivious smile, the one that made my heart slow down or lose track of its beats. So soft, so good, he was. And everyone else was just buried in their own interests and motives. It was just my son and I who were in the grip. We were euphoric, in the grip of God, in the broad palms of the universe.

'We're the only ones who know, you and I, Nicholas,' I whispered tenderly and kissed his downy cheek. But then he began screaming. He kicked his legs. Aurelia looked at me as if I had done something wrong. My heart raced. Ted went on about a crow he had introduced Frieda to the other day: it was a story he was just now recreating for my mother and the wildness of his eyes followed.

'The baby crow sat down and began to pick at Frieda's fingers, practically *bit* her, can you believe it?' Ted said.

'Oh no, how awful, no crow gets to do that to Frieda!' Mother exclaimed, and tugged at Frieda's wrist until she could reach to kiss the back of the little girl's hand. Frieda whimpered and pulled free. Ted got up and something fell from his trousers onto the grass: an envelope he must have carried in his back pocket.

I called out through Nick's screams, while my heart somersaulted in my chest: 'You dropped something, Ted! You dropped a letter!'

He picked it up, pausing in the grass so as to offer us some kind of reaction. Shrugged.

'Oh, it's just an empty envelope,' he said and shuffled inside past the laburnum. I had to shush Nick on my own.

Mother passed me a napkin.

When Mother couldn't see, when she was out on a walk with the children in the pram — then I was able to take Ted's arm and ask. His elbow was resistant.

'This won't do,' I exclaimed. 'Our hearts beat in the same house, but we don't see each other.'

'Calm down, Sylvia. Don't get upset right away. Let's handle this like adults . . .'

Our two hearts in the house, our children's cries, our literary conversations, our conversations about everything, everything else in the world as well, and clinking and laughter from meals we had shared, and neighbours who had knocked at the door and entered without asking — my whims, Ted's quirks, Beethoven's fugues and piano concertos on the gramophone and Ted sitting by the kitchen table at night reciting dramatic works for the BBC, my cries through the house when I came — and now this, since Aurelia arrived: panicky silence.

Ted didn't even want to go fishing.

Ted didn't even want to tickle Frieda until she shrieked.

Ted had even abandoned his gardening books. They lay open here and there, until Aurelia caught sight of them and shut them and crammed them onto our bookshelves (that Ted had built).

Ted didn't even want to make love to me. The last time we did I threw a rose at him – that was the last time.

God, who was ultimately responsible for the mistake that had been made?

There were a bunch of poppies on the kitchen table, like flames, red, vulgar tongues, leaves wilting and falling as they looked at us.

'What is it, Ted? I don't recognise you. Why are you so quiet? Why have you withdrawn into a shell?'

'I'm not the least bit interested in your mother and her games, her way with you.'

'Way with me?'

'What she does with you – it's unbearable, Sylvia. You know it. How she hates me, and how her enormous eye watches over everything and you don't want it, Sylvia, you don't want it!'

'Want what?'

The mailman arrived in the background, a slam from the mailbox, and I started from the sound. What did he mean, what was he on about now? The conversation was not headed in the direction I had chosen.

'You don't want to be a puppet for her fantasies! Just listen to how you disavow your own novel – your own writing – you're not even honest about that, Sylvia!'

His eyes like two hard, judgemental crosses.

I would burn on those crosses. And all I wanted was his tenderness, his understanding, his safe warm hairy stomach to rest on, calm.

'You have no fucking right to come here and sit in judgement of me and my mother,' I said. 'You think you're so perfect?'

'Perfect, Sylvia – I've never been interested in perfect,' the answer quick as the tongue of a snake. Ted poured a glass of blackberry juice for himself, and pulled out a jar of clotted cream from the fridge to smear on a dry scone.

Then he leaned indifferently over the newspaper on the table. Read a bit.

His eyes glowed when he looked up at me again.

'All I ask is to not have to go through the world dishonestly,' he said. 'You're dishonest when you deny your own talent in that way. Dishonest, Sylvia, dishonest when you're ashamed and belittle your own writing. You should ask her to read *The Bell Jar* instead. Christ, I'd admire you if you did that!'

I could do nothing but swallow and remain silent.

So he had heard our conversation on the sofa yesterday? When the children had gone to bed, and I confided in my mother, curled up on the sofa and sat there with my long tanned legs in Bermuda shorts and laid a throw over my feet and stirred my tea. I explained that I had written a novel that would appeal to young women, that it described the kind of *Mademoiselle* experience I'd had, 'But this girl, Esther Greenwood, is far sharper and smarter than I am, so she gets into hot water, and besides she has a rich love life and a kind of confidence that even exceeds my own,' I laughed.

'Is it somehow autobiographical?' Mother asked. She was of course suspicious of the name: Greenwood, translated from her own mother's Austrian name, Grünwald.

'Not in any way,' I had replied.

'My God,' Ted now said. 'My God, how you lied.'

'Fuck you, Ted,' I hissed, but Ted bore no trace of forgiveness or understanding or tenderness. I was engaged in what he termed self-pity.

I was trapped like an animal. Soon, Aurelia would return home with the children. And then I would have to pull out my smile again.

'Besides, you know what?' Ted stood up straight. 'I've started writing again. All spring I was down – half-dead, there was so much with Nick and the house – but now. Maybe right now you're looking at a man who's going to win the Nobel Prize.'

He smiled faintly.

'Is that so?' I said. All at once, all self-pity gone. Doubt vanished. I could see what a small man he was.

'What a fucking joke,' I said. 'The best I've heard all year.'

Then the front door slammed, Aurelia called, 'Hello? Here we are!' and then I rubbed my eyes and straightened my back. Here was my audience, my fans; here was our shared love, the one Ted had just checked out of.

And so everything became fact when the phone rang.

Bright July day, corrosive like hot sugar.

Ted had baked a bundt cake.

Ted had chopped wood at the chopping block.

Ted had crawled around in his overalls and pulled up thistles. Harvested squash and every night we had eaten sautéed spinach, even if I had shuddered from the hay-like flavour. Ted had spoken with my mother. Ted had stuck his stiff dick in me, but I had wiggled myself free since I had sensed the calibre of his efforts: I was not the one he was making love to. The closed eyes were an all-too-clear sign. Ted had played *Grosse Fuge* at the neighbour Percy's funeral, Ted had gone through every chapter of beekeeping with my mother . . .

Ted had locked himself into the studio and written letters.

Now they were to be revealed, these letters, when I picked up the phone receiver, cold in my hand. Nick a little wood-chuck on my shoulder as usual.

'This is Sylvia Plath, to whom am I speaking?' I asked, standing in what was still my kingdom.

Nick on my arm and Mother in the kitchen and Ted, he was a man who disappeared, I never knew where he was. In the garden, on a walk in the hills of Devon, with Frieda by the beehive, at home with Percy's estate.

But I knew he was in the studio.

'Who can I say is calling?' I asked. I could already hear from the voice that there was something strange about it.

No regular person would act like that.

It was someone who was contorting themself.

It was someone who was lying!

And the roof fell down on me at once. Fate. It was that woman . . . I could hear it in the voice. It was that woman who had stepped into our lives just before Aurelia's arrival. She had stepped in beneath the light of the full moon and at that very moment I was no longer safe. The story was taken over to be written by someone else.

This someone else was now calling.

Oh, consuming fire!

She said, clearly and as if in earnest, that she was a man, that it was a certain MR POTTER calling for Ted.

'Mr Potter?' I hissed.

The woman on the phone was not a good man at all. It was Assia Wevill. She was lying. She wanted to get to Ted.

'TED!' I screamed. 'THERE'S SOME STRANGE PERSON ON THE PHONE WHO WANTS TO SPEAK WITH YOU!'

I saw her before me, sharp gaze, sharp tongue, sharp fire that would burn me.

Dead, who invoked my house.

Dead, who enquired regarding my fate.

Dead, who forced herself into my body.

'What was your name again?' I asked the voice on the phone.

'It's Mr Potter calling.'

Ted was down from the studio. He scanned me with quick eyes. He sat down on the stool by the phone. I remained, steady. Let it now be revealed. Let him now show me what he was up to in his lie! Did they really think they could lie their way past me?

Poor dears!

I wanted to laugh out loud.

Ted spoke in a low voice, replied to questions and arranged a meeting. 'Yes, Mr Potter, I want to see you too, we may as well decide on a date at once, please telegraph me if it turns out you cannot make it' – so formal, so formal, more formal than normal!, I thought to myself, merrily, for now I had the upper hand on his lies.

The silence so vast as he hung up. Not even Nick's voice or physical sounds could be heard. Silent as in church. Ted's guilty eyes. And I, raging like a fury, raised myself like an ocean wave above him and reared myself with everything I had. 'You liar!' I screamed. It was one of our life's most decisive encounters. 'You liar, you disgusting liar, you *small* man,' I declared as if I stood high above him, and he was a listener on a square. Our voices did not echo and mother was at a safe distance in the kitchen with Frieda. Ted swallowed.

'What are you up to, Sylvia?' he said. 'What are you talking about? I don't understand.'

I grabbed his wrist, even though I knew it was going too far.

'Tell me who called and distorted their voice!' I said. 'Tell me, unless you assume that I'm an idiot!'

'You're mad, Sylvia,' Ted replied. 'You've gone mad.' He shook me off, ready to go out into the light of the garden again.

'Don't you dare speak to me that way! Don't you dare call me mad! Don't you dare project your lies onto me . . . Don't you dare!'

And Ted, this other human who had appeared before me, looked at me. He had taken another woman's side and with her in his eyes he now looked at me.

ONE THING AND ONE THING ONLY POUNDED THROUGH MY BODY WHEN I TORE THE CORD OUT AND A HOLE APPEARED IN THE WALL OF THE HOUSE ON COURT GREEN, A HOLE IN THE WALL FOR ALL TIME, THAT SOMEONE HAD TO REPAIR AND SPACKLE CLOSED AFTER I WAS OUT OF THE HOUSE. ONE SINGLE THING POUNDED INSIDE ME, OR NO, TWO:

1. I HATE HIM AS I ONCE LOVED HIM
2. I WILL WRITE ABOUT THIS

I stared at the hole that ran into the white hallway wall. I was out of breath. Into the caves, into the deepest most vile caves of our lives. Ted should not be allowed to be such a vile person, I thought, he should not be allowed to appear so vile! Everything I had hidden and stuffed deep down into my darkest caverns of my life, he now tore up, and the path was open for my wretchedness my secrets my diseases my complete exhaustion to now crawl up.

Not now! I thought and stared at the hole. I heard my mother's voice as she spoke with Ted in the kitchen. 'No, Sylvia needs to rest, she's resting in her room I assume,' he said, but that was bullshit: I was sitting here staring into my own hole in the wall. A single thought was in my mind: Not now! Not now, Ted! Not now, when I have no resistance! Not now, I am too exhausted deep down in my bones, I am too tired!!!!!!

The nights.

If the days were his, the nights were mine.

I lay awake at night, I did not sleep.

When Nick woke up I gave him the breast and tried to conjure the calm that could suffice for the impulse in my brain to do its job: I had to be calm, so the milk would come down to him. From me, to him, in our loneliness. Now it was out in the world, I couldn't even feel the warmth of Ted's foot: we had become strangers to each other, now it was in the world.

Only my mother and our children who knew nothing.

I treated them like village idiots during the day – was quiet, quiet and agreeable, then lay and suffered at night.

I gazed at Ted's back. I loved him . . . Him so alone as well, so horribly alone. Him trapped in his fate as well, that small man, even though he believed himself to be so free all at once . . . Trapped in his hopeless fate, full of the worms which would crawl all over his body when he died . . . and birds that would step over him and suck up the worms . . . Don't you see, Ted, that we are deeply connected? Don't you see that you've simply flipped? Don't you see that, if you leave me, you will also leave what you have strived for in life, full enlightenment, a higher truth, the liberation and freedom of thought of the highest caste?

Am I too powerful for you?

Too much fiery poet for you?

Is my joy too wonderful, when it is joyful? Am I too hot and sincere, too *extinguishing* of your life's tentative gravity, so that you cannot have it all to yourself, govern it, in peace? Is my power too comprehensive, when I lay here with my poems at night? Can you not bear that I am a knowing, loving person? Can you not bear that I am real?

I love too, Ted . . . I am also fragile and sincere. You know I am! Why do you do this . . .? Is there no way back, no mercy when truths need to emerge, when you think you are uncovering truths from the corners of your heart! *Assia Wevill is not truth*.

Don't make that mistake, Ted, you're having some kind of crisis, but this is not *true*!

Why are you walking straight into a trap?

At night I could lie and breathe and be in relation to the world without interacting with it, without the threats being present. I could lie and breathe and ruminate. No children called Mommy, no neighbours asked me to smile at them, no husband stood and lied to my face. No one took what I said and screamed: but shut up, why don't you! The sorrow and the madness was only mine, and it was lit up by a meagre moon. How raw and bony life is, I thought. So . . . shrunken. Since no one listens to my joy, no one listens to my intentions. No one will follow my plans . . .

I called out in the madness, but there was no one there to hear.

Daddy, I thought.

Daddy, why have you abandoned me?

For the first time all night my eyes were brimming with salty liquid . . . I shook with tears. Nick moved in his sleep. I cried everything out until there was a lake on the sheet, all the sorrow for my life with Ted there, everything lay spilled before us. Had he been a truly strong man he would wake and hold me, no matter how in love with some other bitch he was. But he was *not* a strong man, he did not wake up. I did not want to lie in that sad little room and be fire and earth and tears, all the elements at once, I did not want to be so alone with everything. But I was. I was alone in my life from now on, and this night late in July was when I realised it, that I would need to manage parenting days nights sorrows the lost love everything alone.

I was summoned.

At five in the morning Nick wanted to suck at the breast again, but there was no milk.

He whimpered and cried for a while and rolled about in the wet my tears had made, but then Ted woke, he woke and grunted and placed his palm on Nick's stomach so his son would calm down.

'Why don't you feed him?' he asked.

I looked straight into Ted's eyes.

'I have no milk,' I said. 'Nothing is coming.'

I could have imagined some kind of sympathy in the face of this – but Ted was mad that Nick was crying.

I cried again, quietly, slowly.

'For God's sake, Sylvia, feed him,' Ted said and turned violently in the bed.

'But there's no milk! Don't you understand . . . No milk!'

Nick, his little writhing body, how he screamed as he had when he was born – hollering and blue in the face, not at all at peace. And he tugged and chewed, kneaded at my nipple with his hard mouth, but nothing came – the impulse did not arise – I couldn't conjure the peace in my body necessary for the milk to come.

IT'S YOUR FAULT, TED! was all I could think.

'What the hell have you done?!' he said as he fumbled

and discovered that my side of the sheet was wet. 'Fucking insane asylum.'

Ted stuck his fingers in his ears and rolled over.

I shivered and I shook. If only I had not lain awake. I really needed to sleep at night. This would not do! But it was my only time! It was my only time when I could be a human being and think! Fucking Ted, I cried (silently and calmly, said nothing).

Then I turned to our son.

'There now, my boy.'

I thought that the words would make the milk come down. If I somehow stilled my body. I knew this was Ted's responsibility, that he was the one who ought to calm us down, but he lay with his back turned to us, fingers in his ears.

I could hardly believe it was true, that I had to experience this.

'There now, my boy. Suck, be patient, Mommy's milk, it will come . . .'

But it didn't.

Nicholas sucked and sucked.

I was too tired and too distressed.

I thought of Assia's voice, how it had sounded on the phone. I saw her before me as she did everything to disguise her voice: place her hands on either side of her nose, stick out her chin and become ugly like a monster . . .

She had ruined our life and my motherhood. She, in cahoots with Ted, he who lay here, whose blood pumped through my son's veins.

It was so disgusting, all of it, as if made out of mud, and it could never be clean again!

In the morning when I woke Ted was gone and I grabbed Mother's shoulder at the breakfast table, said:

'Mother, I'm tired, I haven't gotten any sleep all night, can you take the children on an excursion today?'

Mother didn't object. She grabbed her laundry and hung it on the line Ted had hung between the elm and the oak and came back with a plan for the day. Of course she could take the children to see the goats on the hill and then we can visit your midwife, Winifred Davies, she said.

I yawned and asked her to send my regards.

She took out her curlers, placed them in the basket on the telephone table, and then my mother's eyes found the hole in the wall, where I had yanked out the phone jack yesterday.

'What on earth happened there?' she asked and pointed.

I shrugged.

'Oh, that's nothing. An accident. Ted must've pulled too hard at the cord when he got a call.'

I had prepared the formula and held up the bottle that Aurelia slowly took a hold of. A grim expression on her face. She said, I knew her lines by heart:

'You have to make sure to repair that. Fix the hole before a child sticks their fingers into the electrical outlet and dies!'

I sighed.

'Calm down, Mother. Don't be overly dramatic. We'll call someone who can fix it.'

I could already see the future in my mother's eyes: I could sense death and disaster. If only she wasn't so Austrian, so brash, perfect and hard!

Hard as steel, she was, Aurelia.

As soon as the little party walked out the front door, and I had observed them proceed several yards on the cobble stones. As soon as they were out of sight and I was inside 'resting'.

I ran loudly up the stairs to Ted's attic studio.

One way or another I would cleanse us from writing, from what drove us to death.

I pulled open the door and like a burglar – the movements were familiar to me – I rummaged through the papers and letters that lay scattered on his desk. Some drifted down on the floor, some rustled and were wrinkled by my angry hand. I did not touch his poems – but his letters! His poems I had touched another time, in an attack of envy and despair, but that was another time, there were other questions at stake then and it concerned something I had invented in my mind, but this! This sprang from an actual truth! His own fault! Ted had only himself to blame!

I rushed down with my arms full, my steps infernal, I was so putridly furious, so rotten, I could feel it myself, so much swampy mud rising inside me, as if I were, in actuality, made of mud. Now I had their phantasmatic embryos in my arms, now I was pregnant with their sweet words of love . . . Sent between him and this woman, this other witch who just now held his hand in London. I threw the letters down next to the chopping block, our fire spot, between the lettuce and the red cabbage. Poured a pitcher of water to be ready nearby in the event that something other than the letters should catch fire. I ran inside the house (that smelled musty, ugh, how it smelled in here, you could tell if you came in from the outside, I ran around and held my nose) and fetched matches. Flicked swiftly and hard against the box until a stunted bright flame bounced up. Then the letters were gone in a flash. I had not read them but at this moment I could see the evidence: the name Assia materialised on a strip of paper swallowed by the flames. And the perpetrator this time was me.

I ran down to the tobacconist and bought a pack of cigarettes, to the surprise of the young woman behind the counter.

'*Never get married*,' I hissed at her and smiled.

You could smoke a cigarette.

You could laugh your mother in the face.

You could scream at your husband at night.

Last night he had been well on his way to hitting me.

What was it in me that *appreciated* this fragment of raw reality, as if Ted's own inner demons finally bubbled up and gained momentum?

I loved Ted.

Like a mouth could love a cigarette.

The smoke poisoned me and I felt raw and wonderful, and at the same time traitorous, for what was I actually up to when I shrieked at night and burned up letters belonging to my husband . . . and smoked strong white cigarettes?

But I made love with my cigarette, with my lungs. This was the force I had assumed all my life would appear: Yes, my God, it burns, I thought. Yes, my God, it burns so good.

*

Ted went and kicked at the ashes with his boot; tiny flecks flew through the air.

I sat on the garden chair next to the begonias and puffed in and out: had not yet quite learned how to smoke.

'You move out now,' I said loudly so that it could reach him out in the garden.

'You're mad, Sylvia,' Ted said and walked toward me with large steps. 'Completely and utterly mad. You should be committed somewhere, so you're no longer a danger to me and the children.'

This garden — that we bought last summer. Ha!

Now I flicked my ashes onto it.

'Do you really intend to project your madness onto me? You're sick.'

'Stop saying that I'm sick! It always ends with you saying that I'm sick.'

'Quiet, Mother's inside and she'll hear us.'

'Why the hell are you smoking? You don't smoke!'

'You have no fucking idea what I do and don't do. I'm taking riding lessons in Dartmoor, did you know that too?'

What was it in me that ascended, as if I was the victor?

What was this light that had opened its door into me?

What was this marble chamber . . . Where did my desire come from? Was it the nicotine, that poison they put in the cigarettes . . .?

To smoke in front of Ted, to burn myself up while he watched, to reek of something strong and strange, it was too intoxicating.

'I hate tobacco smoke. Please.' Ted sat down on the garden chair.

I scoffed.

'Not when Assia Wevill smokes.'

My heart beat ferociously. Like a tiny terrified hare looking at its life's first headlights and thinking it was supposed to run straight at them, that was me.

Ted fumbled for my hand, but I had none to offer him. He sighed at my manner of refusing him. He tried to play the part of the reasonable one, since it was daytime, and my mother remained in the house.

At night he had said:

'Look at you, Sylvia. So unsexy, I'm not attracted to you any more, you're like a used-up rag to me, and I have lived in this scorpion's nest for years now, thought you would offer me security in marriage, I see it now, that's why I wanted to get such a beautiful house with you, that's why I agreed to marry you.'

He wept when he said it. His chin tried to make a movement as if of softness, pitiable, so that his profile quivered, but I could see how all of him was actually a spear.

'All my life I've only strived to be safe!'

Here, he sobbed.

His naked hairy belly that no longer belonged to me. On the edge of the bed. That I no longer had permission to reach for.

At night he had said:

'Sylvia, you're right, I've met someone else, and I feel alive for the first time in seven years, believe me, I've been asleep this entire time I've been with you. I'm sorry! Do you get it – *I'm sorry*! I'm sorry I've been asleep, even if it's a completely absurd thing to apologise for. Maybe I should ask you for understanding? A last bit of understanding? Maybe you've also been asleep, maybe we've not at all been in our proper element?'

There was his honesty and I shivered at how the words struck deep, deep inside, and how everything I had also lied about during our years together was roused in me.

The perfection in my perfectly tied bows my ecstasy my particular way of being happy that only Ted saw the bright side of but who can bear it, who can bear to be so sweetly happy, who can bear to display the good side of herself in all states, who doesn't get locked into that task and is soon sucked dry by her own excellent loveliness, who is not left to soulful destitution, apathy and then death death death?

I had no joy left, I thought.

He has sucked out all my joy, drunk off my blood like a vampire.

I had laid down like a board on the bed, like a fallow deer shot and hung from the ceiling of some garage so the blood would be tapped, the meat tender.

During the night Ted had said:

'You're the fucking fascist, Sylvia! I can see it now . . . All my life with you, you've tried to steer everything with your iron hand! Under the auspices of being a victim, because that's how you've made it sound, you've actually been there with your imperialistic American fucking smugness! And drawn everything into little cubes, little measurable cubes, you've wanted to cut me and my strangeness, Sylvia, because you haven't been able to handle it. Your smug, inflated bloody ego! You know, I bought that bit about being a victim, I thought it was true. I felt sorry for you with your history of mental illness, but you know what, Sylvia, you've been the perpetrator this entire time, you're the one who's the fucking fascist.'

And he got up naked and walked with his pretty ass through the room where Nick lay and slept his beauty sleep, our pretty son, ours in common.

And I wept as he walked. He no longer cared that my mother lay asleep in the guest room and may fly up at any second and ask if the house was on fire.

I sat and looked at him and his body, tall and muscular

and no longer mine, as he pulled his clothes off the hook and buttoned his shirt and pants, like so many times before.

Yanked open the closet door and pulled out our tent and his fishing rod and headed out into the dawn to fish in Taw. Wake up beneath the sky instead of next to me.

I lay behind and wept and was liberated and it was if my limbs were subject to electric shock treatment, as if someone wanted to perform an exorcism on me and a demon was finally freed.

Ted is gone now, I wept silently to myself and hugged the covers and the sheet soaked through with my sadness. *Ted is gone now* – and what was that wonderfulness that arrived, why did the sorrow burn so deliciously, why did it feel delightful to be humiliated? Why did I weep so happily? I lay and looked at Nick's back rising and falling in the light of night, and it was as if I was breathing alongside him. Why was it so pleasurable to feel true sorrow? Why so wonderful to be humiliated?

Now, in the garden, Ted was the one who tried to broker, who wanted to take my hand, the one who wasn't smoking.

I did not stare at him, I looked straight into the peonies, as if my gaze was stuck.

'Aren't you going to say something, Sylvia? Aren't we going to talk?'

I moved my arm again, placed the cigarette to my mouth. I had gotten all the way to the butt, it burned against my finger.

'Put out that cigarette now,' Ted said. 'Stop being ridiculous.'

'Watch out so I don't burn you with it,' I hissed.

'Is that a threat? Should I be worried? Should I be afraid of you now?'

'Says the one who nearly hit me last night.'

'I would never hit!'

'Cut it out, you violent shit. I hope you hit Assia as much as you've been violent with me.'

'Here it goes again. Does it have to be completely impossible to have a single conversation with my wife? Can't we talk like mature adults?'

I fired against the matchbox and inhaled a new cigarette roughly.

'So now it suits you,' I said. 'Now. Adult, you! Ha! Good for you that Percy's dead, you didn't have to be a little immature boy in front of him. *Mommy . . . I think I'm in love with another girl . . .* Meow!'

I gave a raw and loud laugh. What was this laughter in me, what was this liberation?

He should always leave me. It was like absinthe, it was like the high of seeing your former lover gasp for air, fumble for society's status and respect.

'You know what, Ted?' I said.

'No, what, my little smoker?'

'I don't look up to you any more. You're a small man to me. You're nobody . . . And I've understood that I've placed you on a slightly too-high pedestal. Sure. I created a story about you. You were godly to me, a large, fantastic man, you were everything. If you only knew what I've called you in my books! My diaries . . .'

I inhaled and exhaled on the cigarette.

'I admit *one* mistake in this entire ordeal. I made you into someone you weren't. But you have no right to betray me because of that. You have no right to say that I should be committed, like you did last night. You have no right to describe reality that way! It's always been one of your specialties.'

'You just said that it was *your* speciality.'

'YOU use words to design your own reality!' I went on. 'You write about it until it suits you. It's common knowledge.

God, I should've listened to you that time when you said POETS ARE INSANE. Never marry them.'

Ted laughed.

'Once again you're talking about yourself . . .'

'I'm talking to you, little man.'

'Stop claiming that I'm a child.'

'Stop being a child,' I said.

'Céline writes in *Journey to the End of the Night*, "That is perhaps what we seek throughout life, that and nothing more, the greatest possible sorrow so as to become fully ourselves before dying . . ."'

'Which means . . .?'

'You've always been so afraid of this happening! It's as if you . . .' Ted rubbed his hands together. Then he caught sight of Frieda, who had toddled out and sat down in the doorway to the porch, in her white dress and white tights, dazed.

Our purity there. Our love.

He got up, walked toward her. 'It's as if you've always somehow wanted for this to happen.'

I put the cigarette out against the garden chair, felt sludgy inside, sick from the tobacco smoke.

'How the hell can you say that?'

'Why else have you, well, conjured this?'

My cheeks were red. I felt my heart pound and the blood rush to my face.

I stood up, prepared to fight or flee, flee from our shared love – Frieda, there, in his arms. Fucking arms.

'So now you're blaming ME for being horny for sluts and teenage girls?'

Ted looked toward the stone wall, quickly placed an index finger against his mouth and hushed me, hard.

'Dammit, Sylvia! Damn you – hell!'

My mother came out in her white teeth and my Bermuda

shorts. She carried a green watering can in her hand, got down to watering all the pots of begonia.

'Everything all right?' she asked.

'Yes, everything's all right, except Ted is about to leave me,' I said and threw the pack of cigarettes deep into the garden.

Ted looked at me with his mad gaze.

I loved it when he looked at me like that, when I had the upper hand.

'What?' I asked him, in an attempt at a kind of whispering. 'I'm not subtle. And besides, you son of a bitch (my mother only pretended she couldn't hear anything, she kept on watering our plants), you're the one committing this assault. Not me! Don't try to make it into me. You're the one abandoning your wife when she's most vulnerable, when she needs you the most, with two little children.'

Now Ted was the one lighting a cigarette.

'We share the responsibility, Sylvia. We're the ones who have unconsciously driven ourselves into this situation. That's why it hurts so much.'

'You have to move out!' I screamed and pointed toward the cemetery, toward the road beyond the wall that led away, toward Crediton, toward Okehampton, away. He needed to get out now, he needed to disappear now.

Ted took a few steps toward the door further down the wall.

BUT TED COULD NEVER BE THE ONE TO LOSE. Ted could not lose. I knew his path through life, I knew his ego was always bigger. In relation to my feigned female role my ego was enormous but Ted always won, his ego was monstrous behind his saintly talk of insight and spirituality.

Instead of stepping right through the door he walked up to me and grabbed my free arm. I recognised his scent, his hot breath in my ear when he whispered:

'Sylvia Plath. I wish you were dead.'

And so he was able to leave me, leave my body that all of a sudden was emptied and limp. I was a kind of clothing fluttering in the wind.

'Bye, Aurelia, see you later, I'm going for a walk,' Ted called to my mother.

Mother and I. It was the last time we saw each other. The last time ever. The last time in life. My mother's heels against asphalt. With every step she crushed me like a cockroach. And Ted walked alongside her like a soldier. The asphalt was their stage; the train would soon be Aurelia's. Wherever they travelled they had a stage.

My mother had pretended for a week already that she was staying with Winifred Davies, the midwife, because it was 'more practical that way'. My mother did not like dirty cups and poorly written stories. There had to be a happy ending, true love, wool fabric, sturdy silks and proper soap. Better to be ashamed in silence and grin and bear it than to love in distraction and madness.

She left.

I walked with tired empty steps to catch up with them on the asphalt. It almost looked like my mother was married to Ted. That was the mistake I had made. She was right about that. She had asked me to reconsider. But I chose Ted, I chose the unstoppable brain, I chose love and art.

My mother had never dared: she chose someone in the academy. A bore but a safe bet. Otto. A stern man with deep knowledge, but a boring interior.

Oooooooh, I wanted to live! I wanted to escape her

conformist American suburban life and flit around in higher heels than hers. In Paris, London, Spain! A good-looking lipstick-shaped gorgeous gazelle with a lightning-sharp brain, as marvellous as Ted's!

And this is what came of it.

This fall I'd turn thirty; the entire summer I'd dreamed of had turned to nothing. But I was not bitter. I would succeed without him.

'Goodbye, Mother,' I said even though it was several minutes until the train would depart.

She looked at me sternly and like an Austrian.

With her, I had always wished I was someone else.

Shit, Sylvia, I thought, I don't want to be humiliated! Never again will I be humiliated.

Ted looked at me pityingly with that new gaze he had, since just a few weeks back, that said I was a nobody.

I desired his naked body. I wanted to lie with him at night, or no, I didn't want to, I hated him, I regretted that I had given myself to him at all, given and given of my body.

We stood on the platform. I put my arms out and hoped to give her a hug.

She was warm and steady, shoulders hard like a hanger; she held her daughter now, held her mistake, and I wanted to fall into her arms and explain everything, but at the same time I knew I couldn't, for my mother could not comfort, only worry.

I thought of a song she sang two Christmases ago, *Edelweiss, bless my homeland for ever*, and there was a pull deep down inside me that would like to pack myself up in her bag and go home to America with her. The light, the dignity. But those were the stones in my heart. I needed to solve this conflict on my own.

My mother bent down to our children, Nicholas the only one to smile just a bit.

'Goodbye, my girl,' Aurelia said and hugged me a final time. I looked up at her. It was almost as if she was weeping. My mother, weeping? It had never happened, but there was a dampness in the corners of her eyes. Still, it stirred nothing in me. I was petrified. She gently caressed my cheek. 'Take good care of yourself now, my good girl.'

The soldier stood and looked on and scraped at the asphalt with his shoe. Looked at something he thought was despicable. Our love. Mine and my mother's. So that was what had been a template for our marriage, I knew he thought to himself. An immature, shallow, American, disoriented love.

And inside me I said, my tongue pressed hard against my teeth: Damn you, Ted. Don't ruin this moment, too.

Then that moment also passed and she assaulted the grandchildren, with their less complicated love.

I was alone in the house, standing bent over a cold roast in the kitchen.

My mother, Ted, the children: all of them had gone.

Now I understood why we had bought a house so close to the headstones on the other side of the garden.

Our house was a headstone as well, if a far less majestic one.

I thought of everything that had been dragged through my body since then, since our arrival exactly one year ago.

A hurricane had passed through our lives and left me washed up on the shore.

A tiny moon had hung up above in the sky, innocently, in its smallness, and shone down on us.

Silly moon that I'd used in my poems!

My idiotic, laughable novel, that I'd placed my faith in.

It was all a wreckage!

Nothing was true!

My body, ripped through the middle only because the moon deigned to place a child in there that then needed to come out.

January seventeenth he arrived.

And now it was August seventeenth, Ted's birthday.

And his wife lay washed up and gasping for breath.

I once asked the rector for the keys to the church on the other side of the garden, but he did not want to give them to me.

I asked for them so I could go there every once in a while and get some light, some sustenance.

See if I in the end could be enlightened by faith.

In Ted's words:

You're like a fundamentalist without a religion.

And in another mood, he had translated those words and swapped them out for:

Sylvia, you're a fucking fascist!

I cried, I cried, I cried, I cried.

Soon I was nothing but taut, salty, stiff cheeks.

I had always been drawn to death, what Ted said was true, just not in the way he made it sound, to the rotten, to my father's amputated foot, the cadavers, the anatomy, the physician's scalpel, the equal sign between moon and flesh. Animal and human.

It seemed to me that Ted had left me not simply for egotistical reasons – it also felt like a kind of education – you should be educated! Get a hold of yourself, Sylvia! Become the person you've always wanted to be! It's beneath you to make yourself smaller than you are!

He had wanted to blow life into me, and at the same time he was the one who had turned me into a doll . . .

A doll, for now I had no more force left in my body, was I about to develop a fever again? Where was the thermometer?

OOOOOOOOOOOOOOH, I got up out of the lonely bed and whirled around on the floorboards in my nightgown. I slapped myself on the cheeks, my hair fluttered about in the air like dried seaweed, please Sylvia, kill the image of Ted in you, shoot it with a gun! (I said to myself). I tried my voice in the room, let it rise – higher, higher. Now I was speaking, loudly and clearly, in the bedroom with its open window. SYLVIA! I said. YOU HAVE TO QUIT LETTING LIFE BE DICTATED BY TED. SUCK HIM UP IN THE VACUUM CLEANER, NOW! I laughed at the simile. Haha, how small he was that he could fit there, in a vacuum cleaner bag. ANYWAY, JOY HASN'T FIT INTO THE LIFE I'VE HAD WITH YOU, TED. I'VE ONLY FELT SHAME AND DESPAIR THROUGH AND THROUGH. I'M RELEASING YOU NOW, LIKE WHEN YOU LET YOUR TEETH FALL OUT IN A DREAM. DEAD, DEAD, OUT OF MY HOUSE! NOW I AM FREEDOM PERSONIFIED!

I had a few more months of being alone in the house, alone in the large tomb with my children – then everything would be evacuated, the tenants would move in and I would be far away, in Ireland, in London. If only I could figure out what to do. What were you supposed to do?

Well, you called every number you had on a list (the phone was fixed now, a repairman had come and installed a new jack). Elizabeth Compton could help me – that friendly soul who was watching my children at that very moment – but I also needed someone more regular. A nanny. I wound the phone cord around my fingers and tried to convince myself to forget how I had held the phone cord then, that time, when Assia hissed with her voice that was like steam passing through the receiver, poison gas enveloping Ted.

I got a lead, a friend's sister's teenage daughter could help with babysitting a few evenings a week. Bingo! I would write then, I would ride, I would be liberated, I would be alone.

It was time to get myself together, time to be a human being.

Time to move out of this old dusty house! This crypt he had left me in.

When I had asked the rector for the keys to the church but he hadn't wanted to entrust me with them . . . What had

I been thinking? That I'd lay down flat in there in the icy cold and die a slow death, see if anyone came looking for me? Drama queen. Now it was time to rise out of the ashes. Now it was time to harvest the garden.

I called the woman with the horses. I was going to take riding lessons, yes, hell, I was going to be free. I needed to somehow dash across the expanses, let an animal larger than myself, an animal larger than Ted, take charge of reality. I would use Devon for this, I would get myself out of the crypt and sit on horseback and see expanses rise before me, the ones that had wanted to trick me and lock me in their labyrinth. I would see the Devon Hills from above, from atop a horse.

The girl who met me in the stable was young and aloof. I, who had already announced my riding lessons to Ted, now they became a reality. Entirely as it should be.

'You can have this horse,' said the girl.

I was afraid of horses.

Horses reminded me of being a girl.

I had a heart that pounded, I was tired, I was a mother of two, but still – still: could I become a girl? Even I?

The horse turned around, her brown eyes, a mare, a back for me.

'What's her name?' I asked, looking into the brown velvet eye.

'Ariel,' said the horse girl.

I laid my palm against her warm stomach. The coat was flat and mute.

The girl showed me how to fasten the saddle, how to step up and sit down.

'You're not afraid of horses, are you?' she asked.

'I'm not afraid of anything.'

★

I was supposed to trot, we were going to dedicate this first
hour to trotting, and the horse girl would lead me and Ariel
around a circular track, round, round, while she held us on a
rope.

'Can I gallop?' I asked. 'I feel like Ariel doesn't want to
trot.'

The horse girl looked at me stiffly, did not know which
expression to opt for when she looked at me.

I understood her. I understood her – my God, I was not
the easiest person to select an expression for – me, with my
divine thoughts and hyper-intellectual solutions to life's difficult questions!

I felt consumed by this thought, ecstatic.

So she had no answers.

I slid down Ariel's neck, grabbed the bridle the horse girl
held on to with her rope, and then I slowly pulled the length
of rope toward me until she let go.

There was no one holding me – it was just me and Ariel.

So I pushed her. I had done this before: somewhere deep
inside me I knew how to do it, in approximately the same
way as when you gave birth to a child – the knowledge was
deep inside! And people thought it was special, boring horse
girls who could just sit on horseback. Pah! Not in my case.

Ariel and I rode through Devon's undulating landscape, across
sloping fields with grazing animals as far as the eye could see,
and somewhere over there a horizon. The billowing hills
covered me like heavy blankets. Nowhere in England was it
more than seventy miles to the ocean, but which ocean? It
was not my ocean. I rested my stomach against her spine,
against Ariel's God-given heat that was enough for all of me
and made my muscles relax, the rhythm of Ariel's hooves as
she made her way through the ancient landscape with me
like a king on her back. No helmet – only an invisible halo.

If she threw me off, I would fall, Frieda and Nicholas would no longer have a mother, but in that case it was the will of the Devil and the irony of fate and I could not do anything about it.

I laughed inside at the simple secret that Ariel revealed to me and which I understood made it possible for English horse girls to remain boring for ever, to not have to advance through life like I did: it was lovely to sit on a horse, it evoked the familiar tingling feeling between my legs that sooner or later leads to orgasm. Pathetic horse girls could sit here and rub against the animal, up and down, that was enough; they rode and so they needed no men, no dicks. So now I knew that as well!

'Ariel, I love you,' I said when I returned several hours later. Her hooves scraped against the gravel. The sun had set on North Tawton and my mouth was dry from the wind that had blown through me. The children must have fallen asleep at Elizabeth's by now. My God, what a mother I was!

The stable was empty, the lights off.

The horse girl sat with her back to the barn. I thought she should get herself together, not sit there and sleep! My God, if I was paying for my experience, I didn't want to trot round, round in a boring outdoor track. I wanted to move through life like the goddess life had denied me the chance to be.

I rummaged through my pocket for some cash to give her.

'Here's your money,' I said to the tired horse girl in the dark and tossed the bill at her. I saw that she had tears on her lower lip, that her face would not let her look at me, there was something she was mulling over.

'But what IS it?' I asked her. 'Am I not allowed to gallop? That's what I'm paying for!'

The girl trembled:

'I was just worried something had happened. We didn't agree that you would leave with the horse. Not this first time.'

'Geez, I'm sorry, then,' I said, leaning forward to kiss Ariel on the neck. I patted her, thanked her for the freedom she let me feel.

Always these hucksters down on the ground who wanted to deny me my freedom, diminish the happiness I felt.

'Besides, in the future, we'd like you to wear a helmet.'

I laughed out loud at the homely stable girl who wanted to assert herself against me, a twenty-nine-year-old mother of two with a husband and a profession – my poem *Three Women* would be broadcast on the radio in just a few days. Turned my mouth up in the air, like a neigh.

'Damn, it stinks here, by the way!' I said and held my nose all the way to my black car.

Awakened by dreams: my entire chest was filled with cornflakes, rustling when I tried to breathe. Sat up and coughed, bent like a swan, and the body ejected its infection. The lump of mucus was yellow in my hand. I smeared it onto the sheet, could not bear it. It was the summer guests, the ones I was always going to invite and invite, now I had invited intruders again and they had stayed in my house and now.

Sat here with the flu as if it were 1918.

I thought of that time when we made love and I whispered to Ted, 'Please, say "Oh, Sylvia", as if I was pitiable.'

And Ted began to say,

'Oh, Sylvia. Oh, poor Sylvia.' And it got me going.

I had the thermometer in my armpit in the sweaty night-gown and a stink of sludge rose from me.

I thought: Why don't I just write about that? I'll write a novel. I'm going to write, my God, it's not even difficult, I have everything in my head, here is the entire world for me to just evoke, I'll write about Ted's whims, his idiocy that makes me seem like I'm a lower-standing human being, someone who does not even deserve her husband.

Here I was: all of America's progress, I was time that could not be stopped, the wars were over, we were heading into the new unarticulated and I would be the one to articulate it, be the New Woman for him – but now the disease prohibited it. If Ted came here now, and he would, for he needed to help me with the children when I lay here drenched in fever – he would only see my wreckage.

I lay on my side and gasped, like when I was pregnant.

I lay here and was shot to death. A duck.

This was marriage: a question to the world. Can these two young people love each other, even in a crisis? Even when they are no longer young and beautiful, when the movement, the hurtling forward, at the moment has been stopped, when someone has been prevented from living their life in freedom; when the plans to move to Europe and then to America and then to Australia or some other thrilling continent are halted, because the body demands a halt, sometime, or because someone did not get a job and there was not enough money – yes, there was always something stopping that forward motion.

And Ted came, and Ted was a worse father than I had thought. Ted did not take my word for it when I said Nick needed to be strapped into the pram. Nick fell like a bowling ball onto the concrete hallway floor, an incident that would play over and over in my head all of September–October. Do you want to make our son an imbecile, Ted? Do you want him to die?

Ted came, and in my thin voice I explained from the bed that I had the flu. I happened to say I probably had the rabbit flu and then he laughed a raw laugh and thought I was ridiculous, and then when I heard him talking to other people on the phone or in the doorway, with neighbours, he repeated that very term and giggled –

'She thinks she has *rabbit flu.*'

He came in like a freshly fucked hunk and stood in my doorway and looked at what he saw—

Yes – me – me, in my sweaty sheets, the awful smell of bacteria oozing from my mouth.

'Do you need anything?' he asked.

And he came with white powder in water that tasted like metal and a hot water bottle, though I kicked it away. 'Are you an idiot, I'm already hot enough for an entire expedition to the North Pole,' I hissed.

'Fine, sorry.'

'I have a fever of nearly one-oh-three, you know.'

'Are you okay with me taking the kids out to the garden and picking the cabbage?'

I nodded, I sobbed, I wanted him there always, standing right there, in my trap, in my female trap, in my arms, but then I wanted him to be content, not to feel trapped.

Besides, I doubted my ability to write anything, since I hadn't been able to figure out this one person, this human mystery – Ted.

Tired of marriage tired of captivity tired of the monster I apparently was – I had miscalculated everything, even myself.

'Poor thing, Sylvia,' Ted said.

His body disappeared from the doorway. I heard their sounds down there, Frieda's crying, her happy exclamations a moment later, shoes clattering against the hallway floor, Ted's calming voice in response to Nick's whimpering and a door that flew open so there was a cross breeze.

At last, I slept. I slept with my cornflake lungs and dreamed that I wrote a novel—

I'm so fucking healthy, I wrote to my psychiatrist in a letter, underlined the three last words, sucked on the tip of the pen. I had just recovered from the rabbit flu, and Ted who was going to help me – I had to tug at all his threads, and he did not help me anyway. Stop blackmailing me with your health! as he said.

I'm so fucking healthy, I wrote. And it was true: I was the one who stayed with the children. Through illness and distress: I was the one who surrounded them with a wall of peace and dignity. All I needed was some help, and I would probably get it now, from the psychiatrist and from the new babysitter, Susan, who was about to start coming regularly in the mornings so I could write.

It was so nice to be healthy, well and on my own. And so damn sensible: I was the one who took care of motherhood, home ownership and gardening. The trees stood beyond the gap between the curtains and bent in the wind: seventy-two of them and they were mine. It would be autumn and I would gather honey from the beehive. I was the one who would harvest chard and red cabbage, I would take care of our apples. That was my life: Die, and rise again.

And I stuck the letter to Dr Beuscher in an envelope and licked it shut. Then my fingertips tingled to write more and

I picked up a fresh sheet of stationery and started writing an intro to my mother.

Nothing calmed me down like writing a letter to my mother.

Then, in the letter, life was manageable and possible to manoeuvre again.

She could not be *here*: she could not stand and breathe over my shoulder and have eyes and opinions, and her own relationship with my children.

It was impossible.

But when she loomed as a chance for love. A choice you could make. Someone I could still perform for, and make her believe it was true. There was nothing more precious.

And to beat out the most wonderful feeling on earth, I put the proofs for *The Bell Jar* in a folder, ran up to the attic and found one of Ted's large envelopes to put them in, then licked it closed with my tongue and tasted the future run down my throat. I would give the American editors a try, they could use it; a new brain on the other side of the earth, someone preoccupied with things they themselves could only dream of. Autobiographical fucking insight, when all they had was surface and engraving to put on display. Poetic truth. Mother would see.

The envelope was heavy and I addressed it to Knopf, Broadway, Manhattan; sending my dreams of the world back to where they began, my pain to its source, the midnight-black street in New York and the gloss of asphalt.

Here was the strategy: Ted was the crazy one, the one who was ill, who had grown wildly mad. He was the one who lived as if there were only hotel beds. He was the one who had become – I spelled out the word for myself and blocked the letters in my head – M A N I C.

'But little darling,' I said to Nick, curled up by my breast in bed, 'the pain we feel in the morning doesn't belong to us, Nicholas. We're not the crazy ones. And we'll take good care of ourselves. We'll make our way, my sweet boy.'

His lips worked at my breast, and I had regained the milk that dried up in August, before the flu. Calm down, calm down. I still had the potential to realise myself and my life. Thirty was a new beginning. I'd have a birthday in a mere month. How to celebrate? The thought fluttered away in a sigh and the rhythm of nursing. My beloved little child . . . Who had begun to crawl, who had no father.

Later, when he would have fallen asleep, I would have to get up and walk through the rooms and check on Frieda, who was sitting in the playroom bent over a toy train and the blocks I heard her continuously demolish and rebuild. I would have to deal with the dishes that accumulated in dirty little mountains in the kitchen, covered in dried food. I would have to open the windows and air out the house, gather laundry and soak it in the washbasin. Then it would begin all over again: Nick would wake up, and we would have to go for a walk . . .

I washed with warm water and soap, rubbed and rubbed at dirt on the plates, and Frieda hobbled after me and wanted to stand and do dishes next to her mother.

Well, it's a job as good as any, as long as she doesn't whine, I thought.

I tied on her apron.

This pain doesn't belong to us, I thought. Ted was the one who left and pulled his own pain out by the roots and applied it to us. This pain was his, and it was so damn unfair that he smeared it over us, like an idiot spreads his semen on innocent little teenage victims. He was v i l e in that way, I thought to myself. He was d e s t r u c t i v e, goddammit.

The water came rushing out and soaked Frieda; she whined that she would have to change clothes. Stood there on the chair with both arms stretched straight up as if to God, as if I were God. I tore off the wet-warm clothes, the feeling of wetness against my fingertips . . . I looked at her, straight into those blue-light eyes, and then I said, 'Let's go to the ocean for a while.'

Frieda nodded. Stood there happy with her bare stomach, nodded and smiled.

Beloved child.

'Yes, let's go to the ocean for a bit!' I said. 'Let's go to Ireland!' There was a glow in me, it radiated inside, a kind of phosphorescent green light. Yes. The ocean. Ireland. Not this backward idiot English ocean which more resembled a fjord or river or large lake, which Ted had tried to lure me to while I sat and sulked in the car. This never became the real, wild, open ocean I grew up with. This ocean did not suit me. That was what Ted hated. Nothing was good enough. But that was because EVERYTHING WE DID WAS PERMEATED BY

HIS PAIN! HIS WAY OF HIDING AND CONCEALING
HIS PAIN!

My eyes burned with the sudden realisation.

'Yes, I'll be damned,' I convinced myself, dried the dishes
with a clean towel and stacked clean white plates, one after
the other. 'We're going to Ireland.'

I kissed Frieda on her soft cheek.

It could be good for my writing – it could be good for the
illusion that something within me was alive, that there was a
future that did not have to do with his pain! The ocean in
Ireland was a hell of a lot better than all of England's crumbly
seal beaches. There, the wind gusted; there, it was green and
beautiful and glorious, Richard was also there: a decent man
I had awarded a prize. His poetry was poetry that merited a
prize from the committee *I* had sat on; that way I was *above*
him, therefore I must write to him now.

I wrote to Richard Murphy and poured out the plans,
nearly forced them upon him.

I knew I had told Frieda that she could come along, but
she didn't understand anything, anyway, that brat, that darling,
whatever. I was going to Ireland. I was going to Ireland – Ted
and I – one last trip, a trip where I was the one who called
the shots and made the plans – one last trip where I really
was in control, and where he got to see what it was he had
left. Yes!

Before the trip to Ireland, I would buy a new suit in
Exeter and I would scrape together the money and be extrav-
agant and never someone you sat on, yes, totally immune to
vulnerability; I would be as healthy and daring as the ocean.

It was as simple as it sounded.

I mailed the letter down in the village that evening.

And as if by a miracle, I managed, with my cunning, to get Ted to go with me to Ireland!

I was beyond myself with happiness. Now life was beginning again.

I was waiting for him in the kitchen in a light-blue suit and heels. Car keys, passports, tickets, the children delivered to the new sitter in collaboration with my old midwife – a lovely combination. Perfect. Now it began!

Of course I should have cut my hair.

This was the trip when Ted would get to know maturity and decency. He would regain his senses and UNDERSTAND that nostalgic feeling of lost youth combined with the confusion that arises after having two children and dealing with a wife for a couple of years . . . Naturally, it could result in crazy antics where you got it into your head that you loved someone else!

My pack of Lucky Strikes was on the kitchen table with the lighter on top.

This was before The Beatles, this was before JFK was shot, this was before Simone de Beauvoir's greatness and Bob Dylan had not yet sung his songs: I was so far ahead of my time, I was so beautiful as I stood there in my high heels and butterflies in my stomach because I was waiting (just one last time) for Ted. It had not yet happened that I had taken my suitcases and packed them in anger and hope (both co-existed simultaneously) in order to travel slightly closer to the feeling of America, away from the awkwardness of southern England back to London, where Frieda was born.

I wore a suit, light-blue like the ocean. It was the middle of September and a few apples for my husband lay red and swollen in a basket. A gift of love. It was a notch in time, one last journey, a journey of reconciliation, oblivion and fire. A real trip to the ocean.

I waited. I had taken my last steps through the house in those high heels, really pattered across the floor, so the house would echo with childlessness and anticipation. For my husband to come here now – it would be audible. That I was alone, in possession of a life of my own – it would be audible. It would be audible like a heart, one that beats for ever. My heart. My big painted heart there on my lips.

So the handbag, the suitcases, the tickets, the car keys, the notebooks and the umbrella – everything had taken on a life of its own. It was my life that pushed into the shadows, behind, that would be crowded out by the things that now enveloped me, which I now brought to Ireland to negotiate with.

But I did not know that yet.

That was fate.

The green island and us.

A magpie had been sitting in the tree feasting on a small bird, and I would ask Ted about it when he arrived – aren't magpies vegetarians?

I thought so!

We would laugh; we would talk; it would all be about ordinary things.

He entered the room like a pair of scissors. Cut something in my face, some skin, like a barrier, some of my mood.

'Oh hello, darling,' I said, and he looked straight through me, he just wanted to set the trip in motion.

'We have a long way to go,' he said, rushed. 'I ran over a hare on the way here. Come on, Sylvia—'

He was already out the door. Asked me if I had everything, tossed his head in a youthful way. It was another Ted and now I became little sister, I became girl.

Me and my silly high heels that I had put so much stock in! I tore them off; stood on the hall floor in my nylon stockings. Brown, flesh-coloured heels. Here: we had stood here so many times.

I swallowed. Sat in the front seat of the car. Our car that he left for me. I was nobody. I had the handbag on my knees like any old lady. It was really still summer in September here in southern England. I wanted to look sexy to him. So what was missing in his gaze? Was it time, which was not yet created for our love? Was it the odds that were against us – the gold somewhere in the fields that the two of us never found?

The ocean, I thought, the ocean!

While Ted went on about practicalities. Lectured while he drove away in savagery and apathy – drove us jerkily, drove slowly, drove quickly over the hills – a lecture on the importance of choosing one's own life, of following one's own inner compass, that 'life has chosen a mission for everyone, Sylvia, now I know, because I've explored my mission, and my mission is *freedom*, Sylvia, what's yours?'

I held on to him tightly as we boarded the boat, and on to the wet railing. Stumbled in those high heels, the wind gusting in my hair. Goodbye, children. Goodbye, confinement that I thought was a law of nature. Hello, adventure; hello, raw, gusty winds straight from the ocean. Hello, my father. Hello, Poseidon, King of the Ocean, my father, you.

Ted was buying a beer.

I had turned down his offer of a drink.

'You're not pregnant, are you?' he smiled and sat down next to me, right on top of the box of life jackets. I laughed a laugh, happened to nudge his stomach. It was just like it used to be, and at the same time so sheer; it all hung on a thin clothesline, it was broken and could never be whole, but we performed. We performed this trip.

And it was the expression on Ted's face that made us perform: hard and watchful, he judges me, I thought, with every glance he has judged me. Hard and for ever.

Were it not for Ted's betrayal, I would lay spread on his lap, my head there in his warmth, gazing up at the sky where seagulls flew, crying their cries, billowing above us.

Ted sipped on the bottle and started to guzzle. The more I looked at him, the more I wanted a beer.

And the ocean was the ocean and the ocean made me tired: it was just salt, rutting seaweed and waves. Nothing. Nothing was as it was in my head, that was the whole problem: in my head the ocean was magic and paradise because it was a fixed image and I, Sylvia, loved to direct life like that, wasn't it wonderful, wasn't it wonderful, for in my head I held the whole truth.

And in reality, seagulls shat and roaring oceans boomed until my ears throbbed and an old-lady girl like me said no to beer and regretted it a minute later when she saw her husband put his lips against the rim of the bottle. And I put on my sunglasses and let this fact bloom like a wound inside me, and then all the energy of reality was wasted. It was so pathetic! The force of reality was so pathetic!

My illness arose when I could not order reality and give it the shape of words: and now, as I looked over the railing out at the sea, I was suddenly homesick, wanted to go home to America, home to Court Green, home to our old routine relationship – oh, if time could be turned back! I wanted to go home and write.

And if it was Ted who was the beer drinker on board with his own internal force, and I the dejected, waiting woman (even though I was no Penelope), it was now, as we stepped across the threshold of Richard's summer house in Connemara, I who must take charge.

I threw my arms out. Clean floor, clean scent, beautiful flowers, sun. Now it was me, now it was me. Married woman about to turn thirty! My laughter was all over my face and as usual Ted collapsed. I was guilty of the fact that Richard was now invaded by two poets, and I must pay him back with my entire being. NO OUTSIDER SHOULD EVER SUSPECT THAT SOMETHING WAS WRONG.

Ted had checked out; he could not stand my exaggerated smile. Had once said: 'That'll give you crow's feet, Sylvia. That'll freeze your face.' And now, just as I stood by Richard's arm and went off in a monologue of fandom, where I said things like, *What a dream that we get to spend a few days in your sweet cottage in Connemara, how great to be able to make a living off tourists and then just write!!!*

And Richard did not know; he still believed in us as though we were real.

Then Ted took me by the arm because he was about to vomit. He already had half of it inside him somewhere; his dreams eddied across his face, his puppiness stood out like a stiff erection. Grabbed me and whispered, while Richard carried flower pots out on the patio: 'Sylvia, stop it!'

The sun flowed. I jerked my arm away. He may not grab me like that.

We had travelled all day me and my heels and now I walked around as if I had done nothing but walk in Richard's poor little house, which had been forced to take our destiny into its hands.

'LET'S WRITE!' I said, with such speed and conviction that even Richard laughed a little strained laugh.

'My God, Sylvia,' Ted said in the evening as we each had a cigarette in the cool night on Richard's patio, where you could see all the way to the Irish mountains.

'You talk like you were aboard the *Titanic* and shut your eyes to your own fate!'

I looked into his despairing eyes.

Despair: now I could see it.

Ted had – surprise! – made the beds; yet again, he had to prove what a damn good man he was. And I was permitted to sleep in the same room as him.

Our door read marriage.

Now it was as if time had acquiesced to our great love, the lifelong bond we once swore to cherish for ever. Maybe something would happen in this bedroom just as it had before the future was destroyed.

I picked up my towel and walked to the bathroom, I was no longer wearing those high heels, it was my bare feet against the floor. Rinsed my face beneath Richard's faucet while the two gentlemen chatted in the kitchen. Ted had made a private phone call and so be it! He was a free man! And so was I, though a woman and a mother. I would tell him how much I loved him when he came back.

Because I had not said it enough.

I remembered once in the spring (Oh, this damned spring, when I was so involved in the struggle with Nicholas, when our love took shape) as I breathed beside my husband in the dark and lay silent for a long time then said:

'Ted, you are my heart.'

And meant every single word I said.

As if the sound rose from the darkness, took root and began to bloom.

Ted's voice trembled then.

He said:

'Sylvia, it warms me. My entire being becomes warm when I hear you say that.'

And I lay there, content.

Then I thought: Have I not done this often enough? Showed myself, exposed my love. Is that the mistake I made? Have I dug a pit for our love, a trench for each of us? Is it Nick who, with his arrival, dug them for us?

Because I had felt it, the distance.

And it was as if someone started playing a wonderful Parisian song in our room. Ted crawled closer to me. And I kept myself from getting lost in the questions. Let it be blank, let myself be a blank page.

Breathed with him in the dark, held his warm blank hand.

How would I show Ted that I loved? was the question I armed myself with now. Pulled the towel off the hook, scrubbed it across my face. I looked myself in the eye. Hollow-eyed, blank this time as well. And still so full. Where was everything, where was it, what I had in me and forced onto paper at three-thirty in the morning?

I stepped out of Richard's bathroom washed and clean. The scent of soap on my hands. Ted was not there; I pulled off the bedspread, lay down on top of it and felt around. The beds had a nightstand between them. Of course it would be possible to move. I stood up and tugged at the table with my ass facing the door when he suddenly came in, asked what I was doing, what are you doing, Sylvia, *we're not going to sleep next to each other*. (He whispered when he said it.)

'We're not?'

Ted looked surprised.

'You mean that you want to?'

'Sorry. That was stupid.'

I moved the table back, lay down on the bed. It has to be exquisite, I understood that now, Ted was like a woman that way, he wanted to be surprised, caught off guard with flowers handed to him, I had to shock him with my love.

'That was stupid of me.'

He sat down on the bed and began to undress. The shirt, against his t-shirt. It was the last time I saw him naked in front of me; off with his undershirt and there was his stomach covered with hair. The skin that once belonged to me, now just a memory deep down inside.

'But how can we reconcile if we can't get close to one another?'

I knew what I had written to Dr Beuscher: I would not fall for his gestures of love and I would not sleep with him again. Just as she had told me. But I was horny, twenty-nine years old one month more and utterly horny, like an animal that saw nothing but. There was no morality, just people to perform in front of. Richard had seen me – Ted had seen me – I had been seen today, in my lipstick-red mouth and it had, in short, made me horny. Horny.

'I want to make love with you one last time,' I managed to say.

Ted . . . Ted laughed. Not in a way that dismissed me. He laughed because I was hopeless. This drama queen, housewife, suddenly turned into a chic mother of two on holiday (as if I denied my own motherhood) in a light-blue suit and with hunger. Heels, hat. A new morality.

Ted never said no to a fuck, did he?

Yes to everyone else but no to me?

'Don't you like me any more?' I asked, pushing the night-gown off my shoulders.

Ted asked me to stop, stop humiliating yourself now, Sylvia, it's pointless, you don't want to play the fool in front of Richard and then humiliate yourself like this . . .

That the purpose was so unclear, that our relationship was so unclear, that I somewhere inside me hoped with all of my cursed heart that he would return.

My returnee, Ted, dammit.

'That this is your way of showing vulnerability, Sylvia,' Ted said and got up to caress my cotton-thin arms while I sat there, on the bed. They trembled, I trembled like a little girl. He opened the curtain inside me that I had pulled tightly shut. Ted could do it. Ted did it, as the only one.

Ted, you were my heart.

I wanted to say it to him again.

I wanted to go out and drink beer and not give a shit about anything; toss my hair; after all, we were in Ireland, on free ground. Neither my country, nor his. Let's make something of that, now.

'Hold me, touch me,' I cried.

Ted stood close; his crotch and legs were against my head. I drilled my way in.

'There, there, Sylvia,' he said, his arm on my strong shoulder, down my spine.

'There, Sylvia, cry,' he said. 'You can cry. You get to be needy. You get to. Let it all come out . . . come on.'

He squatted down in front of me and kissed me. It was my salty tears that tasted so acrid in our kiss. My lips swollen, humiliated, horny. He ate them. One last time. I was set loose in my body. He let go of the hug, got me on the bed. Ended up on top of me. So much there in our connection. We had never erased that. We had a pattern. Now here was his cock entering into me as it had entered into other women. It returned. He was at home, moving inside me. Mild and tender, much closer because I was sad. I could feel it more. I had no resistance. He came sincerely, on my stomach so that I would not get pregnant. Ted's deep moans. Turned heavy next to me. I breathed like a little hare. Wet stain on top. I was clubbed, broken, it was a delicious feeling. I had longed for him to drive himself inside me. Then it was done. That was the last time. My body was alive, warm. I kissed him on the forehead.

'You are my heart, Ted,' I said. The words just came out. Straight out into everything that was so quiet.

Four-thirty in the morning I woke up. Got up, rummaged through my bag for my notebook. Pen and paper. It was a cool morning and yesterday I had fucked. I washed myself in the bathroom as fast as I could without waking anyone. Here came a poem. In my head, while the water flowed. It was the energies, of truth and love, that was what made the soul split open and turn into poetry. An entire syntax that arose. And I was inside it, deep inside it. What, then, emerged? I had to rush out, before I woke anyone, before hunger tore a gaping hole in my stomach, before the feelings caught up with me, before chores and duties summoned me, me, the chosen one. The blue hour of dawn was so restorative. Not a single human being in the entire world demanded anything of me. I felt like the first human, or God. My cheeks wore roses. There was a seed of self-assurance and hope in me. Maybe it even felt good to fail. To dare to be hurt, dare to let the world be torn to pieces and turn ugly. I always demanded the beautiful and enduring, dignity in everything. I, with the disturbingly high expectations. Now it collapsed, now my husband lay there in the room next door and everything had collapsed. Maybe he would really become my ex-husband. Maybe everything would fall. And in that darkness I rose, in a new reality. It was an opportunity. A new vintage. Ted was so kind to me last night . . . I went out into the cool breeze on the stone slabs on Richard's patio, and blushed as I put the tip of the pen to paper. Got the marks down on paper. It had to do with something, I didn't even think of what. Just a tone in me. I didn't need to control things so much. I was just an initiator of series of events. Trust life, Ted had once said. Now I tried it myself: Trust life. I wanted to be someone who trusted life. And now, when I was in Ireland, when I was a newly fucked wife, when I had regained my feminine benchmarks and ambitions. When I was just awake and sat on the patio with a poem in my hand and it all just was. And Ted slept inside. It was almost like 1956, 1957, our honeymoon years before motherhood began. What did it do to me? What, exactly, had been done? What was that storm I had been in? Look, my hands. Feel, my mouth. Slowly, my body returned to me and then I had to escape.

Richard was up at breakfast; the sun had risen with him.

'Well, aren't you up early, Sylvia!' he sang. Cheerful, carefree.

'Thank you again for letting us stay here with you,' I said. We pecked each other on the cheek.

'Of course. You're my esteemed poet guests,' Richard replied. 'Do you want coffee? Juice?'

'Both,' I said, sneaking into my room, where Ted lay asleep.

But Ted was not there. His bed was hollow, abandoned. I went to the bathroom to jostle the handle. No one there, either.

'Is Ted up?'

My voice stuttered a little when I raised my voice to the kitchen to ask Richard.

'Haven't seen him yet!'

A faint sound within, of something falling.

Now I picked up my pace. Stalked around all the rooms. Ted had apparently torn away from me completely. Of that I was wholeheartedly jealous. You're not the only one who wants to tear yourself away from me, Ted! I do too! The difference between us is that you have the option to do it!

I ran through the house like a ferret. Richard wondered what was with me.

'Why are you rushing around, Sylvia?'

'Because my husband is nowhere to be found.'

'What are you saying?'

I grabbed his arm and turned him toward the sight of Ted's bed: empty as the grave, but he had lived there. The sheets were clues of his presence; the heavy numbness in my crotch full of him, his mark.

All I could not control – Ted!

I cried against Richard's shoulder until he pushed me away with a look of dismay and I suddenly realised the deeply inappropriate fact of being a married woman demanding something – an embrace, a caress – from another man.

Things here in Ireland were Catholic.

And I thought Ireland meant freedom! Wherever I went I had a new morality to wrestle with; a new betrayal! I was persecuted by my betrayal, by my feelings, my grief, my father, Poseidon, my old man who refused to let me be free of complexity and ancient wounds. Awful!

So Richard could not save me, either.

'I have to call Mother,' I said.

We all searched, until we understood that the escape was orchestrated by Ted, had been a long time in the making. A boat receipt left behind and confirmation from the telephone operator that the number Ted dialled in the kitchen last night was to an Assia Devil – in Spain. (I had started calling her that now.)

In the evening, Richard asked me to consider taking my things and heading home the next day.

I was beside myself with grief and this was what he asked of me?

'Let me process this! Let me gather myself somewhere – I

have a ticking bomb in my heart, Richard, don't you understand?'

But he did not understand what was incomprehensible about me, only Ted understood.

Ted, out of everyone.

And now – no one.

This was the end of me as I had been so far. Now it was time for me to begin to burn. I needed to renegotiate the entire contract with myself, the entire constitution.

So I said:

'I'll leave when I want to leave. Just. Like. Ted. I'm not going to care about the rest of you any more. I don't give a damn about you. I'm sleeping here until I feel like going home. I'm loath to shrivel up into a tiny apple core and lie here and rot, just because you say so. You have to put up with me, Richard, I'm sorry.'

The tears were packed tightly in my throat when I said it.

Crying, I still packed my bags and went home to England the next day. It was beneath me to remain with a man who despised my company, left by a husband who had fled me. Who were these people? Did they not care at all about my greatness, the one I knew I possessed?

On the night boat home from Ireland, something happened to me. I nursed a drink for a long while and saw a young woman being seduced by a man on the dance floor. Jazz music was playing. I sucked at the swizzle stick and observed her short hair, how it lay in small curls at the neck. She appeared to be Finnish: as soon as she opened her mouth a gurgling sound came out, a long harangue. I could not take my eyes off her. One day, I would also be vulgar and perched high like that – soft and hard at the same time, like a taut string on a cello as she aimed herself, her entire torso, toward him, the older man, tall and handsome – a cool couple embracing in a silly dance.

And I was young.

I was still young, still lovable, and if I jumped off at the port and showed the conductor my train tickets and then left this ordinary life, fled somewhere and refused the two messy baby butts waiting for me at home . . .

But my heart was pounding with eagerness as I lay down in my cabin. I piled my hair on top of my head and looked in the mirror to see if the style would suit me.

Yes, I would be short-haired. This fall I would be the vulgar woman I never dared to be when I was young, because I had my mother's breath on me all the time. I was long since free of her. Would never see her again. And now also from

Ted – my black-clad husband with dictator eyes – oh, the difficult years, oh, the difficult bitter years with my poet!

They were over now; the ocean rocked me to sleep in my cabin. I slept a hollow, dreamless sleep. It felt like there was no boat there, only the ocean and I, my body laid flat on top of the waves.

I still had the jazz tune in my head when I awoke and got up with the first streak of sun through the cabin window.

Underwear, jumper, a splash of perfume and the prim skirt – I would go home and be mother (because I would never be able to forget the kids and go to hell, NO. No matter the tingling at the mere possibility. NO).

I would have coffee and then I would sit down with a notebook – and when I sat there with a big cup of coffee at the round table by the bar, I suddenly felt as if the wind blew straight through my heart.

My arms were as thin as paper. I had barely emerged from the whole hysterical business of giving birth and breastfeeding children and having mental breakdowns and the flu and mastitis and arguing with a man who was a lunatic – I had lost nine kilos just in August and September! – and here I sat, empty.

If I formed my mouth to make a sound, perhaps silence was the only thing to come out.

No one paused by me and asked; no one confirmed to me that I was really here.

Only the notebook.

When I got off the night boat at dawn, when the boat had attached itself to the old country of England and the misty autumn winds blew up from the furious Atlantic British side of the pond – then I already had several pages full of words on them, without me having noticed.

★

On the train back to Exeter, I thought of circus animals. And I thought of the married couple I read about in *Ladies' Home Journal*, the ones who had an abusive relationship, and how the woman had emerged from the pain and said to the audience: *It felt like he woke me up when he hit me. It felt like I needed it.* And the man said: *If I did not flog her, she just lay there like a vegetable and felt like a victim. As soon as I hit her, she got into gear.*

Circus animals in chains.

I thought of Anne Sexton, too. Circus animal. Her latest poetry collection was a good model, goddammit: that woman was full of fire.

Competitor or no competitor — now it was important to stay on good terms with everyone in the literary world — I would write her another letter when I got home.

I sighed as I glanced at myself in the window, homeward bound. I knew that freedom had a price — but now there was no stopping. All I could do was start dancing.

A flock of jackdaws sat on the thatched roof and shrieked; they rose into the sky when I unlocked the door to Court Green. I was alone now. It was dark here. My thousand efforts to conjure feelings of decency and modernity out of this majestic house over the past year had swirled away like dust in a corner.

I let my hair down, but still the sense of liberation didn't arrive. I fell into a fresh, forced weeping, only because I realised I could not shout out his name any more.

His name in my mouth; it had been such a grace. And now the sorrow over what I had lost washed over me with full force.

What have I done? I cried. What have I done to deserve this?

Ted, why don't you love me any more?

I picked up postcards from the mailbox, cut open envelopes; nothing was important at the moment. Paper that fell to the floor without my blessing.

And about this life, I thought I would write a novel. Life in North Tawton, Devon.

Blah!

I took off my socks and walked barefoot across the cold floor.

So much to bring home; children to be reunited with, love to try to forget.

I need to repair who I am, I thought.

That was a line I had to save for a poem.

Oh, despair!

Despair when I stepped out into the living room and threw open the door to the garden, where the grass stood tall, nearly three feet, and I was the one who had to walk the lawnmower to cut it. Check the lawn.

Ted, scrape out the sink, Ted, you take the kids, Ted, will you pour me some coffee, Ted, we have laundry to hang, Ted, I can't open this jar, Ted, we have to plan the week, Ted, can it be my turn to write now, Ted, should we say yes to that dinner this weekend, Ted, do you have something planned on Thursday – please say you have nothing, because the midwife's coming. Ted, have you seen that damn bill I put on the table?

And Ted came, Ted came with his face rooted around and kissed me lightly and fleetingly on the lips, then disappeared just as quickly.

This was Ted in the void of my memory.

The rest was gone; it was like a tomb, a barrel I stepped into, filled with water, and my hair would assume snake-like form; this house in the countryside in Devon would be a horror film, it would be October here and sheer horror.

How would I manage?

Soon the nanny would come with my little ones.

There was only one answer, there was only one answer to everything and it was words, words to write with, words to clog the silence, words to carve out of silence, words to burn everything up in remorseful flames. I could – I had the ability – I had the opportunity to resuscitate the life that once unfolded here.

★

It was with hiccups and dried tears that I opened my arms to the children when the nanny left them in my hall. They stood there like two aliens: Where are we? Who are you, Mommy? Frieda, warm, wonderful lump to let my ego be crushed by and with whom I could turn a stiff grin into juicy laughter! Daughter I had missed so much!

And Nicholas, you should not have been given the chance to grow so big and sensible while Mommy was gone!

I kissed him on the nose, on the forehead, on the cheek; his gaze that had always been dark and amazed looked at me so that it stung deep inside. So palpably sad now that Daddy was gone. Complete focus. Eight months and so accusatory. For a while we were strangers to each other. The nanny noticed it, stepped into the kitchen, leaving us alone to get acquainted again.

I shook him a little. Felt how thin I was – not a motherly woman for him.

Frieda got to play with the music box I bought on the boat home from Ireland, a tune that livened her up and she didn't have to ask for Daddy, Daddy.

At night I could not fall asleep.

'Beloved Nicholas,' I whispered, trying to force the breast on him, which he after some tentative nuzzling accepted and let himself be consumed by.

'You will discover a creeping emptiness, a discomfort. You will realise, when you are older, that your daddy actually left us.'

There was in fact no actual milk in my breast. I simply needed to fall asleep and took one, two, three sleeping pills in order to pass out next to my little children.

I had just been by the ocean, and now? Now I was locked in the jaws of this house again. In a completely unguarded moment; *anything* could happen to me. I knew that all too well – history as a mental patient, a fragile psyche, now it was a free-for-all for the demons to sink their teeth into me, a free-for-all for thunderstorms and all the lightning to appear in the grim darkroom of this house . . .

Imagine lying here on the floor, fallen, a perfect creation without any muscle strength. A picture to look at. A picture of me—

But to think that I would never again ask for permission to write. That was what I had done. I had measured myself against his greatness and if he was the yardstick, the great one, the ideal, who could I then ever become?

Who?

This was a question for God.

And there was no God!

This, too, was a relief for me. My pulse was racing. Soon the children would be home from babysitting . . . Soon they would thunder in and exhaust me during round two and make me long for my ex-husband again. My ex-husband Ted Hughes their daddy, Ted Hughes. Ted Hughes Ted Hughes Ted Hughes.

Oh, this exquisitely beautiful name, now this curse. Stop growing on my wall, on my body, in my brain, on my paper-thin skin!

If Ted was the one who could help me navigate lunar landings, solar eclipses, earthiness and the celestial pitches . . .

Then I had no one for that now.

No child, no nurse, cleaner, gardener. There was me.

Was just one thing to do, one thing left to worship, now that Ted did not exist:

The writing.

The writing.

The novel.

ME.

At this thought, I lay down breathless.

My pulse stilled. I fell asleep.

Sunday roast! The realisation woke me up, my chest shot straight out of bed and my breath sharpened. I would cook her Sunday roast! What tingled like soda in my legs suddenly speeded up, got enough air to rise. I would cook the nanny a Sunday roast! Such a perfect impulse. It was Sunday. And then we would chat about my wonderful children and I would tell her about my plans. Hallelujah! (If only I was a believer; but still – such a very good word sometimes.) Susan O'Neill, that is. The woman who got along so well with my children. Oh, perfect impulse. Oh, meat. I would go down to the butcher and bring home this piece of welcome meat for me, her and our children. I would enjoy being alone, free of my husband and soon truly divorced. I would talk to her about how cool I would become, a divorced mother of two – and I would really show her how much I understood of her position: a young twenty-two-year-old who cared for someone else's children. (I had once been like that.) How I observed the husband and the woman in the house then, how he treated her in front of me, what their intimacy appeared like when viewed through my gaze. Their contract – yes. Because that's the kind of thing you enter into, I thought now, in marriage – it was nothing less than a contract. Not a relationship at all. And now he had burned the contract into ashy crumbs.

When we clattered with our pieces of lamb late on Sunday afternoon and Frieda asked Susan to cut her meat – I should be the one she entrusted with such a task but it was a signal: you haven't been home in a while, Mommy, now Susan is the one who does this – when I drowned my plate in the gravy and served the peas and carrots and pale little round potatoes, more salt because it tasted so good, then I said straight out that she was such a damn good nanny.

Susan looked at me a little strangely, where she sat. A silent second while she cut and composed a bite.

'Hallelujah, I'm just saying!' I said. 'What good fortune that I have you!'

And Susan responded by putting an arm around my daughter, who smiled.

'What good fortune that we have Susan,' I emphasised in a hint to Frieda, because I really wanted her to feel that she was in the middle of our circle.

Now that the circle had just been redrawn.

I wanted her to know that she was more beloved to me than that snake Ted Hughes.

We ate and the peas tumbled around in my mouth as I delivered statements about my new life to Susan; I need to repair who I am, I said, I have an identity to restore.

Susan did not understand such poetry but she nodded nonetheless, and ate of my food.

What a success I was! Invited her for Sunday roast!

As one should.

'I've wasted too much time on Ted,' I said. 'He cut through my life like an axe and I didn't understand while it was happening, but now I have to gather the wreckage myself, you understand that, Susan: do you understand that?'

Susan pushed a curl behind her ear and said she probably did not understand, but somehow understood anyway, if you understand . . .

We laughed.

'And sometimes I really wish I was deeply religious,' I continued with my long monologue. 'Ted actually said that to me. He said I was like a fundamentalist without a religion . . .'

The tone between us continued to waver; it was as though Susan really tried to understand me, and as though I relished the fact that she couldn't.

'Of course it's not like that at all,' I continued. 'It was just Ted's way of trying to assume power over me. He would always tell stories about how I was, the analyses rained down on me.'

I laughed, and my hair hung down to the plate, it was so long now, I really had to cut it.

I twisted a loop between my fingers and tossed my hair over my shoulder. Ate.

'And by the way, I plan to get a haircut, get ready for this new woman that I am. What do you think about that? What do you think that would say?'

I asked Frieda to get up and stand behind me and hold up my hair.

'Do you see, now? Do you see what it would look like if it was short?'

Susan narrowed her eyes at me, looked at my hair, made small polite motions to try to appear interested.

What's going on with her? I thought. Is it that I'm not asking her enough questions? I have to be interested in her, too, of course, I realised.

'I'm sure it'll be nice,' Susan said. 'Of course, you'll be very beautiful even with short hair.'

There was such an awkward, sad mood in the room, even though everything was supposed to be GOOD.

So I asked her:

'What are your plans for the future then, Sister Susan?'

She laughed at the nickname.

She looked at Frieda anxiously. Then she placed her hands around Nicholas's waist, since he was attempting to crawl out of the high chair.

She put him in her lap.

'No, but the truth is, Sylvia,' she said, 'that I can't be your nanny any more.'

I swallowed.

Frieda heard that something was shifting in the room. She looked in my direction. Hard and fast I stretched out my arms to take Nicholas back to my lap.

'What are you saying?'

Kissed his scalp, the soft fluff, and the scent, the lump of warmth with me, he would always be here, him they could not take away from me. He was mine.

'My God, what are you saying, Susan?'

Everyone who left me ruined my life and they didn't so much as shrug.

My nanny sat completely, mercilessly still.

Like a wax doll.

Susan wiped her mouth with the napkin, patted Frieda's cheek.

'Stop that!' I roared, suddenly appalled by my own reaction to what had happened, but still. I still had to show that I was angry.

Susan got up, pulled out her chair.

'Please, Sylvia,' she said in an angelic voice. 'Please, Sylvia, don't get angry. It's just that I have a life in London waiting for me.'

Yes, who hadn't had that?

Who hadn't had that?

My forehead fell into Nicholas's weak back, all my resilience, all my show, Sunday roast and the cleaning of half the house earlier today. To entrust someone with important details about your life, it took so much energy.

All the effort I put in – I did it so that it would last! For the final peace to arrive at last. When all the exertion was over. When I could just start to repair my self. Then all the people near me came and ruined just that . . .

It always happened when I was the most vulnerable . . .

The least prepared.

When I had revealed myself.

When she had eaten my food. My meat. Lamb.

Little lamb with a knotty bone sticking out. I wished that I was the one lying there charred on the plate . . .

The only thing I could do was run away like a little girl up to my room, and I did, for my heart fluttered wildly in my chest.

Susan knocked at the door, wanted to try to comfort me.

'But Sylvia,' she said. 'Maybe I can stay for a while longer. The month out. Okay?'

I dreamed that I rode, galloped across the ocean, on a pretty white horse. I was struggling with his ocean waves. Tidal wave, on the Atlantic Ocean.

I opened my mouth; these were tears.

Like a clenched fist from within, that rotated up through my stomach and wanted to get out through my throat.

That was how he drummed through me.

The children who slept so loudly, their breathing drove me crazy, that the hours when they gave me respite and rest soon were in the past.

Damn, I was out of breath, I was drenched in sweat, this sheet was not enough for me, I was like an ocean to be contained.

It was October. I was alone in this house. The summer had set all around me like a sun that has been extinguished. I would never get to see summer again. In a way, I knew this. October with its greedy little birds that pulled the fattest worms out of the earth, the pheasant that built a nest elsewhere for the winter, hoarded nuts. The swallows migrated. Soon it was just me and the rats and the kids here!

With my dreams . . .

I went to the toilet and was close to vomiting across the cold white enamel, my body crouched in an arch and sobbing emptiness, emptiness.

Damn damn Daddy, I said.

I had dreamed . . .

About him.

He was the one who did this to Ted and me. Everything is your fault, Daddy! I rested my elbow against the edge of the toilet and cried. It smelled like piss and tears. I cried . . . Damn you, Daddy! You thought I would be able to struggle all my life . . . Now, when I need my strength the most, I have no strength left . . . It's gone!

I wiped my face with a piece of toilet paper, threw it in the toilet bowl's clear water. Got up and opened the door to October and went out, alone in the dark dawn. It took a while before it brightened here. How could I be fooled into bringing my life and my story here, I thought, leaning against an icy, wet brick wall. I'm so tired . . . Devon has sucked the life out of me . . . He gets the kids, he can come and take them, I don't care about them any longer . . .

I folded my arms across my chest and sharpened my mind. If there was anyone I had to keep fighting for it was them. But I had been left during a vulnerable time. I had written to my mother, speaking of my longing for Ireland: I cannot handle one more winter in England.

I already knew, I knew. I knew.

I had also written:

I'm so fucking healthy.

Because if Ted was whoring around with secretaries, fans and girls with marble uteruses, who'd had abortions several times over, I was standing here in my tall October grass that no one ever cut, with a harvest to gather in the evenings before the frost settled, and seventy-two apple trees to make jam and cider from. Frieda and I gathered a big basket, yet the worms had already begun to eat them.

Now it was just a matter of surviving as clean and vulnerable naked honest and exposed as I was.

Oh, Amazons, what was your weapon? Cunning?

I stepped inside again, wishing I was someone who managed to take care of herself, someone who held herself and life in high regard, who made tea for herself, put on sheepskin slippers and wrapped a robe around her, sat down on the throw on the couch and opened the morning paper before breakfast . . .

Instead, I was a disgusting poet whose head hammered with poetry; I have to write about my father; if that were to happen at some point it should happen right now; in the flame of a fucking candle – that was all.

I pulled out a kitchen chair. It was four in the morning. I sat down naked, I was shivering but that was how it was, I thought, a poet's work; in reality you froze your ass off as a body and as a human but the poem did not care, readers for all of eternity and all of the future did not care! To them it was just a successful poem on a piece of paper!

I had paper now, a pen; I scribbled down the words.

DADDY pounded like doom in me, or rather, a doom that would become reality if I did not put the words down, the hammering that sounded in my head.

If I did not manage the act of writing now, if I missed the chance to really put my finger on everything just the way it felt inside me, then I was done for ever, then I was not worth being called a human.

Then Ted was probably right.

If I didn't cry this out my fucking innermost my heart and soul, all my eternal shit collected here, if I didn't manage it but instead let it turn into flat similes and godawful ugly words and thoughts that were interrupted before they were even considered – well, then. Well, goddammit, then I wasn't worth my own name – Sylvia Plath.

I wrote until my insides were hollowed out, until all of me felt like my body was an arch that threw my soul out like the kind of innards that would lurch into a toilet. Here was the toilet, here was the salvation – here was the paper. I glowed, I was hunched over from shortness of breath. Don't look at the words. Don't look, not until they were written. Just stay in the writing. Don't listen to sounds. A crow cried in the garden – don't listen to it. The crows always wanted me to interrupt the event I was creating – one of life's most beautiful poems – and instead think of something more earthly. I refused! I held the pen tightly and it banged out the words like ammunition against reality! Bang! Bang! Bang! Bang! I didn't even suck at the tip of the pen because there were no breaks! Everything was just one thought and now it was being born! Now I was birthing all the words that damn well belonged together and creating something larger and more true than reality could ever conjure! Now I was conquering reality! Here was what was even higher! What lurched, fused bridges, healed internal wounds and bent open the most firmly locked chambers of the heart! I was going to break into them! Into hearts! Into people!

I wrote until I wept.

Wept, and received a smile.

'Daddy' was the title of the poem.

I felt like opening the fridge and lapping from a bowl of cream.

I stumbled upstairs and lay down next to Frieda, who had moved over to the big bed, and I hugged her warm little body. She didn't wake, only jerked a little at my touch. I crept closer to her, little frog. Little frog, and me! Me, the predator, mixed up in such strong, terrible forces! Who was I, even?! Who was I to manage these forces?!

The one with the task to comfort and warm me was herself a little child.

A thought came to me, kept me awake that entire morning: did I in fact feel responsible for my father's death?

The thought had never before reached me.

I was eight years old – did I think it was my fault? Did I begin to compensate by being good and exceeding at aesthetic beauty? Winning all the awards . . . writing the most beautiful of the beautiful . . . painting, playing the piano (but that I was lousy at and quit).

An image of my mother rose before my mind's eye. Did we all try to cover it up, somehow – that the great man grew weak and died, that even his body began to rot?

Did we all use me in some way – a young, beautiful promise to cover up the rotten, the dead?

I would halt death, I would be even more life, I would shine and glow, I would be the all-American girl, the promise of a better future; everything depended on me.

Was that how it was?

Was I sent to keep death at bay?

Anyone can see: it's a charge no one can shoulder.

No one should have that charge!

Soft, yellow October, the point when I entered the world, and now I was about to be born all over again! That was the feeling I had! That was the feeling I wrote with! And I had a steady plan in my head: it was still called Ireland, it was still called London in December, and I was set on visiting the capital in order to see the state of my destiny!

I walked around in the garden in order to gather everything scattered there before Ted was delivered in a cab. This black son, black-clad with sorrow in his eyes who would arrive this afternoon to gather apples to bring back to London.

To check in on the children.

To enquire about how I was doing.

Fucking fire of hell, gangrene of my soul!

Yes, he was on his way. He would arrive in a few hours. And I stood here in the middle of a birth, was in the process of becoming, and I didn't want him here. (But could at the same time not turn him away.)

And this damn transience that ruled Court Green. If only I could be born alone . . . Like when I was allowed to write my poems at four in the morning. If I could remain undisturbed by the world and be born and hatch my grand plans in peace . . . if He didn't exist, if He didn't come and poke and prod at me. If He wasn't their father. If He didn't come and slap a mirror in my face so I could see how ill and malnourished I ACTUALLY was. Oh, this *actually*! They were trapped in their actually! There was no actually! I had my own truth here, don't come and pick at it!

My back hurt. I shuffled across the floor to pick up a piece of paper and pen to write a message to Susan. I wrote the nanny a note:

'Dear Susan, the children and I have gone for a walk, Ted is coming at 4, please make him some tea and converse with him and for God's sake toss this note so he never sees it. I'll be back at 6, then he can have an audience with the children while I hand him a basket of apples, then that's the visit. I'm eternally grateful if you tend to him. Thanks!!! Sylvia.'

I piled the children into heavy October clothes since October in England could be particularly raw. I brought a pair of binoculars, a book on mushrooming and an umbrella, and told them that now Mommy is going to take you out on an excursion, won't that be lovely? We walked far from the town, climbed the hill where you could gaze out across Dartmoor and where I had ridden bareback on Ariel. Frieda fed the goats dead grass that they refused and Nick fell asleep in the pram. There was a light rain but I was safe here, beneath the grey sky, I was safe here from he who wanted to profit from my birth, he who risked stealing my entire truth from me. He who would say, my, haven't you gotten thin, Sylvia, watch out so you don't get cystitis or the flu again, I'm worried about you, you look like a bird, please darling Sylvia don't write so much, make sure to rest when the sitter is actually here – don't wear yourself out with the writing, it'll work out eventually, your thing about a career . . . Trust life, Sylvia, trust life!

And at the top of the hill we found a dead blackbird that

lay abandoned with its orange beak beneath an oak tree. Frieda was horrified, she gasped, 'Bird dead, Mommy, bird dead?' and had I been in the mood I would have buried it for her, but I just sat down on a rock.

I sat down completely cold on the wet rock until Nick woke up and Frieda tugged at me and wanted me to return to reality. She was like everybody else, they tugged and pulled at me and no matter the price wanted to get me to back away from my euphoria, away from the bliss of my heart. I was not allowed to be happy, I was not allowed to believe in my own life.

I was tired and nauseous when I slammed open the door to the house and there he was, deep in conversation with Susan. For a moment everything was almost as before, when our eyes met. A faint ray of light passed between us. And the same fatigue now as then, in my muscles. 'Where have you been?'

'We've been out picking mushrooms.'

He looked at me suspiciously but Frieda passed him a basket with some worm-eaten morels in it.

'And this was all you found?'

A dense silence, which I interrupted by saying:

'And now you're going to say that everything would've been better if you'd come along, because you're the mushroom expert?'

I tossed the keys on the table.

'Well, here you are.'

Frieda and her father were close with each other in that habitual way; there was something both glorious and sorrowful about how they moved, the kisses he gave her that revealed there had been no father's kisses there for a while.

She wanted to tickle him; he landed on the floor. Had a gift to give her. A doll.

My tears throbbed behind my eyelids, but no one heard or saw.

A *doll.* I was torn to pieces by the thought of the doll bed I had decorated with stars and hearts last Christmas, when Frieda was one year old. So my husband was going to deny us the joy of having a domestic life where we together witnessed our daughter grow and grow and begin to play with – *dolls.*

So my husband would not give our children the same love that I got until I was eight years old.

But Ted did not think of this, Ted only thought of the present, this blazing second when he placed a doll in Frieda's hands and wondered what would happen next. In that way he was carefree, did not dwell. Instead, he let others take care of that detail – the ruminating. I could swear Assia Devil was the same type of ruminator.

And then my heart was sliced open some more.

When he went to Nicholas.

Nicholas whimpered; he was just at the age when he was seriously attached to Susan O'Neill and to his mother, and then the father who made his son fatherless couldn't simply come around and demand love at set times.

It just would not happen.

Nicholas struggled over to me, stretched out his little chubby arms.

'There, there, little one,' I said as Ted looked at us mournfully. He had collapsed and lost his posture, stood there hunched by the chair.

I kissed Nicholas. He was still chilly since he had slept so long in the pram in the cold weather.

I warmed his cheeks with kisses.

The pain I feel doesn't belong to me, I tried to think. The pain he's trying to force on us is not ours. That was his shit, everything was his shit (I squinted with one eye and saw how

Ted easily took to the nanny again, now he had already forgotten the wound he bore in Nicholas), his devilishness, but it did not affect us, because we had each other, didn't we, Nicholas?

My nine-month-old son was fat and heavy and lovely in my arms. A cherub.

I showed him to Ted – now he smiled from my hip.

'Look!' I said. 'In any case, it seems we have a little chub here in the family. Mommy has lost several kilos but they've stuck to you instead!'

Ted had already looked away, he was flipping through the mail for letters.

The empty wind gusted and gusted through my heart. It was the October wind. I would turn thirty years old in this wind. It was going to happen in a couple of days. This spring, Assia Devil asked what kind of party I would have. Now I knew I would be alone on the day I turned thirty. Alone, my children and I and the house with the garden facing the cemetery. Perhaps I would at best be able to fry them some sausage.

'We're tired now,' I said, rocking Nick on my hip, even though it tore at me when I said it. 'You have to go now.'

'And by the way, happy birthday,' Ted said guiltily and blew me a kiss across the room.

He got his apples and was gone.

Now it was all about London! Writing. My own life, which I had committed so deeply to neglecting! I was standing with Susan in the kitchen with the groceries that would soon be cut up and become Blessed Dinner before I left, and I told her that, for so long, I had not lived – but now, now I was alive!

Susan, twenty-two years old, laughed.

Blonde and beautiful.

The October sun peeked in through my window and I loved my new black-and-white checkered floor – now I wanted to grab Susan for a spin and dance across the floor with her!

We danced until Frieda laughed so hard that she gasped for air, with her most adorable two-year-old laughter. She sucked on a piece of carrot and laughed and now I was a mother who was IN MY DAUGHTER'S LAUGHTER and I could be because I was on my way away from her now. I was going to London. London London London! I would be like Ted; I would be freed from Ted and thus BECOME LIKE TED, or, simply: I would take the liberties Ted took on a daily basis just by waking up, just by being a man and liberated and not first and foremost FATHER.

'All this time, I've been such a fucking mother,' I said. 'I've been the mother monster, I've been the mother where Ted has wavered in his fatherhood, I've carried the children inside me, I've dragged them around until my arms have stiffened, I've forsaken my writing, yes, everything! I've done everything for them.'

We stopped dancing and I grabbed a celery stick, stuck it in my mouth.

With the money I'd received from Aunt Dotty, I had bought clothes in Exeter and now I ran out of the kitchen and let Susan chop the vegetables while I eagerly put on the new clothes.

Walked a fashion show for her and Frieda in the kitchen while Nick sat and slammed saucepan lids on the floor.

'Et voilà!' I almost screamed, twirling around.

A black sweater and a blue tweed skirt that fit perfectly around my ass, made me sexy, delicious, good-looking, fuckable!

'You should see my red skirt too, I practically become a stop sign in it,' again, I was talking in a way that made Susan giggle – she did not understand me, but she let me hold forth.

'You look great, Sylvia!'

I picked up the kitchen knife to chop the onion and cut a few sticks of celery so Susan did not have to do everything herself – and in too-swift a movement, the knife went straight through my thumb and red blood began to pump across the cutting board.

'Susan!' I yelled.

She was quickly at my side.

Soon it was November, the anniversary of my father's death, and my hair was braided and my thumb infected beneath its bandage, and in a way it matched so incredibly well with who I wanted to be right now—

Free—

Infected—

True.

I lingered by the glasses at a writers' night in London, in the safe custody of a waiter who poured bubbly for the guests and could easily entertain the lost, neatly dressed lady who was me, and who had no one to talk to.

I showed him my infected thumb.

'Why don't I live here, in a world of high-rise buildings?' I complained. 'Oh, why am I trapped in a Devon village?'

He laughed at me, said I looked like a writer.

'You, if anyone, ought to live in London,' he said. 'You look like you're made for the world.'

You have to spread it on thick when you are in the big city, you have to brag. So I started gossiping about Ted.

'"Life in the country will do us good," my husband claimed when we moved . . . "London has mounted barbed wire in my head," he said too . . . Oh, I could cough up my ex-husband's nonsense like small balls of mucus in the sink!'

Suddenly I had lost my company.

And the hot critic Al Alvarez at *The Observer* would think, when he saw me walk up to him on my big stage – London, the epicentre of writers' evenings – that my freedom was a reactive freedom.

All the expressions of freedom she makes in reaction to Ted, he would think when I approached him like some kind of widow and tremblingly held on to my glass. I showed him my thumb too, told him how it throbbed terribly.

And Al Alvarez pecked me on the cheek as usual, sensed far too strong a scent of perfume behind my ear, thought:

She's too dressed up.

She's practically a widow, of sorts.

She acts as if her husband is dead.

She's here to laud her own excellence, I can see through it, she wants to tell me how good her poems are, and why then is there something inside me that whimpers and writhes? It's like I feel *sorry* for her.

And Al Alvarez would stand there all the while with his sharp blazer sleeve next to me, so that we almost touched, and we would converse, whisper in each other's ears, and I raised my voice a little too loud, levied my speech carelessly.

It had been a long time since I'd been to London. Now the impressions rinsed over me, and I had to catch up with myself, the pace – I needed some time to acclimate. As if I had forgotten what to do, there were many people here I did not recognise, the world of writing rotated and was replaced and began to teem with new people who wanted something and all of them believed they had a voice, that was it.

I told Al Alvarez that I was going to record poems for the BBC the next day.

And once again he thought: She is *copying* him. She does everything just the way he does. I understand that Ted wanted to hurl himself away from her. Whoops – if he writes plays for the radio, well, then she suddenly writes for the radio. So damn generic.

He cleared his throat.

'So, Sylvia, what kind of poems are you writing for the BBC? Can I hear something?'

I laughed and stayed near him because he was a large and protective man to stay close to. In this networking situation, I didn't want to lose his interest so that he would slip away to talk to some other talent – no, I had to live in front of him right now, he needed to feel how I vibrated.

So I laughed and laughed again.

'They're dawn poems,' I said. 'Quite good, if I may say so myself. For the first time, I've . . .'

Al was interested: he wanted to hear the rest.

'For the first time, I've used autobiography, yes, goddammit! It's true.'

Al laughed, he was amused by me.

So I went on.

'I think Ted was right when he said I always used to *imitate*, that I tried, that I forced things out that I did not actually have the mental coverage for. You know what I mean?'

Al Alvarez nodded. Again – it was about Ted; she is obsessed with Ted, he thought. Why? I had to switch tracks.

'So now I try to just rush out the poems, at another pace, as if I was intoxicated.'

'How about that.'

'I've stopped struggling.'

'That's interesting.'

'Really, I've stopped struggling.'

And Al Alvarez, who was a man I also idealised, saw that I was serious, that something had happened to me and it warmed him inside, built a kind of wall around his understanding of me.

He seemed to be happy for me.

And yet – by my appearance – the wrinkles on my face, my slim, thin, bony body's weight loss – and the hair I braided in a far-too old-ladyish, prim hairstyle and the smile with the yellowed teeth and the hysterical eyes that lacked any kind of guard—

Still, he was worried.

She is a widow. It's like Ted died for her.

And who wants to fuck a widow?

'The recording is going to happen at the British Council,' I said, not to lose face.

I had just read 'Daddy' for him.

It was such a crucial event.

He drew his breath.

Then he said:

'It's intense, Sylvia. It's violent. You have become really, really good.'

Something popped in me.

I had won. I knew it. And I fell in love with Alvarez when he said it. When he said something about my poem that I could not say myself.

I slept so well that night, without sleeping pills, because I had bared my soul to someone, to Al; and he judged that it was good, it held up, it was lovely.

Filled with the silence that can only come after you have spoken, as though satiated, I rested after the recordings at the British Council and gazed up at the ceiling.

It was love I felt. I knew it.

I had lost track – rode the waves of life too hard, away from America and into Cambridge life where I was the Other, the one with the bicycle, the American, the one whom Ted saw also wrote.

But now. Afterwards; now I saw love more clearly.

November light; sometimes it felt like spring light, like light sifted through glass. It was all the lightning from the skyscrapers to my room here in the hotel, the fifth floor.

Its soft pardon.

Now I was also soft.

I undressed completely, allowed myself to stand naked in the room, remembered other rooms where I wanted to be naked but hadn't been able to: Richard's stupid room in Connemara, the hospital in London last spring when I was admitted. And at home in Court Green, where I always had to be someone decent who waited on others, prepared for the next unexpected visit from a neighbour.

I had lost weight, I was barely visible, I could barely recall who I was, where was I. So this was how it felt, to be afflicted with self-starvation, to deny yourself your food your joy your stability. Your own body, yes.

Now I was happy in London – right now, yes – but I was bitterly familiar with the recoil, was familiar with the mechanism that sent someone happy back from the heights.

Even I was afraid of it.

Even I – despite the fact that I hated it when my mother put it that way in letters, that of everyone, I would be in trouble, that what was happening was awful for my health, that I had to be damn careful now—

Even I understood.

I do not think I want to be in England for one more winter, as I wrote in confidence to my mother in a letter in August.

Hopeless Mother: if only it were possible to be candid, be equal! If I was not for ever and ever her daughter, in that horrible way. If my joy or misfortune just didn't set off all of heaven and hell in *her*. If she could just listen, collected and confident.

Sometime.

But she could not.

So the rest of the world had to listen to me.

I picked up the book I had with me; that was it, now I needed to catch up. *The Art of Loving* by Erich Fromm, the little book that Dr Beuscher had asked me to read. Read it, and try to get along with your own longing and your feelings, especially when you experience the sharp lurching between hope and despair, when your security seems to be in jeopardy, and try to see through the idealised images you have erected of your mother and of Ted. Find yourself in all this, Sylvia, and be free.

I knew I had a lesson to learn, that I had neglected my own inner work for so long, and see how it had turned out, look at the result of that denial – single mother (just like mother!) left by the child's father, destitute, left to my own literary efforts, solitude was not strength and ooooooooaaaaaaaaaiiiiiiiiih how I knew it and how it hurt and burned. So afraid of disease so afraid of death so afraid of wounds so afraid of vulnerability so afraid of weakness just as my father never ever revealed to himself and his surroundings that he was ill when he was in fact dying – my big strong man in life, DADDY, that he should be weak, that he should be snatched away from me, that he should even be POSSIBLE to amputate, that his foot shrivelled up. That he died.

'Try not to feel like everything has to be perfect,' Dr Beuscher wrote in a letter. 'Practice acceptance. This is how things turned out – they do not always have a simple explanation, life sometimes just is what it is, without patterns or destiny, it is not always a matter of responsibility. Things become, things happen, it's beyond your control, try to tell yourself that.'

And if she had sat in front of me in a session I would have replied:

'But I'm afraid of imperfection. Then I don't dare to live. It's scary.'

And she would have asked me:

'What's scary?'

And I would have sat quietly for a while. Then I would have rubbed my long narrow fingers against each other in a kind of dance of the hands you stage in front of your psychiatrist in order to look like you're thinking and to gain time; to look small, look like someone vulnerable without being vulnerable.

And then I would have said:

'It feels like if I don't hold the reins, I can't live. It's worse than death for me. Then I lose control . . .'

'And what's so dangerous about that?'

And I would answer:

'That's what I'm trying to come up with! I have no good answer . . . I guess my writing is a kind of answer . . . There's something about myself that I don't understand.'

Silence.

'I guess . . .'

'What do you guess?'

'I guess death hit me as a child at a point when I was unprotected, I was in someone else's hands completely. And still, he died. I should have been prepared. I should have known better.'

And she would shake her head lightly and say:

'Do you realise what's about to happen right now? You have imagined that you have control over everything, in a way that makes you blind to when things slip out of your hands one more time.'

I would sit stock-still, not even my hands would move against each other this time.

I would be able to really feel the pain of what she said. And with large, guilt-ridden eyes ask:

'So it's my fault? You're blaming me?'

And Dr Beuscher would deny the accusation with a sharp that's-enough expression.

'Cut it out, Sylvia. This is your ego talking. Don't feed your ego! You bear no responsibility at all in this – the ego loves guilt, feeds on guilt – what I'm saying is that you're exposed to the very mechanism you think you can stay away from. But no – the uncontrollable will return, without exception.'

I was freezing now. If I did not have to think these thoughts and could only wallow in the self-love you felt three minutes after someone loved your poem.

That dark-eyed guy at the British Council – oh, how grand I was in front of him! Really sauntered around the office with my voice, reciting to myself before I was placed at the microphone. The microphone – my rightful place, the airwaves – my true shelter in the world. I would thrive there for ever, Amen. And so wonderful later, to be done, to loudly shut one's notebook and just dash into the London Underground and head home, to the hotel, where a bed with two blankets was waiting for me, and a shower in the bathtub and a book that would enlighten me about my self-love, called *The Art of Loving*.

I did not open the book. In fact, I did not. So afraid of the truth, so afraid of being confronted with myself, yes, but let me rest, I thought, let me be filled with the love that arises after reading two of my best poems at the British Council. Read and been loved for it, been praised for my voice. Dark strong voice. Let it go this time, Sylvia. You have your entire life to get to know yourself!

I stared up at the ceiling and lay quietly breathing until I felt the cold occupy my entire body. I was cool as a corpse. My skin shone like mother of pearl. And it was me and no one else.

Then, when life had temporarily left me and I felt how alone I was in every pore in my entire body, I lifted my hand and placed it on top of my secret.

My secret, my sex.

The language for all that we had carried together, but did not have left.

He had had me – I had realised his children – our love had flowed between my legs.

And I still carried this secret, this dark cave of life, the female sex, the hole, the damage, to constantly walk around with the vulnerability.

Carry the living damage at the core of my body.

Always.

I placed my hand over my secret which was my sex and

moved my finger up and down until it felt like velvet, the tissue and secretions together. I spat on my finger. I sent it into the cave that was me. That was my entire outer space, my question. The strange fruit of the universe. The question that was impossible to answer: But what WAS a female sex? What DOES it mean to walk around with it?

And why was he now fucking Assia Wevill?

I had not thought she would endure; I thought it was 'her and other women', that she was one in the crowd; but NO. It *was* her. He was faithful.

I sat with my hands clasped in my lap on the London Underground. It looked like a ridiculous prayer. So I let go, let my fingers slip homeless down across the cold fabric of my skirt and gazed out into the dark tunnels. Soon – a sun that rose over Primrose Hill – a woman who rose out of the underworld – the trains that kept running deep down there, for her sake, if she just chose it – and the light above the colourful facades here in London's Primrose Hill, where I was once born as Frieda's mother.

Nobody looked at me in the train car but fine, I thought, it was November, they would look at me later; this was preparation, something I did to become immortal, to let my strong sense of reason take centre stage, to be remembered later as the most proper and at the same time coolest poet of all time. Ted faded like a soiled and wrinkled shirt in comparison.

I emerged from the tunnels and once outside it was as if a wind grabbed my coat and carried me forward. Here was a hairdresser, here was a small shop for when I needed to feed my children's mouths, a stone's throw away the library and then the park and the galleries . . .

This was going to be the weekend when I cut my hair.

Primrose Hill, and this is where I once was the most alive. What was wrong with resting on old laurels, or just resuscitating what had been lost?

Who the hell could blame me for that?

Abundance, I thought, crushing the cigarette beneath my shoe. I had read it in the book I was reading now, the one Dr Beuscher recommended to me about the brain; I did not remember the title – some people think they live in utter scarcity, and everything they then focus on is negativity, averting disasters. Other people (and I had no desire to divide Ted and I into any of the categories, but I wasn't stupid, either: even I understood things) – other people; that is to say, the rest of the world; those who were not me – other people mostly saw the abundance, they lived in a constant state of feeling that there was enough for everyone, of love, of permanence, life was like a cake that would suffice even for them.

The walk from Primrose Hill took me less than five minutes and there were sadder houses here, uglier colours on the facades, the cars looked dull but I could not see it. I inhaled icy black London air and swallowed. I had arrived at 23 Fitzroy Road.

Abundance, I thought, and climbed the stairs to the brown door beneath the blue sign that informed me that the poet W. B. Yeats had lived here as a child. My Yeats, my love poet, my Irish role model; I wanted to bask in the splendour of his name, the cold green ocean, its abundance, the ocean that cooled and sufficed for everyone and wanted to encompass everything.

My element – the ocean, the all-consuming, the dangerous, the fire-extinguishing, roaring, the large waves I one day long ago had wanted to swim out into, with Mel, my friend when I was nineteen years old, and he screamed and worried that I would want to die there, in the green waves, swim out and never return. Maybe he was right that time; but regardless, what a difficult task: to die, what a damn difficult task it was.

I had turned around, spat out the water in my mouth, laughed at his anxiety.

Life just flooded you with its livability.

Forced you to remain.

I knocked on the door – one, two, three times. Here stood a young woman in her prime and waited to be admitted.

London. Yeats's house. I had found it. I would never again live lonely, bitter, abandoned in a disgusting house in the countryside that reminded me of all my losses and the qualities no one understood.

I was not going to be forgotten.

I did not intend to become a scrap, a phase of life to be checked off.

I did not intend to be frigid and used like a pair of socks.

I thought I was in my prime.

Now I'm in my prime, I thought. I have my poems, I have my recordings for the BBC, I have my author name, Sylvia Plath, I have given birth to my kids and here I am waiting to be admitted to the apartment that will give me my life back.

Ted was forgotten now, he was swept away like a piece of seaweed on a strip of beach. Swept out into the ocean. I was the ocean. I was the waves. He had just forgotten. I was the future. I bore it in my chest. I was time, I was life itself, I was the primordial mother, I was the one who took care of the children.

Oh, I shivered and froze because no one opened, couldn't it unfold as I had hoped, did the moon not shine tonight to guide me home, back to the hotel where I had slept last night, had the people here forgotten about me too?

After what felt like ten minutes, someone opened the door

slightly ajar. And I was shown in by an elderly gentleman. There were two apartments to choose from. One belonged to an elderly man – 'don't mind him, but he's kind, you might need a reliable fellow in the house' – and I giggled, that was how you were in your prime; you giggled, were quick to play, easy to deal with.

The man showed me the way to my dream apartment. It was rundown, of course, dark, but now I did not see the darkness, I did not see how worn it was, I just saw the potential – or else I saw the worn-down and was seduced by just that: how it resonated in me, the decayed, what needed to be repaired and sewn, the wallpaper curling from moisture and misery, the toilet that looked shabby and which at the moment could not be flushed.

'We have to look this over, but don't worry, once the water gets going, it'll be fine. I'll call the plumber on Monday, so you don't have to do that,' said the man.

My eyes gleamed. I held on to the door frame, I felt a faint smell of mould and filth but I also saw – my eyes served me now – I saw a kind of light, an air I could live with; how the windows admitted this light I once lived with, the Primrose Hill light.

The very first spring light of the sixties, full of baby skin.

That's what I wanted.

'I'll take it,' I said, extending my hand to him. He was not even done with the showing yet, we were standing in the kitchen and in the kitchen it flared up in me, a feeling of being so completely rooted and at home in my own house, my own time, and the future, even.

This was mine.

Mine – and my children's.

Ted would come here and take them to the museum and the zoo and for a walk. I wanted to come back here to the birthplace, Frieda's arrival into the world, how happy we were then, how I stood tallest at the top just as I this spring would be at the top again, when the novel was published, the fantastic *The Bell Jar*, and when the new poems had a publisher.

The stranger took my hand. He could see that I in that moment made up my mind. There were no doubts.

Late November at Court Green, one of the final times.

It was me, alone, in my room, which had been my bedroom with Ted.

Stood there digging for clothes in the closet. Now everything had to go. And I had to decide, manage so many tasks. While the children had their last babysitting session with Susan, I had to catch up on everything. So many decisions – so much purging to do – so much future to shape – so much love to decide on.

So this was me, then. So these were my old clothes. Ugly, disgusting! And all the while I had walked around and thought that the clothes had felt *good* inside the closet, when I put a bag of lavender in there to make the clothes feel comfortable and smell good, but in fact the little monsters had been there gnawing on our silk, our wool.

Damn disgusting lie I lived right at the centre of!

Now I tore everything out, now I tore down the hangers.

I was no longer a consequence, subordinate, I was not the incentive for someone to be able to live their life. I was not the beginning for someone else. I was the beginning for me.

So how did this beginning begin? How did it take shape? What did it look like?

I had put a pile of old clothes from the closet on my bedspread; that's where it began, too – a beginning as good as any. They lay there dusty and crawling with carpet beetles that had eaten away at them. Large holes where my love had been. The deepest question was: How would I make do with the love I had?

Who would give it to me now?

Love.

Who would build the great shelter I needed in the world?

LONDON, baby. London all on its own. I had seen the prospect – Yeats's house, with the blue sign – I had seen fate inscribed there in the aged stones in the walls of the house: My fate. The end. My house.

There it was, waiting for me all the while. The house that would untangle me from these claws that had their pincers in me – Ted's crow claws, his raven ways, far out in the English countryside.

Like a helium balloon, I would rise into the sky if I did not anchor myself, get a hold of a door to lock behind us, beds to put the kids in.

Yeats's old house.

Had been waiting for me all along.

Every day this fall felt like my birthday.

I dusted off the clothes, folded them one by one and placed them in a bag. A large, deep bag for my old clothes that once kept me warm. The memories of these clothes when Ted and I were in windy York together, when his parents saw our future in me, as I now saw my future in Yeats's house. They had seen that I was an opportunist and that I was dubious. It was not clear that I would be enough for Ted.

It would be clean when I left Court Green and rented

our rooms out to strangers, you wouldn't be able to track us down here. We would be purged, the house would be freed of us.

The deepest question was (and I brought it with me to the city): How would I be deeply loved?

Who would love me deeply?

Who, if not Ted?

If not Ted, who else could truly love me?

Ted's betrayal had reminded me of this, and it pushed a deep screw tip into the red flesh that was my heart: that he had never loved me, never deeply, never sincerely during the course of our seven years.

It was just as he had told me: fake. Fakery and poetry, never reality. He loved me as a motif. He loved the picture of me. He loved the type. The American, the emotional one, the poet. He loved my high demands (and hated them). He loved having a thinking wife. He loved having a wife. He loved that I was thinking and grinding my own thoughts, then there was nothing left of them later in the writing. He loved that I tried but failed. That I got up and was stabbed, like a goat. That I was not who I wanted to be. He loved my imperfection, and I stood in the middle of it and tried to be perfect.

In that gap, neither of us could love.

Now I knew.

So what should I do now, when I left for London?

Who would love me now?

I had the children; but I was also embarking on an entirely new era, an entirely new time, a new term. It was totally unknown. I knew that. And yet – it was right. That's why – it was right. It was right because I would not be in the foetal position and a victim any longer. I would become real, I would become text, I would become an acclaimed author,

I would make waffles for my kids during the day and go to London publishing parties at night. I would belong to my own elite. Not his – I would be MY OWN.

The self-love I had previously denied myself, I would economise with now. Give to myself. I would give, I would give, I would give!

So who would love me now?

Me.

I went and got the letter from the drawer, the letter I was so ashamed to receive last week. It was Dr Beuscher who had written to me to say that I should not put my life in the hands of Ted's love, the love he did not intend to give to me anyway. I should not build a model of love with Ted. He should not be my substitute father, nor my mentor, either. Not my editor, not my first and final reader as we had said before, not the big brother I had always longed for, not . . . my maternal substitute.

He should be nothing to you now, Beuscher wrote. Put no weight in him. No meaning. He's paper. Crumble him now. Construct your own little ritual! Try. Play, for once. Try to grind him into powder in your hand.

I was so embarrassed by what she said because I understood that it was also what I had done – with *myself*. Even if she was sitting on the other side of the Atlantic, Beuscher – she knew me, she knew how I operated. How could she read me like that? That was the kind of man I could have used: a man who let me take my time and my space, a man who knew that a woman could not grow and become a mother at the same time; for at that moment she submitted herself to the universe, she came to belong to everything, never her own again.

I should have had a man who understood me that way.

And who loved me, in the same breath.

So, crumble him in a ritual. I fished out Ted's ugliest sweater that was already torn, large holes, and which I thought he was so disgusting in. It was a sweater Ted pulled on over a shirt when it had enough stains – that was the one, the one I would crumble.

I pulled at the hole and started unravelling it. Thread by thread, all of Ted would be pulverised, just as he had turned me into air. Made me a useless mycelium, thread by thread but nothing whole, nothing valuable.

Now he lay in threads on the floor.

I felt so fucking empty and enormous.

I crawled up on the bed among all the clothes which had not yet been thrown into the bag; crawled around in them, regretted what I had just done, put the jumper from 1959 over my eyes and let myself be transported by the smell, to Yaddo, the summer in the cottage in Saratoga Springs, we wrote, we still had the world fresh and damp in front of us, I had a life in my stomach. Pregnant with Frieda, our first.

Now I cried beneath the sweater.

It was dark to lie beneath old clothes and cry – and I should not be here, I should be determined and proper, know what I was doing because soon Susan would return with the children, it was the last session before she quit, and I had rented an apartment in London and decided on a departure date and packed things – and it was thick November out there, grey and cold. I wanted to greet them with the smile of life when they returned, the roasted glorious love that children were entitled to here in the world and that only I had to give them.

I did not want them to be greeted by a weeping monster that lay in a pile of clothes and remembered, and that the weeping monster would be me.

I wanted to give myself the love I would then give them.

But my God – how do you give yourself love? How to love yourself?

Dr Beuscher asked me to read Erich Fromm specifically for that reason – self-love – that I would find a way to find self-love, and that would be the starting point of my beginning. My new life.

Oh, crying, nasty enormous overwhelming crying – what was crying even worth, when there was no one to mourn in front of?

In a way, I would be happy if Susan stomped in here and I could break down in front of her, if she could be my caretaker in the same way that she now was the children's protector; I also wanted to give in and release myself from my own claws, also just be taken care of.

I would like to be loved that way—

And then, then I would have to show myself.

Such was the essence of love.

I got up, stood in front of the mirror on the wall, struck my palm hard against my own cheek until it stung. Then the other cheek, and back against the first one again. I slapped myself until it burned and my cheeks glowed pink. There was no peace to uncover. No silence to be found. It just was not in me. No safe harbour. No peace. No redemption. No pleasure.

I realised it now, when I looked at myself.

I was a lost cause.

You should give me CPR. There had to be some fucking air-blowing machine on me for me to have some kind of stability and direction. I had no direction. Not even when I decided, when I was ready for something, when I had found an address where I could flee: London, 23 Fitzroy Road. Not even then.

I tore Ted's clothes out of the bag.

This is what I would do instead: I would pack a bag for

Ted, full of his old clothes. Then he could decide for himself, if he came, whether there was anything to save.

I would not decide his fate.

I no longer controlled Ted!

It was a relief.

I retrieved the brown suitcase from the storeroom, opened it and neatly folded all of Ted's clothes (except the sweater).

It was nice for our clothes not to have to be in the same bag.

Deeply loved.

That's how you became deeply loved – you let others take care of their shit, you didn't take too much responsibility for others. Ted's clothes for Ted. My clothes for oblivion. I would just buy new ones with all the money I would get in January when the novel came out.

How liberating it was to close the bag on Ted's shirts and his old worn sweaters, the ones I once loved.

This is how you became deeply loved: you thought in abundance, did not wallow in old injustices, ate vitamins and stayed healthy, slept while the children slept. This is how you were deeply loved: you bided your time, you wrote your poems, you stuck to routines, you found ways to try to love yourself.

I exhaled. The grip released, anxiety rode out of the room. I remained – I was breathing, I was here. I dragged myself up. I could hear them now. They were returning; now the door slammed. They were my children, still! I was still their mother!

I rushed down the stairs, my steps boomed, they had me there – Mommy! – Mommy! – and I embraced their little bodies, thin glorious, my flesh for their flesh, my blood for their blood.

We warmed each other. I did not want to release them, even if Frieda wanted to start chatting. She talked so much now! And Nicholas, how he babbled with his words, he would soon turn one, oh my God how quickly could a year pass, how much awfulness and love could a year hold?

'Come,' I said to Nicholas. 'Come on, my boy. Come and sit here.'

Now I would just give the little ones a meal. Because I was their mother. And the little boy fit on me, on my hip.

And now London, for a weekend.

The last week in November had passed, and wasn't that what was so grand about London – the big city obscured all the harsh seasons, winter did not become as palpable here. I would fill Yeats's childhood home with balloons and light-blue wallpaper.

And my mother knew, on the other side of the Atlantic, or she felt it deep in her stomach, that it was when I uttered the words *Once I settle in this apartment I shall be the happiest person on earth—* and then, when I settled in the apartment: *And rest assured that I have never been happier—*

That was when her daughter was really in trouble.

The city was shrouded in mist, I could not see my hand when I held it up in front of me on the way to the phone booth, and it was nice to be enveloped, to disappear into a multitude and turn into smoke that way.

The children and I had temporarily installed ourselves at Susan's boyfriend, in Camden. There were so many odds against me and I worked as hard as a Marine. Now they wanted references from me. A rock-hard lady (it was always ladies) spoke to me from a red phone booth in the fog; her giraffe voice told me that I was not a safe bet for them, I had no fixed income, I was young, I was an American – yes, she locked me into all these types. Then I spat on the iron floor, where I stood flat as a pancake and short-haired and with red swollen lips.

Life never ended.

I stood there for ever, forever young, forever fighting for my future. Unseen, in my little cage, hidden by the fog, I fought. Completely without anyone else's involvement – the war took place only in my little life. I was the one who remedied the disasters, who found my way through the fog, who rented out houses and hired and fired nannies, wiped snot and vomit off children.

I told the giraffe lady that I had a mother at home in America who could guarantee the rent.

'What does your mother do for work?' she asked then.

'She's a professor,' I bit off.

Professor: where did that come from? My heart began pounding up a pulse that raged and became the loudest of the living in London; but it could not be heard right now, in that voice I offered the giraffe lady in the phone booth. She had no clue that my mother practically fell ill that summer in the aftermath of her visit with us. She became ill and was fired from her job. Destroyed, with a lousy pension. With stomach problems. That was what this 'professor' actually looked like.

Oh, this damn 'actually' that I avoided like the plague!

There was no actually.

Actually, I was also in fact just a tired and abandoned mother of young children, who soon had no money, emaciated in the wake of childbirth and harbouring illness in my throat.

I gurgled and asked her to take me, now you just have to take me, I said, I need this house, it's my dream apartment, my insurance for the future and I AM GOING TO HAVE IT, can you hear me?

I'm going to live at 23 Fitzroy Road.

I went out into the fog and I could barely see, my brown coat melted into the street. If I stepped down off the sidewalk that was already crowded – here it was crowded with people in hats and coats everywhere – then it would already be over, in a moment.

A car could run over my functioning body and that was it. That was it for me.

Oh, awful thought.

I went up to Susan, who had settled in with the children in her boyfriend's apartment a few blocks away. She drank tea and listened to jazz in the arms of her beloved. I did not want to interrupt their 'actually', did not want to disturb them, but I had to pour my shit on her for a while when the children were asleep for the night. I said:

'I think I remedied the disaster by claiming that my mother is a professor.'

Susan's boyfriend looked up, I saw in his eyes that he looked out at a monstrous, beat-up face, and I attempted to cover myself, for this body was mine, I was the one who walked and lived exactly as tired and emaciated as I looked, in reality.

This was me.

And the only thing that kept me from letting them see me exactly as stripped-down and naked as I was, was the words, was the dream of the future, was that I was a success, was that I now held the reins of this runaway horse, I had just taken my future and kissed it, blessed it.

Soon only the fruits were left to harvest.

Fruits: novel 1 (soon it would arrive on the scene in England, and what an entrance – reading groups everywhere would want to discuss it, and mental health would be what everyone cared about – I set the tone!). Novel 2 (as a matter of course following the first success, it would be released the following year, and then the rights to films and plays would sell themselves, since I was *actually* a prose writer, I was such a damn talent; or – I was nearly there in so many places; I was one big actually!).

Actually, I was this, actually, I was that! Actually, I was not alive! Actually, I was not dead at all! Actually, I was a primordial force you brought with you into eternity! Actually, I was like the ocean!

You see: all my poems were crammed full of these actuallies, they were everywhere. Actually, this word meant this; actually, this word meant that. So many meanings to my word choices, so many ambiguities, so many ACTUALLY!

So crammed with symbolism.

Actually, I was just a gorgeous writer queen who sat here on Susan and her boyfriend's couch, and they did not know what a magnificent woman I was, made for great works and wonders, who had birthed two wonderful little children into the world. They could not have come from another woman.

And actually, everything was fine.

What was a little fatigue, compared to owning everything? Yes, all of life and its grand destiny unfolding here and now. Taking shape. I made the giraffe-voiced hag in the London phone booth receiver realise her shortcomings here in the world (who was she? A simple landlord) and give me the right to rent the apartment I since a few weeks back longed for so deeply. Now the hucksters would be put in their place. Now I would finally get to show them who they were dealing with.

The world was ready now.

I could care less what my mother huddled behind the Atlantic and worried about. I hated it when she sat on her high horse and had the nerve to worry about me. What did she have to worry about? What was her whole fucking identification with me about? She had to stop it, and I would prove her concern wrong – that was my highest goal right now; I would show her who was the most successful in the world. Show her how insanely well I took care of myself. Period.

'It's going to be sunny tomorrow,' Susan said. 'Maybe we should take the kids to the zoo?'

I LOVED HER!

Then I got up from the couch, happy in my short, brown hair which in the glow of the fire assumed a kind of red lustre – and dove into her spell with her boyfriend to give her a kiss on the forehead.

'I adore you, Susan,' I said. 'So happy to have you here. You help me become the queen I've always been.'

Susan laughed and asked me to shush, no big words like that now!

'It's just an idea,' she giggled.

'It'll be perfect!' I went on, threw out my hands. 'Oh, it's so wonderful here – this is my place – and I was welcomed so warmly by the woman in the grocery store downstairs, and by the butcher, even! They recognised me, and the woman remembered my name! My God, I was so tired of all the bovine types in Devon that I had nearly forgotten what cultured, educated beings feel like. I nearly started thinking that everyone who lives and breathes in the world is more like an animal – sluggish, incapable of finesse and . . . *language.*'

The boyfriend sipped from his teacup. I had my audience. They waited for my next word, for the next thing that would fall out of my red mouth. I looked tired, I had wrinkles, my smile was petrified and faded – but I did not know, I still thought what I said was true, that I embodied my own reality.

That what I put on display was what they saw.

But that just was not the case.

I was already dead.

I had moved on, I did not know I was the highest bidder on my own coffin.

That it was my own cemetery plot I actually signed a lease for.

That I gave my last money to.

That I asked my mother to guarantee.

This was what she worried about; she felt it in the pit of her stomach in Boston, and I hated her for it.

No one was allowed to stop me. Oh, I was so tired. Oh, could no one see the signs? No, I was unstoppable. Susan and her boyfriend were too young to read the signs; they thought I was funny. Damn funny. I entertained them. What. Is. That. Mad. Woman. Doing?

Sylvia Plath: it was still nearly me.

In one week, I would move my things into Yeats's house, a blank page, and we would initially live there without any actual furniture. It would arrive later! Just a crib for the time being, and a single bed for me and Frieda. (Yes, she got to sleep with me now. Her warm, hopeful body. Like a celebration of us being born here, both she and I; just a block away lay the apartment where I gave birth to Frieda, and where she made me a mother, the happiest one.)

Damn, she looks like an old woman, Susan thought to herself. And her boyfriend, he yawned: *What more can she come up with to bother us about now?*

I felt the sudden shift in the room and shoved some bills at Susan.

Her boyfriend could see how well I paid.

'Oh, thank you very much,' she said.

'I'm thanking you,' I replied curtly, and went to undress and lie down with the children.

One last look in the mirror before my bra was unfastened. I loved myself. I did. Life was unstoppable. My mother could not blame me for anything else.

If anyone slipped in here and took a photo of me now I would reveal myself just as I was.

Regardless of poems. Regardless of voice.

That was the goal: to show myself exactly as I was. To own the narrative. I would just make myself *deserve* that kind of treatment first. Soon, soon. Soon they would all discover me and my white skin. They would stand in line to snap their pictures. What would it be like to kiss my mouth? My story: they would all read it. Page upon page upon page. The text was ready at the publisher's, and I had made the recordings. When I got back to Devon, I would actually entertain myself by writing a list of why I truly did not want to die. It would be good for me, to be able to look at when I needed it the most. Days like that would come. I knew it. But what could make me want to die? Now? During my victory lap?

I unfastened my bra, laid it down in front of me. Here I was with the pearl necklace and my new short hairstyle. The white, extracted marble skin. A sweet little white bunny, and two bunny children asleep.

I pulled out the hairpins. I thought for a long time, until a warmth, a comfortable deep warmth, like a warm wave all the way from Winthrop, washed over me.

Well, if Ted got Assia pregnant, I thought, and buried the thought by putting on my nightgown the next moment. Horrible, senseless thought. If he should squirt his semen into her barren womb, and plant a sibling for my children.

That would decide the matter.

Such eternal luck then, I thought, and crawled into the warm bed that Susan and her loverboy loaned me, that there were no such prospects. That Assia Devil's womb was sealed like a grave.

Ted nudged at a dead womb every time they lay down. Ha!

The thought made me soft and supple. I was tired – so damn tired. No fucking poems were written during this move, no sleeping pills were needed, either; but as sure as anything,

I had already written my most striking poems, and there was the novel, and the reviews, the readings, my voice on the BBC through all of eternity.

And the children. The children. If only I had them next to me I could fall asleep like an exhausted baby bunny. I had run all day, and now I had peace.

Elin Cullhed
28 February 2020

ACKNOWLEDGEMENTS

From the depth of my heart, I would like to thank Jennifer Hayashida, Christina Cullhed, Gunnar Ardelius, Maria Såthe, Astri von Arbin Ahlander, Rachel Åkerstedt, Therese Cederblad, Sara R. Acedo, Lena Endre, Amanda Bergquist, Matilda Fogelström Johnsson, Jamie Byng, Hannah Knowles, Leila Cruickshank, Aa'Ishah Hawton, Lorraine McCann and Rafi Romaya for creating the pillars of this novel. A very special thank you to Jennifer Hayashida for merging Sylvia Plath's tone with my own within your exact and fine language; and for doing so with such empathy and care. Thank you to Mom for reading and translating Sylvia Plath together with me and thank you Dad for binding all my diaries that would one day turn into a novel. Thank you Astri von Arbin Ahlander for your delicate and dedicated handling of *Euphoria* and thank you Maria Såthe for our friendship and your willingness to stand by me in this publication and to always push it in the right direction. Thank you also Sara Parkman and Hampus Norén for creating the music I listened to while writing, leading me into deep inner forests of feeling and reality. Thank you, posthumously, Sylvia Plath and Ted Hughes for living and writing so courageously and with such honesty, and for letting us hear your voices through eternity. Thank you to Lana Del Rey for directing one song to Sylvia Plath and thank you

Patric Kiraly for posting this song on my Facebook wall when I most needed it. Moreover, thank you Marie Darrieussecq for writing so engagingly about Paula Modersohn-Becker, lending her 'more life' and inspiring me with the courage to do likewise. Thank you Sveriges Författarfond for trusting me with the grant that took me to North Tawton, and thank you to all my lovely readers – how could I have guessed that you would become so many? Thank you lastly to all who in their writings have contributed to my knowledge of Sylvia Plath and who are out there constantly keeping the arrow in motion: Karen V. Kukil, Heather Clark, Peter K. Steinberg, Rebecca Alsberg, Carl Rollyson, Frieda Hughes and more. Of course, the gratitude I feel towards my children and Gunnar, the love of my life, has no end – thank you for being there with me in the story as well as outside of it, in the grace and glory of life.

PERMISSION CREDITS

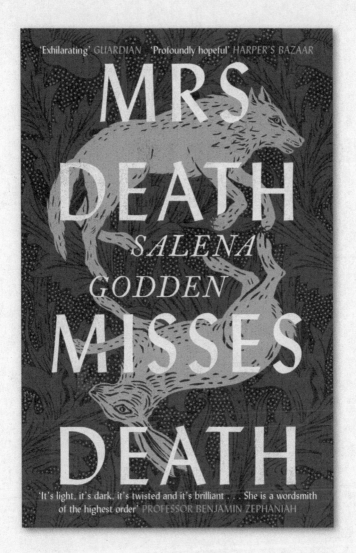

MRS
DEATH

SALENA
GODDEN

MISSES

DEATH

'Exquisite'
Irenosen Okojie

CANON▌GATE

RUTH
OZEKI

The Book
of Form &
Emptiness

'If you've lost your way with fiction over the last year or
two, let *The Book of Form and Emptiness* light your way home'
David Mitchell

'Deeply affecting and uplifting'
Guardian

CANON‖GATE